Lost Man's Lane

A Second Episode in the Life of
Amelia Butterworth

Anna Katharine Green

To

ELIZABETH D. SHEPARD
COUSIN AND FRIEND
THIS BOOK
IS AFFECTIONATELY INSCRIBED

CONTENTS

Preface vi

BOOK I
THE KNOLLYS FAMILY

I   A Visit From Mr. Gryce 2
II   I Am Tempted 3
III   I Succumb 9
IV   A Ghostly Interior 16
V   A Strange Household 19
VI   A Sombre Evening 22
VII   The First Night 25
VIII   On the Stairs 28
IX   A New Acquaintance 30
X   Secret Instructions 35
XI   Men, Women, and Ghosts 38
XII   The Phantom Coach 44
XIII   Gossip 48
XIV   I Forget My Age, or, Rather, Remember It 51

BOOK II
THE FLOWER PARLOR

XV   Lucetta Fulfils My Expectation of Her 58
XVI   Loreen 60
XVII   The Flower Parlor 65
XVIII   The Second Night 70
XIX   A Knot of Crape 75
XX   Questions 78
XXI   Mother Jane 81
XXII   The Third Night 84

BOOK III
FORWARD AND BACK

XXIII   Room 3, Hotel Carter 90
XXIV   The Enigma of Numbers 95
XXV   Trifles, But Not Trifling 100
XXVI   A Point Gained 102
XXVII   The Text Witnesseth 105
XXVIII   An Intrusion 107
XXIX   In the Cellar 109
XXX   Investigation 111
XXXI   Strategy 113
XXXII   Relief 118

BOOK IV
THE BIRDS OF THE AIR

XXXIII	Lucetta	122
XXXIV	Conditions	130
XXXV	The Dove	131
XXXVI	An Hour of Startling Experiences	134
XXXVII	I Astonish Mr. Gryce and He Astonishes Me	144
XXXVIII	A Few Words	146
XXXIX	Under a Crimson Sky	148
XL	Explanations	154
	Epilogue	158

PREFACE

A word to my readers before they begin these pages.

As a woman of inborn principle and strict Presbyterian training, I hate deception and cannot abide subterfuge. This is why, after a year or more of hesitation, I have felt myself constrained to put into words the true history of the events surrounding the solution of that great mystery which made Lost Man's Lane the dread of the neighboring country. Feminine delicacy, and a natural shrinking from revealing to the world certain weaknesses on my part, inseparable from a true relation of this tale, led me to consent to the publication of that meagre and decidedly falsified account of the matter which has appeared in some of our leading papers.

But conscience has regained its sway in my breast, and with all due confidence in your forbearance, I herein take my rightful place in these annals, of whose interest and importance I now leave you to judge.

Amelia Butterworth
Gramercy Park, New York.

BOOK I

THE KNOLLYS FAMILY

A VISIT FROM MR. GRYCE

Ever since my fortunate—or shall I say unfortunate?—connection with that famous case of murder in Gramercy Park, I have had it intimated to me by many of my friends—and by some who were not my friends—that no woman who had met with such success as myself in detective work would ever be satisfied with a single display of her powers, and that sooner or later I would find myself again at work upon some other case of striking peculiarities.

As vanity has never been my foible, and as, moreover, I never have forsaken and never am likely to forsake the plain path marked out for my sex, at any other call than that of duty, I invariably responded to these insinuations by an affable but incredulous smile, striving to excuse the presumption of my friends by remembering their ignorance of my nature and the very excellent reasons I had for my one notable interference in the police affairs of New York City.

Besides, though I appeared to be resting quietly, if not in entire contentment, on my laurels, I was not so utterly removed from the old atmosphere of crime and its detection as the world in general considered me to be. Mr. Gryce still visited me; not on business, of course, but as a friend, for whom I had some regard; and naturally our conversation was not always confined to the weather or even to city politics, provocative as the latter subject is of wholesome controversy.

Not that he ever betrayed any of the secrets of his office—oh no; that would have been too much to expect—but he did sometimes mention the outward aspects of some celebrated case, and though I never ventured upon advice—I know too much for that, I hope—I found my wits more or less exercised by a conversation in which he gained much without acknowledging it, and I gave much without appearing conscious of the fact.

I was therefore finding life pleasant and full of interest, when suddenly (I had no right to expect it, and I do not blame myself for not expecting it or for holding my head so high at the prognostications of my friends) an opportunity came for a direct exercise of my detective powers in a line seemingly so laid out for me by Providence that I felt I would be slighting the Powers above if I refused to enter upon it, though now I see that the line was laid out for me by Mr. Gryce, and that I was obeying anything but the call of duty in following it.

But this is not explicit. One night Mr. Gryce came to my house looking older and more feeble than usual. He was engaged in a perplexing case, he said, and missed his early vigor and persistency. Would I like to hear about it? It was not in the line of his usual work, yet it had points—and well!—it would do him good to talk about it to a non-professional who was capable of sympathizing with its baffling and worrisome features and yet would never have to be told to hold her peace.

I ought to have been on my guard. I ought to have known the old fox well enough to feel certain that when he went so manifestly out of his way to take me into his confidence he did it for a purpose. But Jove nods now and then—

or so I have been assured on unimpeachable authority,—and if Jove has ever been caught napping, surely Amelia Butterworth may be pardoned a like inconsistency.

"It is not a city crime," Mr. Gryce went on to explain, and here he was base enough to sigh. "At my time of life this is an important consideration. It is no longer a simple matter for me to pack up a valise and go off to some distant village, way up in the mountains perhaps, where comforts are few and secrecy an impossibility. Comforts have become indispensable to my threescore years and ten, and secrecy—well, if ever there was an affair where one needs to go softly, it is this one; as you will see if you will allow me to give you the facts of the case as known at Headquarters to-day."

I bowed, trying not to show my surprise or my extreme satisfaction. Mr. Gryce assumed his most benignant aspect (always a dangerous one with him), and began his story.

II

I AM TEMPTED

"Some ninety miles from here, in a more or less inaccessible region, there is a small but interesting village, which has been the scene of so many unaccountable disappearances that the attention of the New York police has at last been directed to it. The village, which is at least two miles from any railroad, is one of those quiet, placid little spots found now and then among the mountains, where life is simple, and crime, to all appearance, an element so out of accord with every other characteristic of the place as to seem a complete anomaly. Yet crime, or some other hideous mystery almost equally revolting, has during the last five years been accountable for the disappearance in or about this village of four persons of various ages and occupations. Of these, three were strangers and one a well-known vagabond accustomed to tramp the hills and live on the bounty of farmers' wives. All were of the male sex, and in no case has any clue ever come to light as to their fate. That is the matter as it stands before the police to-day."

"A serious affair," I remarked. "Seems to me I have read of such things in novels. Is there a tumbled-down old inn in the vicinity where beds are made up over trap-doors?"

His smile was a mild protest against my flippancy.

"I have visited the town myself. There is no inn there, but a comfortable hotel of the most matter-of-fact sort, kept by the frankest and most open-minded of landlords. Besides, these disappearances, as a rule, did not take place at night, but in broad daylight. Imagine this street at noon. It is a short one, and you know every house on it, and you think you know every lurking-place. You see a man enter it at one end and you expect him to issue from it at the other. But suppose he never does. More than that, suppose he is never heard of again, and that this thing should happen in this one street four times during five years."

"I should move," I dryly responded.

"Would you? Many good people have moved from the place I speak of, but that has not helped matters. The disappearances go on just the same and the mystery continues."

"You interest me," I said. "Come to think of it, if this street were the scene of such an unexplained series of horrors as you have described, I do not think I should move."

"I thought not," he curtly rejoined. "But since you are interested in this matter, let me be more explicit in my statements. The first person whose disappearance was noted——"

"Wait," I interrupted. "Have you a map of the place?"

He smiled, nodded quite affectionately to a little statuette on the mantel-piece, which had had the honor of sharing his confidences in days gone by, but did not produce the map.

"That detail will keep," said he. "Let me go on with my story. As I was saying, madam, the first person whose disappearance was noted in this place was a peddler of small wares, accustomed to tramp the mountains. On this occasion he had been in town longer than usual, and was known to have sold fully half of his goods. Consequently he must have had quite a sum of money upon him. One day his pack was found lying under a cluster of bushes in a wood, but of him nothing was ever again heard. It made an excitement for a few days while the woods were being searched for his body, but, nothing having been discovered, he was forgotten, and everything went on as before, till suddenly public attention was again aroused by the pouring in of letters containing inquiries in regard to a young man who had been sent there from Duluth to collect facts in a law case, and who after a certain date had failed to communicate with his firm or show up at any of the places where he was known. Instantly the village was in arms. Many remembered the young man, and some two or three of the villagers could recall the fact of having seen him go up the street with his hand-bag in his hand as if on his way to the Mountain-station. The landlord of the hotel could fix the very day at which he left his house, but inquiries at the station failed to establish the fact that he took train from there, nor were the most minute inquiries into his fate ever attended by the least result. He was not known to have carried much money, but he carried a very handsome watch and wore a ring of more than ordinary value, neither of which has ever shown up at any pawnbroker's known to the police. This was three years ago.

"The next occurrence of a like character did not take place till a year after. This time it was a poor old man from Hartford, who vanished almost as it were before the eyes of these astounded villagers. He had come to town to get subscriptions for a valuable book issued by a well-known publisher. He had been more or less successful, and was looking very cheerful and contented, when one morning, after making a sale at a certain farmhouse, he sat down to dine with the family, it being close on to noon. He had eaten several mouthfuls and was chatting quite freely, when suddenly they saw him pause, clap his hand to his pocket, and rise up very much disturbed. 'I have left my pocket-book behind me at Deacon Spear's,' he cried. 'I cannot eat with it out of my possession. Excuse me if I go for it.' And without any further apologies, he ran out of the house and down the road in the direction of Deacon Spear's. He never reached Deacon Spear's, nor was he ever seen in that village again or in his home in Hartford. This was the most astonishing mystery of all. Within a half-mile's radius, in a populous country town, this man disappeared as if the road had swallowed him and closed again. It was marvellous, it was incredible, and remained so even after the best efforts of the country police to solve the mystery had exhausted themselves. After this, the town began to acquire a bad name, and one or two families moved away. Yet no one was found who was willing to admit that these various persons had been the victims of foul play till a month later another case came to light of a young man who had left the village for the hillside station, and had never arrived at that or any other destination so far as could be learned. As he was a distant relative of a wealthy cattle owner in Iowa, who came on post-haste to inquire into his nephew's fate, the excitement ran high, and through his efforts and that of one of the town's leading citizens, the services of our office were called into play. But the result has been nil. We have found neither the bodies of these men nor any clue to their fate."

"Yet you have been there?" I suggested.

He nodded.

"Wonderful! And you came upon no suspicious house, no suspicious person?"

The finger with which he was rubbing his eyeglasses went round and round the rims with a slower and slower and still more thoughtful motion.

"Every town has its suspicious-looking houses," he slowly remarked, "and, as for persons, the most honest often wear a lowering look in which an unbridled imagination can see guilt. I never trust to appearances of that kind."

"What else can you trust in, when a case is as impenetrable as this one?" I asked.

His finger, going slower and slower, suddenly stopped.

"In my knowledge of persons," he replied. "In my knowledge of their fears, their hopes, and their individual concerns. If I were twenty years younger"— here he stole a glance at me in the mirror which made me bridle; did he think I was only twenty years younger than himself?—"I would," he went on, "make myself so acquainted with every man, woman, and child there, that—" Here he drew himself up with a jerk. "But the day for that is passed," said he. "I am too old and too crippled to succeed in such an undertaking. Having been there once, I am a marked man. My very walk betrays me. He whose good fortune it will be to get at the bottom of these people's hearts must awaken no suspicions as to his connection with the police. Indeed, I do not think that any man can succeed in doing this now."

I started. This was a frank showing of his hand at least. No man! It was then a woman's aid he was after. I laughed as I thought of it. I had not thought him either so presumptuous or so appreciative of talents of a character so directly in line with his own.

"Don't you agree with me, madam?"

I did agree with him; but I had a character of great dignity to maintain, so I simply surveyed him with an air of well-tempered severity.

"I do not know of any woman who would undertake such a task," I calmly observed.

"No?" he smiled with that air of forbearance which is so exasperating to me. "Well, perhaps there isn't any such woman to be found. It would take one of very uncommon characteristics, I own."

"Pish!" I cried. "Not so very!"

"Indeed, I think you have not fully taken in the case," he urged in quiet superiority. "The people there are of the higher order of country folk. Many of them are of extreme refinement. One family"—here his tone changed a trifle—"is poor enough and cultivated enough to interest even such a woman as yourself."

"Indeed!" I ejaculated, with just a touch of my father's hauteur to hide the stir of curiosity his words naturally evoked.

"It is in some such home," he continued with an ease that should have warned me he had started on this pursuit with a quiet determination to win, "that the clue will be found to the mystery we are considering. Yes, you may well look startled, but that conclusion is the one thing I brought away with me from—X., let us say. I regard it as one of some moment. What do you think of it?"

"Well," I admitted, "it makes me feel like recalling that pish I uttered a few minutes ago. It would take a woman of uncommon characteristics to assist you in this matter."

"I am glad we have got that far," said he.

"A lady," I went on.

"Most assuredly a lady."

I paused. Sometimes discreet silence is more sarcastic than speech.

"Well, what lady would lend herself to this scheme?" I demanded at last.

The tap, tap of his fingers on the rim of his glasses was my only answer.

"I do not know of any," said I.

His eyebrows rose perhaps a hair's-breadth, but I noted the implied sarcasm, and for an instant forgot my dignity.

"Now," said I, "this will not do. You mean me, Amelia Butterworth; a woman who—but I do not think it is necessary to tell you either who or what I am. You have presumed, sir—Now do not put on that look of innocence, and above all do not attempt to deny what is so manifestly in your thoughts, for that would make me feel like showing you the door."

"Then," he smiled, "I shall be sure to deny nothing. I am not anxious to leave—yet. Besides, whom could I mean but you? A lady visiting friends in this remote and beautiful region—what opportunities might she not have to probe this important mystery if, like yourself, she had tact, discretion, excellent understanding, and an experience which if not broad or deep is certainly such as to give her a certain confidence in herself, and an undoubted influence with the man fortunate enough to receive her advice."

"Bah!" I exclaimed. It was one of his favorite expressions. That was perhaps why I used it. "One would think I was a member of your police."

"You flatter us too deeply," was his deferential answer. "Such an honor as that would be beyond our deserts."

To this I gave but the faintest sniff. That he should think that I, Amelia Butterworth, could be amenable to such barefaced flattery! Then I faced him with some asperity, and said bluntly: "You waste your time. I have no more intention of meddling in another affair than——"

"You had in meddling in the first," he politely, too politely, interpolated. "I understand, madam."

I was angry, but made no show of being so. I was not willing he should see that I could be affected by anything he could say.

"The Van Burnams are my next-door neighbors," I remarked sweetly. "I had the best of excuses for the interest I took in their affairs."

"So you had," he acquiesced. "I am glad to be reminded of the fact. I wonder I was able to forget it."

Angry now to the point of not being able to hide it, I turned upon him with firm determination.

"Let us talk of something else," I said.

But he was equal to the occasion. Drawing a folded paper from his pocket, he opened it out before my eyes, observing quite naturally: "That is a happy thought. Let us look over this sketch you were sharp enough to ask for a few moments ago. It shows the streets of the village and the places where each of the persons I have mentioned was last seen. Is not that what you wanted?"

I know that I should have drawn back with a frown, that I never should have allowed myself the satisfaction of casting so much as a glance toward the paper, but the human nature which links me to my kind was too much for me, and with an involuntary "Exactly!" I leaned over it with an eagerness I strove hard, even at that exciting moment, to keep within the bounds I thought proper to my position as a non-professional, interested in the matter from curiosity alone.

This is what I saw:

"Mr. Gryce," said I, after a few minutes' close contemplation of this diagram, "I do not suppose you want any opinion from me."

"Madam," he retorted, "it is all you have left me free to ask for."

Receiving this as a permission to speak, I put my finger on the road marked with a cross.

"Then," said I, "so far as I can gather from this drawing, all the disappearances seem to have taken place in or about this especial road."

"You are as correct as usual," he returned. "What you have said is so true, that the people of the vicinity have already given to this winding way a special cognomen of its own. For two years now it has been called Lost Man's Lane."

"Indeed!" I cried. "They have got the matter down as close as that, and yet have not solved its mystery? How long is this road?"

"A half mile or so."

I must have looked my disgust, for his hands opened deprecatingly.

"The ground has undergone a thorough search," said he. "Not a square foot in those woods you see on either side of the road, but has been carefully examined."

"And the houses? I see there are three houses on this road."

"Oh, they are owned by most respectable people—most respectable people," he repeated, with a lingering emphasis that gave me an inward shudder. "I think I had the honor of intimating as much to you a few minutes ago."

I looked at him earnestly, and irresistibly drew a little nearer to him over the diagram.

"Have none of these houses been visited by you?" I asked. "Do you mean to say you have not seen the inside of them all?"

"Oh," he replied, "I have been in them all, of course; but a mystery such as we are investigating is not written upon the walls of parlors or halls."

"You freeze my blood," was my uncharacteristic rejoinder. Somehow the sight of the homes indicated on this diagram seemed to bring me into more intimate sympathy with the affair.

His shrug was significant.

"I told you that this was no vulgar mystery," he declared; "or why should I be considering it with you? It is quite worthy of your interest. Do you see that house marked A?"

"I do," I nodded.

"Well, that is a decayed mansion of imposing proportions, set in a forest of overgrown shrubbery. The ladies who inhabit it——"

"Ladies!" I put in, with a small shock of horror.

"Young ladies," he explained, "of a refined if not over-prosperous appearance. They are the interesting residue of a family of some repute. Their father was a judge, I believe."

"And do they live there alone," I asked,—"two young ladies in a house so large and in a neighborhood so full of mystery?"

"Oh, they have a brother with them, a lout of no great attractions," he responded carelessly—too carelessly, I thought.

I made a note of the house A in my mind.

"And who lives in the house marked B?" I now queried.

"A Mr. Trohm. You will remember that it was through his exertions the services of the New York police were secured. His place there is one of the most interesting in town, and he does not wish to be forced to leave it, but he will be obliged to do so if the road is not soon relieved of its bad name; and so will Deacon Spear. The very children shun the road now. I do not know of a lonelier place."

"I see a little mark made here on the verge of the woods. What does that mean?"

"That stands for a hut—it can hardly be called a cottage—where a poor old woman lives called Mother Jane. She is a harmless imbecile, against whom no one has ever directed a suspicion. You may take your finger off that mark, Miss Butterworth."

I did so, but I did not forget that it stood very near the footpath branching off to the station.

"You entered this hut as well as the big houses?" I intimated.

"And found," was his answer, "four walls; nothing more."

I let my finger travel along the footpath I have just mentioned.

"Steep," was his comment. "Up, up, all the way, but no precipices. Nothing but pine woods on either side, thickly carpeted with needles."

My finger came back and stopped at the house marked M.

"Why is a letter affixed to this spot?" I asked.

"Because it stands at the head of the lane. Any one sitting at the window L can see whoever enters or leaves the lane at this end. And some one is always sitting there. The house contains two crippled children, a boy and a girl. One of them is always in that window."

"I see," said I. Then abruptly: "What do you think of Deacon Spear?"

"Oh, he's a well-meaning man, none too fine in his feelings. He does not mind the neighborhood; likes quiet, he says. I hope you will know him for yourself some day," the detective slyly added.

At this return to the forbidden subject, I held myself very much aloof.

"Your diagram is interesting," I remarked, "but it has not in the least changed my determination. It is you who will return to X., and that, very soon."

"Very soon?" he repeated. "Whoever goes there on this errand must go at once; to-night, if possible; if not, to-morrow at the latest."

"To-night! to-morrow!" I expostulated. "And you thought——"

"No matter what I thought," he sighed. "It seems I had no reason for my hopes." And folding up the map, he slowly rose. "The young man we have left there is doing more harm than good. That is why I say that some one of real ability must replace him immediately. The detective from New York must seem to have left the place."

I made him my most ladylike bow of dismissal.

"I shall watch the papers," I said. "I have no doubt that I shall soon be gratified by seeing in them some token of your success."

He cast a rueful look at his hands, took a painful step toward the door, and dolefully shook his head.

I kept my silence undisturbed.

He took another painful step, then turned.

"By the way," he remarked, as I stood watching him with an uncompromising air, "I have forgotten to mention the name of the town in which these disappearances have occurred. It is called X., and it is to be found on one of the spurs of the Berkshire Hills." And, being by this time at the door, he bowed himself out with all the insinuating suavity which distinguishes him at certain critical moments. The old fox was so sure of his triumph that he did not wait to witness it. He knew—how, it is easy enough for me to understand now—that X. was a place I had often threatened to visit. The family of one of my dearest friends lived there, the children of Althea Knollys. She had been my chum at school, and when she died I had promised myself not to let many months go by without making the acquaintance of her children. Alas! I had allowed years to elapse.

III

I SUCCUMB

That night the tempter had his own way with me. Without much difficulty he persuaded me that my neglect of Althea Burroughs' children was without any excuse; that what had been my duty toward them when I knew them to be left motherless and alone, had become an imperative demand upon me now that the town in which they lived had become overshadowed by a mystery which could not but affect the comfort and happiness of all its inhabitants. I could not wait a day. I recalled all that I had heard of poor Althea's short and none too happy marriage, and immediately felt such a burning desire to see if her dainty but spirited beauty—how well I remembered it—had been repeated in her daughters, that I found myself packing my trunk before I knew it.

I had not been from home for a long time—all the more reason why I should have a change now—and when I notified Mrs. Randolph and the servants of my intention of leaving on the early morning train, it created quite a sensation in the house.

But I had the best of explanations to offer. I had been thinking of my dead friend, and my conscience would not let me neglect her dear and possibly unhappy progeny any longer. I had purposed many times to visit X., and now I was going to do it. When I come to a decision, it is usually suddenly, and I never rest after having once made up my mind.

My sentiment went so far that I got down an old album and began hunting up the pictures I had brought away with me from boarding-school. Hers was among them, and I really did experience more or less compunction when I saw again the delicate yet daring features which had once had a very great influence over my mind. What a teasing sprite she was, yet what a will she had, and how strange it was that, having been so intimate as girls, we never knew anything of each other as women! Had it been her fault or mine? Was her marriage to blame for it or my spinsterhood? Difficult to tell then, impossible to tell now. I would not even think of it again, save as a warning. Nothing must stand between me and her children now that my attention has been called to them again.

I did not mean to take them by surprise—that is, not entirely. The invitation which they had sent me years ago was still in force, making it simply necessary for me to telegraph them that I had decided to make them a visit, and that they might expect me by the noon train. If in times gone by they had been properly instructed by their mother in regard to the character of her old friend, this need not put them out. I am not a woman of unbounded expectations. I do not look for the comforts abroad I am accustomed to find at home, and if, as I have reason to believe, their means are not of the greatest, they would only provoke me by any show of effort to make me feel at home in the humble cottage suited to their fortunes.

So the telegram was sent, and my preparations completed for an early departure.

But, resolved as I was to make this visit, my determination came near receiving a check. Just as I was leaving the house—at the very moment, in fact, when the hackman was carrying out my trunk, I perceived a man approaching me with every evidence of haste. He had a letter in his hand, which he held out to me as soon as he came within reach.

"For Miss Butterworth," he announced. "Private and immediate."

"Ah," thought I, "a communication from Mr. Gryce," and hesitated for a moment whether to open it on the spot or to wait and read it at my leisure on the cars. The latter course promised me less inconvenience than the first, for my hands were cumbered with the various small articles I consider indispensable to the comfortable enjoyment of the shortest journey, and the glasses without which I cannot read a word, were in the very bottom of my pocket under many other equally necessary articles.

But something in the man's expectant look warned me that he would never leave me till I had read the note, so with a sigh I called Lena to my aid, and after several vain attempts to reach my glasses, succeeded at last in pulling them out, and by their help reading the following hurried lines:

"Dear Madam:
"I send you this by a swifter messenger than myself. Do not let anything that I may have said last night influence you to leave your comfortable home. The adventure offers too many dangers for a woman. Read the inclosed. G."

The inclosed was a telegram from X., sent during the night, and evidently just received at Headquarters. Its contents were certainly not reassuring:

"Another person missing. Last seen in Lost Man's Lane. A harmless lad known as Silly Rufus. What's to be done? Wire orders. Trohm."

"Mr. Gryce bade me say that he would be up here some time before noon," said the man, seeing me look with some blankness at these words.

Nothing more was needed to restore my self-possession. Folding up the letter, I put it in my bag.

"Say to Mr. Gryce from me that my intended visit cannot be postponed," I replied. "I have telegraphed to my friends to expect me, and only a great emergency would lead me to disappoint them. I will be glad to receive Mr. Gryce on my return." And without further parley, I took my bundles back from Lena, and proceeded at once to the carriage. Why should I show any failure of courage at an event that was but a repetition of the very ones which made my visit necessary? Was I a likely person to fall victim to a mystery to which my eyes had been opened? Had I not been sufficiently warned of the dangers of Lost Man's Lane to keep myself at a respectable distance from the place of peril? I was going to visit the children of my once devoted friend. If there were perils of no ordinary nature to be encountered in so doing, was I not all the more called upon to lend them the support of my presence?

Yes, Mr. Gryce, and nothing now should hold me back. I even felt an increased desire to reach the scene of these mysteries, and chafed some at the length of the journey, which was of a more tedious character than I expected. A poor beginning for events requiring patience as well as great moral courage; but I little knew what was before me, and only considered that every moment spent on this hot and dusty train kept me thus much longer from the embraces of Althea's children.

I recovered my equanimity, however, as we approached X. The scenery was really beautiful, and the consciousness that I should soon alight at the mountain station which had played a more or less serious part in Mr. Gryce's narrative, awakened in me a pleasurable excitement which should have been a sufficient warning to me that the spirit of investigation which had led me so triumphantly through that affair next door had seized me again in a way that meant equal absorption if not equal success.

The number of small packages I carried gave me enough to think of at the moment of alighting, but as soon as I was safely again on terra firma I threw a hasty glance around to see if any of Althea's children were on hand to meet me.

I felt that I ought to know them at first glance. Their mother had been so characteristically pretty, she could not have failed to transmit some of her most charming traits to her offspring. But while there were two or three country maidens to be seen standing in and around the little pavilion known here as the Mountain-station, I saw no one who by any stretch of imagination could be regarded as of Althea Burroughs' blood or breeding.

Somewhat disappointed, for I had expected different results from my telegram, I stepped up to the station-master, and asked him whether I would have any difficulty in procuring a carriage to take me to Miss Knollys' house. He stared, it seemed to me, unnecessarily long, before replying.

"Waal," said he, "Simmons is usually here, but I don't see him around to-day. Perhaps some of these farmer lads will drive you in."

But they all drew back with a scared look, and I was beginning to tuck up my skirts preparatory to walking, when a little old man of exceedingly meek appearance drove up in a very old-fashioned coach, and with a hesitating air, springing entirely from bashfulness, managed to ask if I was Miss Butterworth. I hastened to assure him that I was that lady, whereupon he stammered out some words about Miss Knollys, and how sorry she was that she could not come for me herself. Then he pointed to his coach, and made me understand that I was to step into it and go with him.

This I had not counted upon doing, for I desired to both see and hear as much as possible before reaching my destination. There was but one way out of it. To his astonishment, I insisted that my belongings be put inside the coach, while I rode on the box.

It was an inauspicious beginning to a very doubtful adventure. I understood this when I saw the heads of the various onlookers draw together and many curious looks directed at both us and the conveyance that was to carry us. But I was in no mood to be daunted now, and mounting to the box with what grace I could, prepared myself for a ride into town.

But it seems I was not to be allowed to leave the spot without another warning. While the old man was engaged in fetching my trunk, the station-master approached me with great civility, and asked if it was my intention to spend a few days with the Misses Knollys. I told him that it was, and thinking it best to establish my position at once in the eyes of the whole town, added with a politeness equal to his own, that I was an old friend of the family, and had been coming to visit them for years, but had never found it convenient till now, and that I hoped they were all well and would be glad to see me.

His reply showed considerable embarrassment.

"Perhaps you have not heard that this village is under a cloud just now?"

"I have heard that one or two men have disappeared from here somewhat mysteriously," I returned. "Is that what you mean?"

"Yes, ma'am. One person, a boy, disappeared only two days ago."

"That's bad," I said. "But what has it to do with me?" I smilingly added, for I
saw that he was not at the end of his talk.

"Oh, nothing," he eagerly replied, "only I didn't know but you might be
timid——"

"Oh, I'm not at all timid," I hastened to interject. "If I were, I should not
have come here at all. Such matters don't affect me." And I spread out my
skirts and arranged myself for my ride with as much care and precision as if
the horrors he had mentioned had made no more impression upon me than if
his chat had been of the weather.

Perhaps I overdid it, for he looked at me for another moment in a curious,
lingering way; then he walked off, and I saw him enter the circle of gossips on
the platform, where he stood shaking his head as long as we were within sight.

My companion, who was the shyest man I ever saw, did not speak a word
while we were descending the hill. I talked, and endeavored to make him
follow my example, but his replies were mere grunts or half-syllables which
conveyed no information whatever. As we cleared the thicket, however, he
allowed himself an ejaculation or two as he pointed out the beauties of the
landscape. And indeed it was well worth his admiration and mine had my
mind been free to enjoy it. But the houses, which now began to appear on
either side of the way, drew my attention from the mountains. Though still
somewhat remote from the town, we were rapidly approaching the head of
that lane of evil fame with whose awe-inspiring history my thoughts were at
this time full. I was so anxious not to pass it without one look into its
grewsome recesses that I kept my head persistently turned that way till I felt I
was attracting the attention of my companion. As this was not desirable, I put
on a nonchalant look and began chatting about what I saw. But he had lapsed
into his early silence, and seemed wholly engrossed in his attempt to remove
with the butt-end of his whip a bit of rag which had somehow become
entangled in the spokes of one of the front wheels. The furtive look he cast me
as he succeeded in doing this struck me oddly at the moment, but it was too
small a matter to hold my attention long or to cause any cessation in the flow
of small talk with which I was endeavoring to enliven the situation.

My desire for conversation lagged, however, as I saw rising up before us the
dark boughs of a pine thicket. We were nearing Lost Man's Lane; we were
abreast of it; we were—yes, we were turning into it!

I could not repress an exclamation of dismay.

"Where are we going?" I asked.

"To Miss Knollys' house," he found words to say, with a sidelong glance at
me full of uneasy inquiry.

"Do they live on this road?" I cried, remembering with a certain shock Mr.
Gryce's suspicious description of the two young ladies who with their brother
inhabited the dilapidated mansion marked A in the map he had shown me.

"Where else?" was his laconic answer; and, obliged to be satisfied with this
curtest of curt replies, I drew myself up with just one longing look behind me
at the cheerful highway we were so rapidly leaving. A cottage, with an open
window, in which a child's head could be seen nodding eagerly toward me,
met my eyes and filled me with quite an odd sense of discomfort as I realized
that I had caught the attention of one of the little cripples who, according to
Mr. Gryce, always kept watch over this entrance into Lost Man's Lane.

Another moment and the pine branches had shut the vision out, but I did not soon forget that eager, childish face and pointing hand, marking me out as a possible victim to the horrors of this ill-reputed lane. But I was aware of no secret flinching from the adventure into which I was plunging. On the contrary, I felt a strange and fierce delight in thus being thrust into the very heart of the mystery I had only expected to approach by degrees. The warning message sent me by Mr. Gryce had acquired a deeper and more significant meaning, as did the looks which had been cast me by the station-master and his gossips on the hillside, but in my present mood these very tokens of the serious nature of my undertaking only gave an added spur to my courage. I felt my brain clear and my heart expand, as if at this moment, before I had so much as set eyes on the faces of these young people, I recognized the fact that they were the victims of a web of circumstances so tragic and incomprehensible that only a woman like myself would be able to dissipate them and restore these girls to the confidence of the people around them.

I forgot that these girls had a brother and that—But not a word to forestall the truth. I wish this story to grow upon you just as it did upon me, and with just as little preparation.

The farmer who drove me, and who I afterwards learned was called Simsbury, showed a certain dogged interest in my behavior that would have amused me, or, at least, have awakened my disdain under circumstances of a less thrilling nature. I saw his eye roll in a sort of wonder over my person, which may have been held a little more stiffly than was necessary, and settle finally on my face, with a look I might have thought complimentary had I had any thought to bestow on such matters. Not till we had passed the path branching up through the woods toward the mountain did he see fit to withdraw it, nor did I fail to find it fixed again upon me as we rode by the little hut occupied by the old woman considered so harmless by Mr. Gryce.

Perhaps he had a reason for this, as I was very much interested in this hut and its occupant, about whom I felt free to cherish my own secret doubts—so interested that I cast it a very sharp glance, and was glad when I caught a glimpse through the doorway of the old crone mumbling over a piece of bread she was engaged in eating as we passed her.

"That's Mother Jane," explained my companion, breaking the silence of many minutes. "And yonder is Miss Knollys' house," he added, lifting his whip and pointing toward the half-concealed façade of a large and pretentious dwelling a few rods farther on down the road. "She will be powerful glad to see you, Miss. Company is scarce in these parts."

Astonished at this sudden launch into conversation by one whose reserve I had hitherto found it impossible to penetrate, I gave him the affable answer he evidently expected, and then looked eagerly toward the house. It was as Mr. Gryce had intimated, exceedingly forbidding even at that distance, and as we approached nearer and I was given a full view of its worn and discolored front, I felt myself forced to acknowledge that never in my life had my eyes fallen upon a habitation more given over to neglect or less promising in its hospitality.

Had it not been for the thin circle of smoke eddying up from one of its broken chimneys, I would have looked upon the place as one which had not known the care or presence of man for years. There was a riot of shrubbery in the yard, a lack of the commonest attention to order in the way the vines drooped in tangled masses over the face of the desolate porch, that gave to the broken pilasters and decayed window-frames of this dreariest of façades that look of abandonment which only becomes picturesque when nature has usurped the prerogative of man and taken entirely to herself the empty walls and falling casements of what was once a human dwelling. That any one should be living in it now and that I, who have never been able to see a chair standing crooked or a curtain awry, without a sensation of the keenest discomfort, should be on the point of deliberately entering its doors as an inmate, filled me at the moment with such a sense of unreality, that I descended from the carriage in a sort of a dream and was making my way through one of the gaps in the high antique fence that separated the yard from the gateway, when Mr. Simsbury stopped me and pointed out the gate.

I did not think it worth while to apologize for my mistake, for the broken palings certainly offered as good an entrance as the gate, which had slipped from its hinges and hung but a few inches open. But I took the course he indicated, holding up my skirts, and treading gingerly for fear of the snails and toads that incumbered such portions of the path as the weeds had left visible. As I proceeded on my way, something in the silence of the spot struck me. Was I becoming over-sensitive to impressions or was there something really uncanny in the absolute lack of sound or movement in a dwelling of such dimensions? But I should not have said movement, for at that instant I saw a flash in one of the upper windows as of a curtain being stealthily drawn and as stealthily let fall again, and though it gave me the promise of some sort of greeting, there was a furtiveness in the action, so in keeping with the suspicions of Mr. Gryce that I felt my nerves braced at once to mount the half-dozen uninviting-looking steps that led to the front door.

But no sooner had I done this, with what I am fain to consider my best air, than I suddenly collapsed with what I am bound to regard as a comprehensible and quite excusable fear; for, while I do not quail before men, and have a reasonable fortitude in the presence of most dangers, corporeal and moral, I am not quite myself in face of a rampant and barking dog. It is my one weakness, and while I usually can, and under most circumstances do, succeed in hiding my inner trepidation under the emergency just mentioned, I always feel that it would be a happy relief for me if the day should ever come when these so-called domestic animals would be banished from the affections and homes of men. Then I think I would begin to live in good earnest and perhaps enjoy trips into the country, which now, for all my apparent bravery, I regard more in the light of a penance than a pleasure.

Imagine, then, how hard I found it to retain my self-possession or even any appearance of dignity, when at the moment I was stretching forth my hand toward the knocker of this inhospitable mansion I heard rising from some unknown quarter a howl so keen, piercing, and prolonged that it frightened the very birds over my head and sent them flying from the vines in clouds.

It was the unhappiest kind of welcome for me. I did not know whether it came from within or without, and when after a moment of indecision I saw the door open, I am not sure whether the smile I called up to grace the occasion had any of the real Amelia Butterworth in it, so much was my mind divided between a desire to produce a favorable impression and a very decided and not-to-be-hidden fear of the dog who had greeted my arrival with such an ominous howl.

"Call off the dog!" I cried almost before I saw what sort of person I was addressing.

Mr. Gryce, when I saw him later, declared this to be the most significant introduction I could have made of myself upon entering the Knollys mansion.

IV

A GHOSTLY INTERIOR

The hall into which I had stepped was so dark that for a few minutes I could see nothing but the indistinct outline of a young woman with a very white face. She had uttered some sort of murmur at my words, but for some reason was strangely silent, and, if I could trust my eyes, seemed rather to be looking back over her shoulder than into the face of her advancing guest. This was odd, but before I could quite satisfy myself as to the cause of her abstraction, she suddenly bethought herself, and throwing open the door of an adjoining room, let in a stream of light by which we were enabled to see each other and exchange the greetings suitable to the occasion.

"Miss Butterworth, my mother's old friend," she murmured, with an almost pitiful effort to be cordial, "we are so glad to have you visit us. Won't you—won't you sit down?"

What did it mean? She had pointed to a chair in the sitting-room, but her face was turned away again as if drawn irresistibly toward some secret object of dread. Was there anyone or anything at the top of the dim staircase I could faintly see in the distance? It would not do for me to ask, nor was it wise for me to show that I thought this reception a strange one. Stepping into the room she pointed out, I waited for her to follow me, which she did with manifest reluctance. But when she was once out of the atmosphere of the hall, or out of reach of the sight or sound of whatever it was that frightened her, her face took on a smile that ingratiated her with me at once and gave to her very delicate aspect, which up to that moment had not suggested the remotest likeness to her mother, a piquant charm and subtle fascination that were not unworthy of the daughter of Althea Burroughs.

"You must not mind the poverty of your welcome," she said, with a half-proud, half-apologetic look around her, which I must say the bareness and shabby character of the room we were in fully justified. "We have not been very well off since father died and mother left us. Had you given us a chance we should have written you that our home would not offer many inducements to you after your own, but you have come unexpectedly and——"

"There, there," I put in, for I saw that her embarrassment would soon get the better of her, "do not speak of it. I did not come to enjoy your home, but to see you. Are you the eldest, my dear, and where are your sister and brother?"

"I am not the eldest," she said. "I am Lucetta. My sister"—here her head stole irresistibly back to its old position of listening—"will—will come soon. My brother is not in the house."

"Well," said I, astonished that she did not ask me to take off my things, "you are a pretty girl, but you do not look very strong. Are you quite well, my dear?"

She started, looked at me eagerly, almost anxiously, for a moment, then straightened herself and began to lose some of her abstraction.

"I am not a strong person," she smiled, "but neither am I so very weak either. I was always small. So was my mother, you know."

I was glad to have her talk of her mother. I therefore answered her in a way to prolong the conversation.

"Yes, your mother was small," I admitted, "but never thin or pallid. She was like a fairy among us schoolgirls. Does it seem odd to hear so old a woman as I speak of herself as a schoolgirl?"

"Oh, no!" she said, but there was no heart in her voice.

"I had almost forgotten those days till I happened to hear the name of Althea mentioned the other day," I proceeded, seeing I must keep up the conversation if we were not to sit in total silence. "Then my early friendship with your mother recurred to me, and I started up—as I always do when I come to any decision, my dear—and sent that telegram, which I hope I have not followed by an unwelcome presence."

"Oh, no," she repeated, but this time with some feeling; "we need friends, and if you will overlook our shortcomings—But you have not taken off your hat. What will Loreen say to me?"

And with a sudden nervous action as marked as her late listlessness, she jumped up and began busying herself over me, untying my bonnet and laying aside my bundles, which up to this moment I had held in my hands.

"I—I am so absent-minded," she murmured. "I—I did not think—I hope you will excuse me. Loreen would have given you a much better welcome."

"Then Loreen should have been here," I said, with a smile. I could not restrain this slight rebuke, yet I liked the girl; notwithstanding everything I had heard and her own odd and unaccountable behavior, there was a sweetness in her face, when she chose to smile, that proved an irresistible attraction. And then, for all her absent-mindedness and abstracted ways, she was such a lady! Her plain dress, her restrained manner, could not hide this fact. It was apparent in every line of her thin but graceful form and in every inflection of her musical but constrained voice. Had I seen her in my own parlor instead of between these bare and moldering walls, I should have said the same thing: "She is such a lady!" But this only passed through my mind at the time. I was not studying her personality, but trying to understand why my presence in the house had so visibly disturbed her. Was it the embarrassment of poverty, not knowing how to meet the call made so suddenly upon it? I hardly thought so. Fear would not enter into a sensation of this kind, and fear was what I had seen in her face before the front door had closed upon me. But that fear? Was it connected with me or with something threatening her from another portion of the house?

The latter supposition seemed the probable one. The way her ear was turned, the slight start she gave at every sound, convinced me that her cause of dread lay elsewhere than with myself, and therefore was worthy of my closest attention. Though I chatted and tried in every way to arouse her confidence, I could not help asking myself between the sentences, if the cause of her apprehension lay with her sister, her brother, or in something entirely apart from either, and connected with the dreadful matter which had drawn me to X. Or another supposition still, was it merely the sign of an habitual distemper which, misunderstood by Mr. Gryce, had given rise to the suspicions which it was my possible mission here to dispel?

Anxious to force things a little, I remarked, with a glance at the dismal branches that almost forced their way into the open casements: "What a scene for young eyes like yours! Do you never get tired of these pine-boughs and clustering shadows? Would not a little cottage in the sunnier part of the town be preferable to all this dreary grandeur?"

She looked up with sudden wistfulness that made her smile piteous.

"Some of my happiest days have been passed here and some of my saddest. I do not think I should like to leave it for any sunny cottage. We were not made for bonny homes," she continued. "The sombreness of this old house suits us."

"And of this road," I ventured. "It is the darkest and most picturesque I ever rode through. I thought I was threading a wilderness."

For a moment she forgot her cause of anxiety and looked at me quite intently, while a subtle shade of doubt passed slowly over her features.

"It is a solitary one," she acquiesced. "I do not wonder it struck you as dismal. Have you heard—has any one ever told you that—that it was not considered quite safe?"

"Safe?" I repeated, with—God forgive me!—an expression of mild wonder in my eyes.

"Yes, it has not the best of reputations. Strange things have happened in it. I thought that some one might have been kind enough to tell you this at the station."

There was a gentle sort of sarcasm in the tone; only that, or so it seemed to me at the time. I began to feel myself in a maze.

"Somebody—I suppose it was the station-master—did say something to me about a boy lost somewhere in this portion of the woods. Do you mean that, my dear?"

She nodded, glancing again over her shoulder and partly rising as if moved by some instinct of flight.

"They are dark enough, for more than one person to have been lost in their recesses," I observed with another look toward the heavily curtained windows.

"They certainly are," she assented, reseating herself and eying me nervously while she spoke. "We are used to the terrors they inspire in strangers, but if you"—she leaped to her feet in manifest eagerness and her whole face changed in a way she little realized herself—"if you have any fear of sleeping amid such gloomy surroundings, we can procure you a room in the village where you will be more comfortable, and where we can visit you almost as well as we can here. Shall I do it? Shall I call——"

My face must have assumed a very grim look, for her words tripped at that point, and a flush, the first I had seen on her cheek, suffused her face, giving her an appearance of great distress.

"Oh, I wish Loreen would come! I am not at all happy in my suggestions," she said, with a deprecatory twitch of her lip that was one of her subtle charms. "Oh, there she is! Now I may go," she cried; and without the least appearance of realizing that she had said anything out of place, she rushed from the room almost before her sister had entered it.

But not before their eyes had met in a look of unusual significance.

V

A STRANGE HOUSEHOLD

Had I not surprised this look of mutual understanding, I might have received an impression of Miss Knollys which would in a measure have counteracted that made by the more nervous and less restrained Lucetta. The dignified reserve of her bearing, the quiet way in which she approached, and, above all, the even tones in which she uttered her welcome, were such as to win my confidence and put me at my ease in the house of which she was the nominal mistress. But that look! With that in my memory, I was enabled to pierce below the surface of this placid nature, and in the very constraint she put upon herself, detect the presence of the same secret uneasiness which had been so openly, if unconsciously, manifested by her sister.

She was more beautiful than Lucetta in form and feature, and even more markedly elegant in her plain black gown and fine lawn ruffles, but she lacked her sister's evanescent charm, and though admirable to all appearance, was less lovable on a short acquaintance.

But this delays my tale, which is one of action rather than reflection. I had naturally expected that with the appearance of the elder Miss Knollys I should be taken to my room; but, on the contrary, she sat down and with an apologetic air informed me that she was sorry she could not show me the customary attentions. Circumstances over which she had no control had made it impossible, she said, for her to offer me the guest-chamber, but if I would be so good as to accept another for this one night, she would endeavor to provide me with better accommodations on the morrow.

Satisfied of the almost painful nature of their poverty and determined to submit to privations rather than leave a house so imbued with mystery, I hastened to assure her that any room would be acceptable to me; and with a display of good feeling not wholly insincere, began to gather up my wraps in anticipation of being taken at once up-stairs.

But Miss Knollys again surprised me by saying that my room was not yet ready; that they had not been able to complete all their arrangements, and begged me to make myself at home in the room where I was till evening.

As this was asking a good deal of a woman of my years, fresh from a railroad journey and with natural habits of great neatness and order, I felt somewhat disconcerted, but hiding my feelings in consideration of reasons before given, replaced my bundles on the table and endeavored to make the best of a somewhat trying situation.

Launching at once into conversation, I began, as with Lucetta, to talk about her mother. I had never known, save in the vaguest way, why Mrs. Knollys had taken the journey which had ended in her death and burial in a foreign land. Rumor had it that she had gone abroad for her health which had begun to fail after the birth of Lucetta; but as Rumor had not added why she had gone unaccompanied by her husband or children, there remained much which these girls might willingly tell me, which would be of the greatest interest to me. But Miss Knollys, intentionally or unintentionally, assumed an air so cold at my well meant questions, that I desisted from pressing them, and began to talk about myself in a way which I hoped would establish really friendly relations between us and make it possible for her to tell me later, if not at the present moment, what it was that weighed so heavily upon the household, that no one could enter this home without feeling the shadow of the secret terror enveloping it.

But Miss Knollys, while more attentive to my remarks than her sister had been, showed, by certain unmistakable signs, that her heart and interest were anywhere but in that room; and while I could not regard this as throwing any discredit upon my powers of pleasing—which have rarely failed when I have exerted them to their utmost,—I still could not but experience the dampening effect of her manner. I went on chatting, but in a desultory way, noting all that was odd in her unaccountable reception of me, but giving, as I firmly believe, no evidence of my concern and rapidly increasing curiosity.

The peculiarities observable in this my first interview with these interesting but by no means easily-to-be-understood sisters continued all day. When one sister came in, the other stepped out, and when dinner was announced and I was ushered down the bare and dismal hall into an equally bare and unattractive dining-room, it was to find the chairs set for four, and Lucetta only seated at the table.

"Where is Loreen?" I asked wonderingly, as I took the seat she pointed out to me with one of her faint and quickly vanishing smiles.

"She cannot come at present," my young hostess stammered with an unmistakable glance of distress at the large, hearty-looking woman who had summoned me to the dining-room.

"Ah," I ejaculated, thinking that possibly Loreen had found it necessary to assist in the preparation of the meal, "and your brother?"

It was the first time he had been mentioned since my first inquiries. I had shrunk from the venture out of a motive of pure compassion, and they had not seen fit to introduce his name into any of our conversations. Consequently I awaited her response, with some anxiety, having a secret premonition that in some way he was at the bottom of my strange reception.

Her hasty answer, given, however, without any increase of embarrassment, somewhat dispelled this supposition.

"Oh, he will be in presently," said she. "William is never very punctual."

But when he did come in, I could not help seeing that her manner instantly changed and became almost painfully anxious. Though it was my first meeting with the real head of the house, she waited for an interchange of looks with him before giving me the necessary introduction, and when, this duty performed, he took his seat at the table, her thoughts and attention remained so fixed upon him that she well-nigh forgot the ordinary civilities of a hostess. Had it not been for the woman I have spoken of, who in her good-natured attention to my wants amply made up for the abstraction of her mistress, I should have fared ill at this meal, good and ample as it was, considering the resources of those who provided it.

She seemed to dread to have him speak, almost to have him move. She watched him with her lips half open, ready, as it appeared, to stop any inadvertent expression he might utter in his efforts to be agreeable. She even kept her left hand disengaged, with the evident intention of stretching it out in his direction if in his lumbering stupidity he should utter a sentence calculated to open my eyes to what she so passionately desired to have kept secret. I saw it all as plainly as I saw his heavy indifference to her anxiety; and knowing from experience that it is in just such stolid louts as these that the worst passions are often hidden, I took advantage of my years and forced a conversation in which I hoped some flash of his real self would appear, despite her wary watch upon him.

Not liking to renew the topic of the lane itself, I asked with a very natural show of interest, who was their nearest neighbor. It was William who looked up and William who answered.

"Old Mother Jane is the nearest," said he; "but she's no good. We never think of her. Mr. Trohm is the only neighbor I care for. Such peaches as the old fellow raises! Such grapes! Such melons! He gave me two of the nicest you ever saw this morning. By Jupiter, I taste them yet!"

Lucetta's face, which should have crimsoned with mortification, turned most unaccountably pale. Yet not so pale as it had previously done when, a few minutes before, he began to say, "Loreen wants some of this soup saved for"—and stopped awkwardly, conscious perhaps that Loreen's wants should not be mentioned before me.

"I thought you promised me that you would never again ask Mr. Trohm for any of his fruit," remonstrated Lucetta.

"Oh, I didn't ask! I just stood at the fence and looked over. Mr. Trohm and I are good friends. Why shouldn't I eat his fruit?"

The look she gave him might have moved a stone, but he seemed perfectly impervious to it. Seeing him so stolid, her head drooped, and she did not answer a word. Yet somehow I felt that even while she was so manifestly a prey to the deepest mortification, her attention was not wholly given over to this one emotion. There was something else she feared. Hoping to relieve her and lighten the situation, I forced myself to smile on the young man as I said:

"Why don't you raise melons yourself? I think if I possessed your land I should be anxious to raise everything I could on it."

"Oh, you're a woman!" he retorted, almost roughly. "It's good business for women; and for men, too, perhaps, who love to see fruit hang, but I only care to eat it."

"Don't," Lucetta put in, but not with the vigor I had expected.

"I like to hunt, train dogs, and enjoy other people's fruit," he laughed, with a nod at the blushing Lucetta. "I don't see any use in a man's putting himself out for things he can get for the asking. Life's too short for such folly. I mean to have a good time while I'm on this blessed sphere."

"William!"

The cry was irresistible, yet it was not the cry I had been looking for. Painful as was this exhibition of his stupidity and utter want of feeling, it was not the one thing she stood in dread of, or why was her protest so much weaker than her appearance had given token of?

"Oh!" he shouted in great amusement, while she shrunk back with a horrified look. "Lucetta don't like to hear me say that. She thinks a man ought to work, plow, harrow, dig, make a slave of himself, to keep up a place that's no good anyway. But I tell her that work is something she'll never get out of me. I was born a gentleman, and a gentleman I will live if the place tumbles down over our heads. Perhaps it would be the best way to get rid of it. Then I could go live with Mr. Trohm, and have melons from early morn till late at night." And again his coarse laugh rang out.

This, or was it his words, seemed to rouse her as nothing had done before. Thrusting out her hand, she laid it on his mouth, with a look of almost frenzied appeal at the woman who was standing at his back.

"Mr. William, how can you!" that woman protested; and when he would have turned upon her angrily, she leaned over and whispered in his ear a few words that seemed to cow him, for he gave a short grunt through his sister's trembling fingers and, with a shrug of his heavy shoulders, subsided into silence.

To all this I was a simple spectator, but I did not soon forget a single feature of the scene.

The remainder of the dinner passed quietly, William and myself eating with more or less heartiness, Lucetta tasting nothing at all. In mercy to her I declined coffee, and as soon as William gave token of being satisfied, we hurriedly rose. It was the most uncomfortable meal I ever ate in my life.

VI

A SOMBRE EVENING

The evening, like the afternoon, was spent in the sitting-room with one of the sisters. One event alone is worth recording. I had become excessively tired of a conversation that always languished, no matter on what topic it started, and, observing an old piano in one corner—I once played very well—I sat down before it and impulsively struck a few chords from the yellow keys. Instantly Lucetta—it was Lucetta who was with me then—bounded to my side with a look of horror.

"Don't do that!" she cried, laying her hand on mine to stop me. Then, seeing my look of dignified astonishment, she added with an appealing smile, "I beg pardon, but every sound goes through me to-night."

"Are you not well?" I asked.

"I am never very well," she returned, and we went back to the sofa and renewed our forced and pitiful attempts at conversation.

Promptly at nine o'clock Miss Knollys came in. She was very pale and cast, as usual, a sad and uneasy look at her sister before she spoke to me. Immediately Lucetta rose, and, becoming very pale herself, was hurrying toward the door when her sister stopped her.

"You have forgotten," she said, "to say good-night to our guest."

Instantly Lucetta turned, and, with a sudden, uncontrollable impulse, seized my hand and pressed it convulsively.

"Good-night," she cried. "I hope you will sleep well," and was gone before I could say a word in response.

"Why does Lucetta go out of the room when you come in?" I asked, determined to know the reason for this peculiar conduct. "Have you any other guests in the house?"

The reply came with unexpected vehemence. "No," she cried, "why should you think so? There is no one here but the family." And she turned away with a dignity she must have inherited from her father, for Althea Burroughs had every interesting quality but that. "You must be very tired," she remarked. "If you please we will go now to your room."

I rose at once, glad of the prospect of seeing the upper portion of the house. She took my wraps on her arm, and we passed immediately into the hall. As we did so, I heard voices, one of them shrill and full of distress; but the sound was so quickly smothered by a closing door that I failed to discover whether this tone of suffering proceeded from a man or a woman.

Miss Knollys, who was preceding me, glanced back in some alarm, but as I gave no token of having noticed anything out of the ordinary, she speedily resumed her way up-stairs. As the sounds I had heard proceeded from above, I followed her with alacrity, but felt my enthusiasm diminish somewhat when I found myself passing door after door down a long hall to a room as remote as possible from what seemed to be the living portion of the house.

"Is it necessary to put me off quite so far?" I asked, as my young hostess paused and waited for me to join her on the threshold of the most forbidding room it had ever been my fortune to enter.

The blush which mounted to her brow showed that she felt the situation keenly.

"I am sure," she said, "that it is a matter of great regret to me to be obliged to offer you so mean a lodging, but all our other rooms are out of order, and I cannot accommodate you with anything better to-night."

"But isn't there some spot nearer you?" I urged. "A couch in the same room with you would be more acceptable to me than this distant room."

"I—I hope you are not timid," she began, but I hastened to disabuse her mind on this score.

"I am not afraid of any earthly thing but dogs," I protested warmly. "But I do not like solitude. I came here for companionship, my dear. I really would like to sleep with one of you."

This, to see how she would meet such urgency. She met it, as I might have known she would, by a rebuff.

"I am very sorry," she again repeated, "but it is quite impossible. If I could give you the comforts you are accustomed to, I should be glad, but we are unfortunate, we girls, and—" She said no more, but began to busy herself about the room, which held but one object that had the least look of comfort in it. That was my trunk, which had been neatly placed in one corner.

"I suppose you are not used to candles," she remarked, lighting what struck me as a very short end, from the one she held in her hand.

"My dear," said I, "I can accommodate myself to much that I am not used to. I have very few old maid's ways or notions. You shall see that I am far from being a difficult guest."

She heaved a sigh, and then, seeing my eye travelling slowly over the gray discolored walls which were not relieved by so much as a solitary print, she pointed to a bell-rope near the head of the bed, and considerately remarked:

"If you wish anything in the night, or are disturbed in any way, pull that. It communicates with my room, and I will be only too glad to come to you."

I glanced up at the rope, ran my eye along the wire communicating with it, and saw that it was broken sheer off before it even entered into the wall.

"I am afraid you will not hear me," I answered, pointing to the break.

She flushed a deep scarlet, and for a moment looked as embarrassed as ever her sister had done.

"I did not know," she murmured. "The house is so old, everything is more or less out of repair." And she made haste to quit the room.

I stepped after her in grim determination.

"But there is no key to the door," I objected.

She came back with a look that was as nearly desperate as her placid features were capable of.

"I know," she said, "I know. We have nothing. But if you are not afraid—and of what could you be afraid in this house, under our protection, and with a good dog outside?—you will bear with things to-night, and—Good God!" she murmured, but not so low but that my excited sense caught every syllable, "can she have heard? Has the reputation of this place gone abroad? Miss Butterworth," she repeated earnestly, "the house contains no cause of terror for you. Nothing threatens our guest, nor need you have the least concern for yourself or us, whether the night passes in quiet or whether it is broken by unaccountable sounds. They will have no reference to anything in which you are interested."

"Ah, ha," thought I, "won't they! You give me credit for much indifference, my dear." But I said nothing beyond a few soothing phrases, which I made purposely short, seeing that every moment I detained her was just so much unnecessary torture to her. Then I went back to my room and carefully closed the door. My first night in this dismal and strangely ordered house had opened anything but propitiously.

VII

THE FIRST NIGHT

I spoke with a due regard to truth when I assured Miss Knollys that I entertained no fears at the prospect of sleeping apart from the rest of the family. I am a woman of courage—or so I have always believed—and at home occupy my second floor alone without the least apprehension. But there is a difference in these two abiding-places, as I think you are ready by this time to acknowledge, and, though I felt little of what is called fear, I certainly did not experience my usual satisfaction in the minute preparations with which I am accustomed to make myself comfortable for the night. There was a gloom both within and without the four bare walls between which I now found myself shut, which I would have been something less than human not to feel, and though I had no dread of being overcome by it, I was glad to add something to the cheer of the spot by opening my trunk and taking out a few of those little matters of personal equipment without which the brightest room looks barren and a den like this too desolate for habitation.

Then I took a good look about me to see how I could obtain for myself some sense of security. The bed was light and could be pulled in front of the door. This was something. There was but one window, and that was closely draped with some thick, dark stuff, very funereal in its appearance. Going to it, I pulled aside the thick folds and looked out. A mass of heavy foliage at once met my eye, obstructing the view of the sky and adding much to the lonesomeness of the situation. I let the curtain fall again and sat down in a chair to think.

The shortness of the candle-end with which I had been provided had struck me as significant, so significant that I had not allowed it to burn long after Miss Knollys had left me. If these girls, charming, no doubt, but sly, had thought to shorten my watch by shortening my candle, I would give them no cause to think but that their ruse had been successful. The foresight which causes me to add a winter wrap to my stock of clothing even when the weather is at the hottest, leads me to place a half dozen or so of candles in my travelling trunk, and so I had only to open a little oblong box in the upper tray to have the means at my disposal of keeping a light all night.

So far, so good. I had a light, but had I anything else in case William Knollys—but with this thought Miss Knollys's look and reassuring words recurred to me. "Whatever you may hear—if you hear anything—will have no reference to yourself and need not disturb you."

This was comforting certainly, from a selfish standpoint; but did it relieve my mind concerning others?

Not knowing what to think of it all, and fully conscious that sleep would not visit me under existing circumstances, I finally made up my mind not to lie down till better assured that sleep on my part would be desirable. So after making the various little arrangements already alluded to, I drew over my shoulders a comfortable shawl and set myself to listen for what I feared would be more than one dreary hour of this not to be envied night.

And here just let me stop to mention that, carefully considered as all my precautions were, I had forgotten one thing upon leaving home which at this minute made me very nearly miserable. I had not included among my effects the alcohol lamp and all the other private and particular conveniences which I possess for making tea in my own apartment. Had I but had them with me, and had I been able to make and sip a cup of my own delicious tea through the ordeal of listening for whatever sounds might come to disturb the midnight stillness of this house, what relief it would have been to my spirits and in what a different light I might have regarded Mr. Gryce and the mission with which I had been intrusted. But I not only lacked this element of comfort, but the satisfaction of thinking that it was any one's fault but my own. Lena had laid her hand on that teapot, but I had shaken my head, fearing that the sight of it might offend the eyes of my young hostesses. But I had not calculated upon being put in a remote corner like this of a house large enough to accommodate a dozen families, and if ever I travel again——

But this is a matter personal to Amelia Butterworth, and of no interest to you. I will not inflict my little foibles upon you again.

Eleven o'clock came and went. I had heard no sound. Twelve, and I began to think that all was not quite so still as before; that I certainly could hear now and then faint noises as of a door creaking on its hinges, or the smothered sound of stealthily moving feet. Yet all was so far from being distinct, that for some time I hesitated to acknowledge to myself that anything could be going on in the house, which was not to be looked for in a home professing to be simply the abode of a decent young man and two very quiet-appearing young ladies; and even after the noises and whispering had increased to such an extent that I could even distinguish the sullen tones of the brother from the softer and more carefully modulated accents of Lucetta and her sister, I found myself ready to explain the matter by any conjecture short of that which involved these delicate young ladies in any scheme of secret wickedness.

But when I found there was likely to be no diminution in the various noises and movements that were taking place in the front of the house, and that only something much out of the ordinary could account for so much disturbance in a country home so long after midnight, I decided that only a person insensible to all sight and sound could be expected to remain asleep under such circumstances, and that I would be perfectly justified in their eyes in opening my door and taking a peep down the corridor. So without further ado, I drew my bed aside and glanced out.

All was perfectly dark and silent in the great house. The only light visible came from the candle burning in the room behind me, and as for sound, it was almost too still—it was the stillness of intent rather than that of natural repose.

This was so unexpected that for an instant I stood baffled and wondering. Then my nose went up, and I laughed quietly to myself. I could see nothing and I could hear nothing; but Amelia Butterworth, like most of her kind, boasts of more than two senses, and happily there was something to smell. A quickly blown-out candle leaves a witness behind it to sensitive nostrils like mine, and this witness assured me that the darkness was deceptive. Some one had just passed the head of my corridor with a light, and because the light was extinguished it did not follow that the person who held it was far away. Indeed, I thought that now I heard a palpitating breath.

"Humph," I cried aloud, but as if in unconscious communion with myself, "it is not often I have so vivid a dream! I was sure that I heard steps in the hall. I fear I'm growing nervous."

Nothing moved. No one answered me.

"Miss Knollys!" I called firmly.

No reply.

"Lucetta, dear!"

I thought this appeal would go unanswered also, but when I raised my voice for the third time, a sudden rushing sound took place down the corridor, and Lucetta's excited figure, fully dressed, appeared in the faint circle of light caused by my now rapidly waning candle.

"Miss Butterworth, what is the matter?" she asked, making as if she would draw me into my room—a proceeding which I took good care she should not succeed in.

Giving a glance at her dress, which was the same she had worn at the supper table, I laughingly retorted:

"Isn't that a question I might better ask you? It is two o'clock by my watch, and you, for all your apparent delicacy, are still up. What does it mean, my dear? Have I put you out so completely by my coming that none of you can sleep?"

Her eyes, which had fallen before mine, quickly looked up.

"I am sorry," she began, flushing and trying to take a peep into my room, possibly to see if I had been to bed. "We did not mean to disturb you, but—but—oh, Miss Butterworth, pray excuse our makeshifts and our poverty. We wished to fix up another room for you, and were ashamed to have you see how little we had to do it with, so we were moving some things out of our own room to-night, and——"

Here her voice broke, and she burst into an almost uncontrollable flood of tears.

"Don't," she entreated, "don't," as, quite thoroughly ashamed, I began to utter some excuses. "I shall be all right in a moment. I am used to humiliations. Only"—and her whole body seemed to join in the plea, it trembled so—"do not, I pray, speak quite so loud. My brother is more sensitive than even Loreen and myself about these things, and if he should hear——"

Here a suppressed oath from way down the hall assured me that he did hear, but I gave no sign of my recognition of this fact, and Lucetta added quickly: "He would not forgive us for our carelessness in waking you. He is rough sometimes, but so good at heart, so good."

This, with the other small matter I have just mentioned, caused a revulsion in my feelings. He good? I did not believe it. Yet her eyes showed no wavering when I interrogated them with mine, and feeling that I had perhaps been doing them all an injustice, and that what I had seen was, as she evidently meant to intimate, due to their efforts to make a sudden guest comfortable amid their poverty, I put the best face I could on the matter and gave the poor, pitiful, pleading face a kiss. I was startled to feel how cold her forehead was, and, more and more concerned, loaded her down with such assurances of appreciation as came to my lips, and sent her back to her own room with an injunction not to trouble herself any more about fixing up any other room for me. "Only," I added, as her whole face showed relief, "we will go to the locksmith to-morrow and get a key; and after to-night you will be kind enough to see that I have a cup of tea brought to my room just before I retire. I am no good without my cup of tea, my dear. What keeps other people awake makes me sleep."

"Oh, you shall have your tea!" she cried, with an eagerness that was almost unnatural, and then, slipping from my grasp, she uttered another hasty apology for having roused me from my sleep and ran hastily back.

I stretched out my arm for the candle guttering in my room and held it up to light her. She seemed to shrink at sight of its rays, and the last vision I had of her speeding figure showed me that same look of dread on her pallid features which had aroused my interest in our first interview.

"She may have explained why the three of them are up at this time of night," I muttered, "but she has not explained why her every conversation is seasoned by an expression of fear."

And thus brooding, I went back to my room and, pushing the bed again against the door, lay down upon it and out of sheer chagrin fell fast asleep.

VIII

ON THE STAIRS

I did not wake up till morning. The room was so dark that in all probability I should not have wakened then, if my habits of exact punctuality had not been aided by a gentle knock at my door.

"Who's there?" I called, for I could not say "Come in" till I had moved my bed and made way for the door to open.

"Hannah with warm water," replied a voice, at which I made haste to rise. Hannah was the woman who had waited on us at dinner.

The sight of her pleasant countenance, which nevertheless looked a trifle haggard, was a welcome relief after the sombre features of the night. Addressing her with my usual brusqueness, but with quite my usual kindness, I asked how the young ladies were feeling this morning.

Her answer made a great show of frankness.

"Oh, they are much as usual," said she. "Miss Loreen is in the kitchen and Miss Lucetta will soon be here to inquire how you are. I hope you passed a good night yourself, ma'am."

I had slept more than I ought to, perhaps, and made haste to reassure her as to my own condition. Then seeing that a little talk would not be unwelcome to this hearty woman, tired to death possibly with life in this dreary house, I made some excuse for keeping her a few minutes, saying as I did so:

"What an immense dwelling this is for four persons to live in, or have you another inmate whom I have not seen?"

I thought her buxom color showed a momentary sign of failing, but it all came back with her answer, which was given in a round, hearty voice.

"Oh, I'm the only maid, ma'am. I cook and sweep and all. I couldn't abide another near me. Even Mr. Simsbury, who tends the cow and horse and who only comes in for his dinner, worries me by spells. I like to have my own way in the kitchen, except when the young ladies choose to come in. Is there anything more you want, ma'am, and do you prefer tea or coffee for breakfast?"

I told her that I always drank coffee in the morning, and would have liked to have added a question or two, but she gave me no chance. As she went out I saw her glance at my candlestick. There was only a half-burned end in it. She is calculating, too, how long I sat up, thought I.

Lucetta stood at the head of the stairs as I went down.

"Will you excuse me for a few moments?" said she. "I am not quite ready to follow you, but will be soon."

"I will take a look at the grounds."

I thought she hesitated for a moment; then her face lighted up. "Be sure you don't encounter the dog," she cried, and slipped hastily down a side hall I had not noticed the night before.

"Ah, a good way to keep me in," I reasoned. "But I shall see the grounds yet if I have to poison that dog." Notwithstanding, I made no haste to leave the house. I don't believe in tempting Providence, especially where a dog is concerned.

Instead of that, I stood still and looked up and down the halls, endeavoring to get some idea of their plan and of the location of my own room in reference to the rest.

I found that the main hall ran at right angles to the long corridor down which I had just come, and noting that the doors opening into it were of a size and finish vastly superior to those I had passed in the corridor just mentioned, I judged that the best bedrooms all lay front, and that I had been quartered at the end of what had once been considered as the servants' hall. At my right, as I looked down the stairs, ran a wall with a break, which looked like an opening into another corridor, and indeed I afterward learned that the long series of rooms of which mine was the last, had its counterpart on the other side of this enormous dwelling, giving to the house the shape of a long, square U.

I was looking in some wonderment at this opening and marvelling over the extravagant hospitality of those old days which necessitated such a number of rooms in a private gentleman's home, when I heard a door open and two voices speaking. One was rough and careless, unmistakably that of William Knollys. The other was slow and timid, and was just as unmistakably that of the man who had driven me to this house the day before. They were talking of some elderly person, and I had good sense enough not to allow my indignation to blind me to the fact that by that elderly person they meant me. This is important, for their words were not without significance.

"How shall we keep the old girl out of the house till it is all over?" was what I heard from William's surly lips.

"Lucetta has a plan," was the hardly distinguishable answer. "I am to take—"

That was all I could hear; a closing door shut off the remainder. Something, then, was going on in this house, of a dark if not mysterious character, and the attempts made by these two interesting and devoted girls to cover up the fact, by explanations founded on their poverty, had been but subterfuges after all. Grieved on their account, but inwardly grateful to the imprudence of their more than reckless brother, for this not-to-be-mistaken glimpse into the truth, I slowly descended the stairs, in that state of complete self-possession which is given by a secret knowledge of the intentions formed against us by those whose actions we have reason to suspect.

Henceforth I had but one duty—to penetrate the mystery of this household. Whether it was the one suspected by Mr. Gryce or another of a less evil and dangerous character hardly mattered in my eyes. While the blight of it rested upon this family, eyes would be lowered and heads shaken at their name. This, if I could help it, must no longer be. If guilt lay at the bottom of all this fear, then this guilt must be known; if innocence—I thought of the brother's lowering brow and felt it incompatible with innocence, but remembering Mr. Gryce's remarks on this subject, read an instant lecture to myself and, putting all conclusions aside, devoted the few minutes in which I found myself alone in the dining-room to a careful preparation of my mind for its duty, which was not likely to be of the simplest character if Lucetta's keen wits were to be pitted against mine.

IX

A NEW ACQUAINTANCE

When my mind is set free from doubt and fully settled upon any course, I am capable of much good nature and seeming simplicity. I was therefore able to maintain my own at the breakfast-table with some success, so that the meal passed off without any of the disagreeable experiences of the night before. Perhaps the fact that Loreen presided at the coffee-urn instead of Lucetta had something to do with this. Her calm, even looks seemed to put some restraint upon the boisterous outbursts to which William was only too liable, while her less excitable nature suffered less if by any chance he did break out and startle the decorous silence by one of his rude guffaws.

I am a slow eater, but I felt forced to hurry through the meal or be left eating alone at the end. This did not put me in the best of humor, for I hated to risk an indigestion just when my faculties needed to be unusually alert. I compromised by leaving the board hungry, but I did it with such a smile that I do not think Miss Knollys knew I had not risen from any table so ill satisfied in years.

"I will leave you to my brother for a few minutes," said she, hastily tripping from the room. "I pray that you will not think of going to your room till we have had an opportunity of arranging it."

I instantly made up my mind to disobey this injunction. But first, it was necessary to see what I could make of William.

He was not a very promising subject as he turned and led the way toward the front of the house.

"I thought you might like to see the grounds," he growled, evidently not enjoying the rôle assigned him. "They are so attractive," he sneered. "Children hereabout call them the jungle."

"Who's to blame for that?" I asked, with only a partial humoring of his ill nature. "You have a sturdy pair of arms of your own, and a little trimming here and a little trimming there would have given quite a different appearance to this undergrowth. A gentleman usually takes pride in his place."

"Yes, when it's all his. This belongs to my sisters as much as to me. What's the use of my bothering myself about it?"

The man was so selfish he did not realize the extent of the exhibition he made of it. Indeed he seemed to take pride in what he probably called his independence. I began to feel the most intense aversion for him, and only with the greatest difficulty could prolong this conversation unmoved.

"I should think it would be a pleasure to give that much assistance to your sisters. They do not seem to be sparing in their attempts to please you."

He snapped his fingers, and I was afraid a dog or two would come leaping around the corner of the house. But it was only his way of expressing disdain.

"Oh, the girls are well enough," he grumbled; "but they will stick to the place. Lucetta might have married a half-dozen times, and once I thought she was going to, but suddenly she turned straight about and sent her lover packing, and that made me mad beyond everything. Why should she hang on to me like a burr when there are other folks willing to take on the burden?"

It was the most palpable display of egotism I had ever seen and one of the most revolting. I was so disgusted by it that I spoke up without any too much caution.

"Perhaps she thinks she can be useful to you," I said. "I have known sisters give up their own happiness on no better grounds."

"Useful?" he sneered. "It's a usefulness a man like me can dispense with. Do you know what I would like?"

We were standing in one of the tangled pathways, with our faces turned toward the house. As he spoke, he looked up and made a rude sort of gesture toward the blank expanse of empty and curtainless windows.

"I would like that great house all to myself, to make into one huge, bachelor's hall. I should like to feel that I could tramp from one end of it to the other without awakening an echo I did not choose to hear there. I should not find it too big. I should not find it too lonesome. I and my dogs would know how to fill it, wouldn't we, Saracen? Oh, I forgot, Saracen is locked up."

The way he mumbled the last sentence showed displeasure, but I gave little heed to that. The gloating way in which he said he and his dogs would fill it had given me a sort of turn. I began to have more than an aversion for the man. He inspired me with something like terror.

"Your wishes," said I, with as little expression as possible, "seem to leave your sisters entirely out of your calculations. How would your mother regard that if she could see you from the place where she is gone?"

He turned upon me with a look of anger that made his features positively ugly.

"What do you mean by speaking to me of my mother? Have I spoken of her to you? Is there any reason why you should lug my mother into this conversation? If so, say so, and be——"

He did not swear at me; he did not dare to, but he came precious near to it, and that was enough to make me recoil.

"She was my friend," said I. "I knew and loved her before you were born. That was why I spoke of her, and I think it very natural myself."

He seemed to feel ashamed. He grumbled out some sort of apology and looked about quite helplessly, possibly for the dog he manifestly was in the habit of seeing forever at his heels. I took advantage of this momentary abstraction on his part to smooth my own disturbed features.

"She was a beautiful girl," I remarked, on the principle that, the ice once broken, one should not hesitate about jumping in. "Was your father equally handsome for a man?"

"My father—yes, let's talk of father. He was a judge of horses, he was. When he died, there were three mares in the stable not to be beat this side of Albany, but those devils of executors sold them, and I—well, you had a chance to test the speed of old Bess yesterday. You weren't afraid of being thrown out, I take it. Great Scott, to think of a man of my tastes owning no other horse than that!"

"You have not answered my question," I suggested, turning him about and moving toward the gate.

"Oh, about the way my father looked! What does that matter? He was handsome, though. Folks say that I get whatever good looks I have from him. He was big—bigger than I am, and while he lived—What did you make a fellow talk for?"

I don't know why I did, but I was certainly astonished at the result. This great, huge lump of selfish clay had actually shown feeling and was ashamed of it, like the lout he was.

"Yesterday," said I, anxious to change the subject, "I had difficulty in getting in through that gate we are pointing for. Couldn't you set it straight, with just a little effort?"

He paused, looked at me to see if I were in earnest, then took a dogged step toward the gate I was still indicating with my resolute right hand, but before he could touch it he perceived something on that deserted and ominous highway which made him start in sudden surprise.

"Why, Trohm," he cried, "is that you? Well, it's an age since I have seen you turn that corner on a visit to us."

"Sometime, certainly," answered a hearty and pleasant voice, and before I could quite drop the look of severity with which I was endeavoring to shame this young man into some decent show of interest in this place, and assume the more becoming aspect of a lady caught unawares at an early morning hour plucking flowers from a stunted syringa, a gentleman stepped into sight on the other side of the fence with a look and a bow so genial and devoid of mystery that I experienced for the first time since entering the gloomy precincts of this town a decided sensation of pleasure.

"Miss Butterworth," explained Mr. Knollys with a somewhat forced gesture in my direction. "A guest of my sisters," he went on, and looked as if he hoped I would retire, though he made no motion to welcome Mr. Trohm in, but rather leaned a little conspicuously on the gate as if anxious to show that he had no idea that the other's intention went any further than the passing of a few neighborly comments at the gate.

I like to please the young even when they are no more agreeable than my surly host, and if the gentleman who had just shown himself had been equally immature, I would certainly have left them to have their talk out undisturbed. But he was not. He was older; he was even of sufficient years for his judgment to have become thoroughly matured and his every faculty developed. I therefore could not see why my society should be considered an intrusion by him, so I waited. His next sentence was addressed to me.

"I am happy," said he, "to have the pleasure of a personal introduction to Miss Butterworth. I did not expect it. The surprise is all the more agreeable. I only anticipated being allowed to leave this package and letter with the maid. They are addressed to you, madam, and were left at my house by mistake."

I could not hide my astonishment.

"I live in the next house below," said he. "The boy who brought these from the post office was a stupid lad, and I could not induce him to come any farther up the road. I hope you will excuse the present messenger and believe there has been no delay."

I bowed with what must have seemed an abstracted politeness. The letter was from New York, and, as I strongly suspected, from Mr. Gryce. Somehow this fact created in me an unmistakable embarrassment. I put both letter and package into my pocket and endeavored to meet the gentleman's eye with my accustomed ease in the presence of strangers. But, strange to say, I had no sooner done so than I saw that he was no more at his ease than myself. He smiled, glanced at William, made an offhand remark or so about the weather, but he could not deceive eyes sharpened by such experience as mine. Something disturbed him, something connected with me. It made my cheek a little hot to acknowledge this even to myself, but it was so very evident that I began to cast about for the means of ridding ourselves of William when that blundering youth suddenly spoke:

"I suppose he was afraid to come up the lane. Do you know, I think you're brave to attempt it, Trohm. We haven't a very good name here." And with a sudden, perfectly unnatural burst, he broke out into one of his huge guffaws that so shook the old gate on which he was leaning that I thought it would tumble down with him before our eyes.

I saw Mr. Trohm start and cast him a look in which I seemed to detect both surprise and horror, before he turned to me and with an air of polite deprecation anxiously said:

"I am afraid Miss Butterworth will not understand your allusions, Mr. Knollys. I hear this is her first visit in town."

As his manner showed even more feeling than the occasion seemed to warrant, I made haste to answer that I was well acquainted with the tradition of the lane; that its name alone showed what had happened here.

His bearing betrayed an instant relief.

"I am glad to find you so well informed," said he. "I was afraid"—here he cast another very strange glance at William—"that your young friends might have shrunk, from some sense of delicacy, from telling you what might frighten most guests from a lonely road like this. I compliment you upon their thoughtfulness."

William bowed as if the words of the other contained no other suggestion than that which was openly apparent. Was he so dull, or was he—I had not time to finish my conjectures even in my own mind, for at this moment a quick cry rose behind us, and Lucetta's light figure appeared running toward us with every indication of excitement.

"Ah," murmured Mr. Trohm, with an appearance of great respect, "your sister, Mr. Knollys. I had better be moving on. Good-morning, Miss Butterworth. I am sorry that circumstances make it impossible for me to offer you those civilities which you might reasonably expect from so near a neighbor. Miss Lucetta and I are at swords' points over a matter upon which I still insist she is to blame. See how shocked she is to see me even standing at her gate."

Shocked! I would have said terrified. Nothing but fear—her old fear aggravated to a point that made all attempt at concealment impossible—could account for her white, drawn features and trembling form. She looked as if her whole thought was, "Have I come in time?"

"What—what has procured us the honor of this visit?" she asked, moving up beside William as if she would add her slight frame to his bulky one to keep this intruder out.

"Nothing that need alarm you," said the other with a suggestive note in his kind and mellow voice. "I was rather unexpectedly intrusted this morning with a letter for your agreeable guest here, and I have merely come to deliver it."

Her look of astonishment passing from him to me, I thrust my hand into my pocket and drew out the letter which I had just received.

"From home," said I, without properly considering that this was in some measure an untruth.

"Oh!" she murmured as if but half convinced. "William could have gone for it," she added, still eying Mr. Trohm with a pitiful anxiety.

"I was only too happy," said the other, with a low and reassuring bow. Then, as if he saw that her distress would only be relieved by his departure, he raised his hat and stepped back into the open highway. "I will not intrude again, Miss Knollys," were his parting words. "If you want anything of Obadiah Trohm, you know where to find him. His doors will always be open to you."

Lucetta, with a start, laid her hand on her brother's arm as if to restrain the words she saw slowly laboring to his lips, and leaning breathlessly forward, watched the fine figure of this perfect country gentleman till it had withdrawn quite out of sight. Then she turned, and with a quick abandonment of all self-control, cried out with a pitiful gesture toward her brother, "I thought all was over; I feared he meant to come into the house," and fell stark and seemingly lifeless at our feet.

SECRET INSTRUCTIONS

For a moment William and myself stood looking at each other over this frail and prostrate figure. Then he stooped, and with an unexpected show of kindness raised her up and began carrying her toward the house.

"Lucetta is a fool," he cried suddenly, stopping and giving me a quick glance over his shoulder. "Because folks are terrified of this road and come to see us but seldom, she has got to feel a most unreasonable dread of visitors. She was even set against your coming till we showed her what folly it was for her to think we could always live here like hermits. Then she doesn't like Mr. Trohm; thinks he is altogether too friendly to me—as if that was any of her business. Am I an idiot? Have I no sense? Cannot I be trusted to take care of my own affairs and keep my own secrets? She's a weak, silly chit, to go and flop over like this when, d—n it, we have enough to look after without nursing her up and—I mean," he said, tripping himself up with an air of polite consideration so out of keeping with his usual churlishness as to be more than noticeable, "that it cannot add much to the pleasure of your visit to have such things happen as this."

"Oh, don't worry about me!" I curtly responded. "Get the poor girl in. I'll look after her."

But as if she heard these words and was startled by them, Lucetta roused in her brother's arms and struggled passionately to her feet. "Oh! what has happened to me?" she cried. "Have I said anything? William, have I said anything?" she asked wildly, clinging to her brother in terror.

He gave her a look and pushed her off.

"What are you talking about?" he cried. "One would think you had something to conceal."

She steadied herself up in an instant.

"I am the weakest of the family," said she, walking straight up to me and taking me affectionately by the arm. "All my life I have been delicate and these turns are nothing new to me. Sometimes I think I will die in one of them; but I am quite restored now," she hastily added, as I could not help showing my concern. "See! I can walk quite alone." And she ran, rather than walked, up the few short steps of the porch, at which we had now arrived. "Don't tell Loreen," she begged, as I followed her into the house. "She worries so about me, and it will do no good."

William had stalked off toward the stables. We were therefore alone. I turned and laid a finger on her arm.

"My dear," said I, "I never make foolish promises, but I can be trusted never to heedlessly slight any one's wishes. If I see no good reason why I should tell your sister of this fainting fit, I shall certainly hold my peace."

She seemed moved by my manner, if not by my words.

"Oh," she cried, seizing my hand and pressing it. "If I dared to tell you of my troubles! But it is impossible, quite impossible." And before I could urge a plea for her confidence she was gone, leaving me in the company of Hannah, who at this moment was busying herself with something at the other end of the hall.

I had no wish to interfere with Hannah just then. I had my letter to read, and did not wish to be disturbed. So I slipped into the sitting-room and carefully closed the door. Then I opened my letter.

It was, as I supposed, from Mr. Gryce, and ran thus:

"Dear Miss Butterworth:

"I am astonished at your determination, but since your desire to visit your friends is such as to lead you to brave the dangers of Lost Man's Lane, allow me to suggest certain precautions.

"First.—Do not trust anybody.

"Second.—Do not proceed anywhere alone or on foot.

"Third.—If danger comes to you, and you find yourself in a condition of real peril, blow once shrilly on the whistle I inclose with this. If, however, the danger is slight, or you wish merely to call the attention of those who will be set to watch over you, let the blast be short, sharp, and repeated—twice to summon assistance, three times to call attention.

"I advise you to fasten this whistle about your neck in a way to make it easily obtainable.

"I have advised you to trust nobody. I should have excepted Mr. Trohm, but I do not think you will be given an opportunity to speak to him. Remember that all depends upon your not awakening suspicion. If, however, you wish advice or desire to make any communication to me or the man secretly holding charge over this affair in X., seek the first opportunity of riding into town and go at once to the hotel where you will ask for Room 3. It has been retained in your service, and once shown into it, you, may expect a visitor who will be the man you seek.

"As you will see, every confidence is put in your judgment."

There was no signature to this—it needed none—and in the packet which came with it was the whistle. I was glad to see it, and glad to hear that I was not left entirely without protection in my somewhat hazardous enterprise.

The events of the morning had been so unexpected that till this moment I had forgotten my early determination to go to my room before any change there could be made. Recalling it now, I started for the staircase, and did not stop though I heard Hannah calling me back. The consequence was that I ran full tilt against Miss Knollys coming down the hall with a tray in her hand.

"Ah," I cried; "some one sick in the house?"

The attack was too sudden. I saw her recoil and for one instant hesitate before replying. Then her natural self-possession came to her aid, and she placidly remarked:

"We were all up to a late hour last night, as you know. It was necessary for us to have some food."

I accepted the explanation and made no further remark, but as in passing her I had detected on this tray of food supposed to have been sent up the night before, the half-eaten portion of a certain dish we had had for breakfast, I reserved to myself the privilege of doubting her exact truthfulness. To me the sight of this partially consumed breakfast was proof positive of there being in the house some person of whose presence I was supposed to be ignorant—not a pleasant thought under the circumstances, but quite an important fact to have established. I felt that in this one discovery I had clutched the thread that would yet lead me out of the labyrinth of this mystery.

Miss Knollys, who was on her way down-stairs, called Hannah to take the tray, and, coming back, beckoned me toward a door opening into one of the front rooms.

"This is to be your room," she announced, "but I do not know that I can move you to-day."

She was so calm, so perfectly mistress of herself, that I could not but admire her. Lucetta would have flushed and fidgeted, but Loreen stood as erect and placid as if no trouble weighed upon her heart and the words were as unimportant in their character as they seemed.

"Do not distress yourself," said I. "I told Lucetta last night that I was perfectly comfortable and had no wish to change my quarters. I am sorry you should have thought it necessary to disturb yourself on my account last night. Don't do it again, I pray. A woman like myself had rather put herself to some slight inconvenience than move.

"I am much obliged to you," said she, and came at once from the door. I don't know but after all I like Lucetta's fidgety ways better than Loreen's unmovable self-possession.

"Shall I order the coach for you?" she suddenly asked, as I turned toward the corridor leading to my room.

"The coach?" I repeated.

"I thought that perhaps you might like to ride into town. Mr. Simsbury is at leisure this morning. I regret that neither Lucetta nor myself will be able to accompany you."

I thought what this same Mr. Simsbury had said about Lucetta's plan, and hesitated. It was evidently their wish to have me spend my morning elsewhere than with them. Should I humor them, or find excuses for remaining home? Either course had its difficulties. If I went, what might not take place in my absence! If I remained, what suspicions might I not rouse! I decided to compromise matters, and start for town even if I did not go there.

"I am hesitating," said I, "because of the two or three rather threatening-looking clouds toward the east. But if you are sure Mr. Simsbury can be spared, I think I will risk it. I really would like to get a key for my door; and then riding in the country is so pleasant."

Miss Knollys, with a bow, passed immediately down-stairs. I went in a state of some doubt toward my own room. "Am I surveying these occurrences through highly magnifying glasses?" thought I. It was very possible, yet not so possible but that I cast very curious glances at the various closed doors I had to pass before reaching my own. Such a little thing would make me feel like trying them. Such a little thing—that is, added to the other things which had struck me as unexplainable.

I found my bed made and everything in apple-pie order. I had therefore nothing to do but to prepare for going out. This I did quickly, and was down-stairs sooner perhaps than I was expected. At all events Lucetta and William parted very suddenly when they saw me, she in tears and he with a dogged shrug and some such word as this:

"You're a fool to take on so. Since it's got to be, the sooner the better, I say. Don't you see that every minute makes less our chances of concealment?"

It made me feel like changing my mind and staying home. But the habit of a lifetime is not easily broken into. I kept to my first decision.

XI

MEN, WOMEN, AND GHOSTS

Mr. Simsbury gave me quite an amiable bow as I entered the buggy. This made it easy for me to say:

"You are on hand early this morning. Do you sleep in the Knollys house?"

The stare he gave me had the least bit of suspicion in it.

"I live over yonder," he said, pointing with his whip across the intervening woods to the main road. "I come through the marshes to my breakfast; my old woman says they owes me three meals, and three meals I must have."

It was the longest sentence with which he had honored me. Finding him in a talkative mood, I prepared to make myself agreeable, a proceeding which he seemed to appreciate, for he began to sniff and pay great attention to his horse, which he was elaborately turning about.

"Why do you go that way?" I protested. "Isn't it the longest way to the village?"

"It's the way I'm most accustomed to," said he. "But we can go the other way if you like. Perhaps we will get a glimpse of Deacon Spear. He's a widower, you know."

The leer with which he said this was intolerable. I bridled up—but no, I will not admit that I so much as manifested by my manner that I understood him. I merely expressed my wish to go the old way.

He whipped up the horse at once, almost laughing outright. I began to think this man capable of most any wicked deed. He was forced, however, to pull up suddenly. Directly in our path was the stooping figure of a woman. She did not move as we advanced, and so we had no alternative but to stop. Not till the horse's head touched her shoulder did she move. Then she rose up and looked at us somewhat indignantly.

"Didn't you hear us?" I asked, willing to open conversation with the old crone, whom I had no difficulty in recognizing as Mother Jane.

"She's deaf—deaf, as a post," muttered Mr. Simsbury. "No use shouting at her." His tone was brusque, yet I noticed he waited with great patience for her to hobble out of the way.

Meanwhile I was watching the old creature with much interest. She had not a common face or a common manner. She was gray, she was toothless, she was haggard, and she was bent, but she was not ordinary or just one of the crowd of old women to be seen on country doorsteps. There was force in her aged movements and a strong individuality in the glances she shot at us as she backed slowly out of the roadway.

"Do they say she is imbecile?" I asked. "She looks far from foolish to me."

"Hearken a bit," said he. "Don't you see she is muttering? She talks to herself all the time." And in fact her lips were moving.

"I cannot hear her," I said. "Make her come nearer. Somehow the old creature interests me."

He at once beckoned to the crone; but he might as well have beckoned to the tree against which she had pushed herself. She neither answered him nor gave any indication that she understood the gesture he had made. Yet her eyes never moved from our faces.

"Well, well," said I, "she seems dull as well as deaf. You had better drive on." But before he could give the necessary jerk of the reins, I caught sight of some pennyroyal growing about the front of the cottage a few steps beyond, and, pointing to it with some eagerness, I cried: "If there isn't some of the very herb I want to take home with me! Do you think she would give me a handful of it if I paid her?"

With an obliging grunt he again pulled up. "If you can make her understand," said he.

I thought it worth the effort. Though Mr. Gryce had been at pains to tell me there was no harm in this woman and that I need not even consider her in any inquiries I might be called upon to make, I remembered that Mr. Gryce had sometimes made mistakes in just such matters as these, and that Amelia Butterworth had then felt herself called upon to set him right. If that could happen once, why not twice? At all events, I was not going to lose the least chance of making the acquaintance of the people living in this lane. Had he not himself said that only in this way could we hope to come upon the clue that had eluded all open efforts to find it?

Knowing that the sight of money is the strongest appeal that can be made to one living in such abject poverty as this woman, making the blind to see and the deaf to hear, I drew out my purse and held up before her a piece of silver. She bounded as if she had been shot, and when I held it toward her came greedily forward and stood close beside the wheels looking up.

"For you," I indicated, after making a motion toward the plant which had attracted my attention.

She glanced from me to the herb and nodded with quick appreciation. As in a flash she seemed to take in the fact that I was a stranger, a city lady with memories of the country and this humble plant, and hurrying to it with the same swiftness she had displayed in advancing to the carriage, she tore off several of the sprays and brought them back to me, holding out her hand for the money.

I had never seen greater eagerness, and I think even Mr. Simsbury was astonished at this proof of her poverty or her greed. I was inclined to think it the latter, for her portly figure was far from looking either ill-fed or poorly cared for. Her dress was of decent calico, and her pipe had evidently been lately filled, for I could smell the odor of tobacco about her. Indeed, as I afterward heard, the good people of X. had never allowed her to suffer. Yet her fingers closed upon that coin as if in it she grasped the salvation of her life, and into her eyes leaped a light that made her look almost young, though she must have been fully eighty.

"What do you suppose she will do with that?" I asked Mr. Simsbury, as she turned away in an evident fear I might repent of my bargain.

"Hark!" was his brief response. "She is talking now."

I did hearken, and heard these words fall from her quickly moving lips: "Seventy; twenty-eight; and now ten."

Jargon; for I had given her twenty-five cents, an amount quite different from any she had mentioned.

"Seventy!" She was repeating the figures again, this time in a tone of almost frenzied elation. "Seventy; twenty-eight; and now ten! Won't Lizzie be surprised! Seventy; twenty—" I heard no more—she had bounded into her cottage and shut the door.

"Waal, what do you think of her now?" chuckled Mr. Simsbury, touching up his horse. "She's always like that, saying over numbers, and muttering about Lizzie. Lizzie was her daughter. Forty years ago she ran off with a man from Boston, and for thirty-eight years she's been lying in a Massachusetts grave. But her mother still thinks she is alive and is coming back. Nothing will ever make her think different. But she's harmless, perfectly harmless. You needn't be afeard of her."

This, because I cast a look behind me of more than ordinary curiosity, I suppose. Why were they all so sure she was harmless? I had thought her expression a little alarming at times, especially when she took the money from my hand. If I had refused it or even held it back a little, I think she would have fallen upon me tooth and nail. I wished I could take a peep into her cottage. Mr. Gryce had described it as four walls and nothing more, and indeed it was small and of the humblest proportions; but the fluttering of some half-dozen pigeons about its eaves proved it to be a home and, as such, of interest to me, who am often able to read character from a person's habitual surroundings.

There was no yard attached to this simple building, only a small open place in front in which a few of the commonest vegetables grew, such as turnips, carrots, and onions. Elsewhere towered the forest—the great pine forest through which this portion of the road ran.

Mr. Simsbury had been so talkative up to now that I was in hope he would enter into some details about the persons and things we encountered, which might assist me in the acquaintanceship I was anxious to make. But his loquaciousness ended with this small adventure I have just described. Not till we were well quit of the pines and had entered into the main thoroughfare did he deign to respond to any of my suggestions, and then it was in a manner totally unsatisfactory and quite uncommunicative. The only time he deigned to offer a remark was when we emerged from the forest and came upon the little crippled child, looking from its window. Then he cried:

"Why, how's this? That's Sue you see there, and her time isn't till arternoon. Rob allers sits there of a mornin'. I wonder if the little chap's sick. S'pose I ask."

As this was just what I would have suggested if he had given me time, I nodded complacently, and we drove up and stopped.

The piping voice of the child at once spoke up:

"How d' ye do, Mr. Simsbury? Ma's in the kitchen. Rob isn't feelin' good to-day."

I thought her tone had a touch of mysteriousness in it. I greeted the pale little thing, and asked if Rob was often sick.

"Never," she answered, "except, like me, he can't walk. But I'm not to talk about it, ma says. I'd like to, but——"

Ma's face appearing at this moment over her shoulder put an end to her innocent garrulity.

"How d' ye do, Mr. Simsbury?" came a second time from the window, but this time in very different tones. "What's the child been saying? She's so sot up at being allowed to take her brother's place in the winder that she don't know how to keep her tongue still. Rob's a little languid, that's all. You'll see him in his old place to-morrow." And she drew back as if in polite intimation that we might drive on.

Mr. Simsbury responded to the suggestion, and in another moment we were trotting down the road. Had we stayed a minute longer, I think the child would have said something more or less interesting to hear.

The horse, which had brought us thus far at a pretty sharp trot, now began to lag, which so attracted Mr. Simsbury's attention, that he forgot to answer even by a grunt more than half of my questions. He spent most of his time looking at the nag's hind feet, and finally, just as we came in sight of the stores, he found his tongue sufficiently to announce that the horse was casting a shoe and that he would be obliged to go to the blacksmith's with her.

"Humph, and how long will that take?" I asked.

He hesitated so long, rubbing his nose with his finger, that I grew suspicious and cast a glance at the horse's foot myself. The shoe was loose. I began to hear it clang.

"Waal, it may be a matter of a couple of hours," he finally drawled. "We have no blacksmith in town, and the ride up there is two miles. Sorry it happened, ma'am, but there's all sorts of shops here, you see, and I've allers heard that a woman can easily spend two hours haggling away in shops."

I glanced at the two ill-furnished windows he pointed out, thought of Arnold & Constable's, Tiffany's, and the other New York establishments I had been in the habit of visiting, and suppressed my disdain. Either the man was a fool or he was acting a part in the interests of Lucetta and her family. I rather inclined to the latter supposition. If the plan was to keep me out most of the morning why could that shoe not have been loosened before the mare left the stable?

"I made all necessary purchases while in New York," said I, "but if you must get the horse shod, why, take her off and do it. I suppose there is a hotel parlor near here where I can sit."

"Oh, yes," and he made haste to point out to me where the hotel stood. "And it's a very nice place, ma'am. Mrs. Carter, the landlady, is the nicest sort of person. Only you won't try to go home, ma'am, on foot? You'll wait till I come back for you?"

"It isn't likely I'll go streaking through Lost Man's Lane alone," I exclaimed indignantly. "I'd rather sit in Mrs. Carter's parlor till night."

"And I would advise you to," he said. "No use making gossip for the village folks. They have enough to talk about as it is."

Not exactly seeing the force of this reasoning, but quite willing to be left to my own devices for a little while, I pointed to a locksmith's shop I saw near by, and bade him put me down there.

With a sniff I declined to interpret into a token of disapproval, he drove me up to the shop and awkwardly assisted me to alight.

"Trunk key missing?" he ventured to inquire before getting back into his seat.

I did not think it necessary to reply, but walked immediately into the shop. He looked dissatisfied at this, but whatever his feelings were he refrained from any expression of them, and presently mounted to his place and drove off. I was left confronting the decent man who represented the lock-fitting interests in X.

I found some difficulty in broaching my errand. Finally I said:

"Miss Knollys, who lives up the road, wishes a key fitted to one of her doors. Will you come or send a man to her house to-day? She is too occupied to see about it herself."

The man must have been struck by my appearance, for he stared at me quite curiously for a minute. Then he gave a hem and a haw and said:

"Certainly. What kind of a door is it?" When I had answered, he gave me another curious glance and seemed uneasy to step back to where his assistant was working with a file.

"You will be sure to come in time to have the lock fitted before night?" I said in that peremptory manner of mine which means simply, "I keep my promises and expect you to keep yours."

His "Certainly" struck me as a little weaker this time, possibly because his curiosity was excited. "Are you the lady from New York who is staying with them?" he asked, stepping back, seemingly quite unawed by my positive demeanor.

"Yes," said I, thawing a trifle; "I am Miss Butterworth."

He looked at me almost as if I were a curiosity.

"And did you sleep there last night?" he urged.

I thought it best to thaw still more.

"Of course," I said. "Where do you think I would sleep? The young ladies are friends of mine."

He rapped abstractedly on the counter with a small key he was holding.

"Excuse me," said he, with some remembrance of my position toward him as a stranger, "but weren't you afraid?"

"Afraid?" I echoed. "Afraid in Miss Knollys' house?"

"Why, then, do you want a key to your door?" he asked, with a slight appearance of excitement. "We don't lock doors here in the village; at least we didn't."

"I did not say it was my door," I began, but, feeling that this was a prevarication not only unworthy of me, but one that he was entirely too sharp to accept, I added stiffly: "It is for my door. I am not accustomed even at home to sleep with my room unlocked."

"Oh," he murmured, totally unconvinced, "I thought you might have got a scare. Folks somehow are afraid of that old place, it's so big and ghost-like. I don't think you would find any one in this village who would sleep there all night."

"A pleasing preparation for my rest to-night," I grimly laughed. "Dangers on the road and ghosts in the house. Happily I don't believe in the latter."

The gesture he made showed incredulity. He had ceased rapping with the key or even to show any wish to join his assistant. All his thoughts for the moment seemed to be concentrated on me.

"You don't know little Rob," he inquired, "the crippled lad who lives at the head of the lane?"

"No," I said; "I haven't been in town a day yet, but I mean to know Rob and his sister too. Two cripples in one family rouse my interest."

He did not say why he had spoken of the child, but began tapping with his key again.

"And you are sure you saw nothing?" he whispered. "Lots of things can happen in a lonely road like that."

"Not if everybody is as afraid to enter it as you say your villagers are," I retorted.

But he didn't yield a jot.

"Some folks don't mind present dangers," said he. "Spirits——"

But he received no encouragement in his return to this topic. "You don't believe in spirits?" said he. "Well, they are doubtful sort of folks, but when honest and respectable people such as live in this town, when children even, see what answers to nothing but phantoms, then I remember what a wiser man than any of us once said——But perhaps you don't read Shakespeare, madam?"

Nonplussed for the moment, but interested in the man's talk more than was consistent with my need of haste, I said with some spirit, for it struck me as very ridiculous that this country mechanic should question my knowledge of the greatest dramatist of all time, "Shakespeare and the Bible form the staple of my reading." At which he gave me a little nod of apology and hastened to say:

"Then you know what I mean—Hamlet's remark to Horatio, madam, 'There are more things,' etc. Your memory will readily supply you with the words."

I signified my satisfaction and perfect comprehension of his meaning, and, feeling that something important lay behind his words, I endeavored to make him speak more explicitly.

"The Misses Knollys show no terror of their home," I observed. "They cannot believe in spirits either."

"Miss Knollys is a woman of a great deal of character," said he. "But look at Lucetta. There is a face for you, for a girl not yet out of her twenties; and such a round-cheeked lass as she was once! Now what has made the change? The sights and sounds of that old house, I say. Nothing else would give her that scared look—nothing merely mortal, I mean."

This was going a step too far. I could not discuss Lucetta with this stranger, anxious as I was to hear what he had to say about her.

"I don't know," I remonstrated, taking up my black satin bag, without which I never stir. "One would think the terrors of the lane she lives in might account for some appearance of fear on her part."

"So it might," he assented, but with no great heartiness. "But Lucetta has never spoken of those dangers. The people in the lane do not seem to fear them. Even Deacon Spear says that, set aside the wickedness of the thing, he rather enjoys the quiet which the ill repute of the lane gives him. I don't understand this indifference myself. I have no relish for horrible mysteries or for ghosts either."

"You won't forget the key?" I suggested shortly, preparing to walk out, in my dread lest he should again introduce the subject of Lucetta.

"No," said he, "I won't forget it." His tone should have warned me that I need not expect to have a locked door that night.

XII

THE PHANTOM COACH

Ghosts! What could the fellow have meant? If I had pressed him he would have told me, but it did not seem quite a lady's business to pick up information in this way, especially when it involved a young lady like Lucetta. Yet did I think I would ever come to the end of this matter without involving Lucetta? No. Why, then, did I allow my instincts to triumph over my judgment? Let those answer who understand the workings of the human heart. I am simply stating facts.

Ghosts! Somehow the word startled me as if in some way it gave a rather unwelcome confirmation to my doubts. Apparitions seen in the Knollys mansion or in any of the houses bordering on this lane! That was a serious charge; how serious seemed to be but half comprehended by this man. But I comprehended it to the full, and wondered if it was on account of such gossip as this that Mr. Gryce had persuaded me to enter Miss Knollys' house as a guest.

I was crossing the street to the hotel as I indulged in these conjectures, and intent as my mind was upon them, I could not but note the curiosity and interest which my presence excited in the simple country folk invariably to be found lounging about a country tavern. Indeed, the whole neighborhood seemed agog, and though I would have thought it derogatory to my dignity to notice the fact, I could not but see how many faces were peering at me from store doors and the half-closed blinds of adjoining cottages. No young girl in the pride of her beauty could have awakened more interest, and this I attributed, as was no doubt right, not to my appearance, which would not perhaps be apt to strike these simple villagers as remarkable, or to my dress, which is rather rich than fashionable, but to the fact that I was a stranger in town, and, what was more extraordinary, a guest of the Misses Knollys.

My intention in approaching the hotel was not to spend a couple of dreary hours in the parlor with Mrs. Carter, as Mr. Simsbury had suggested, but to obtain if possible a conveyance to carry me immediately back to the Knollys mansion. But this, which would have been a simple matter in most towns, seemed well-nigh an impossibility in X. The landlord was away, and Mrs.

Carter, who was very frank with me, told me it would be perfectly useless to ask one of the men to drive me through the lane. "It's an unwholesome spot," said she, "and only Mr. Carter and the police have the courage to brave it."

I suggested that I was willing to pay well, but it seemed to make very little difference to her. "Money won't hire them," said she, and I had the satisfaction of knowing that Lucetta had triumphed in her plan, and that, after all, I must sit out the morning in the precincts of the hotel parlor with Mrs. Carter.

It was my first signal defeat, but I was determined to make the best of it, and if possible glean such knowledge from the talk of this woman as would make me feel that I had lost nothing by my disappointment. She was only too ready to talk, and the first topic was little Rob.

I saw the moment I mentioned his name that I was introducing a subject which had already been well talked over by every eager gossip in the village.

Her attitude of importance, the air of mystery she assumed, were preparations I had long been accustomed to in women of this kind, and I was not at all surprised when she announced in a way that admitted of no dispute:

"Oh, there's no wonder the child is sick. We would be sick under the circumstances. He has seen the phantom coach."

The phantom coach! So that was what the locksmith meant. A phantom coach! I had heard of every kind of phantom but that. Somehow the idea was a thrilling one, or would have been to a nature less practical than mine.

"I don't know what you mean," said I. "Some superstition of the place? I never heard of a ghostly appearance of that nature before."

"No, I expect not. It belongs to X. I never heard of it beyond these mountains. Indeed, I have never known it to have been seen but upon one road. I need not mention what road, madam. You can guess."

Yes, I could guess, and the guessing made me set my lips a little grimly.

"Tell me more about this thing," I urged, half laughing. "It ought to be of some interest to me."

She nodded, drew her chair a trifle nearer, and impetuously began:

"You see this is a very old town. It has more than one ancient country house similar to the one you are now living in, and it has its early traditions. One is, that an old-fashioned coach, perfectly noiseless, drawn by horses through which you can see the moonlight, haunts the highroad at intervals and flies through the gloomy forest road we have christened of late years Lost Man's Lane. It is a superstition, possibly, but you cannot find many families in town but believe in it as a fact, for there is not an old man or woman in the place but has either seen it in the past or has had some relative who has seen it. It passes only at night, and it is thought to presage some disaster to those who see it. My husband's uncle died the next morning after it flew by him on the highway. Fortunately years elapse between its going and coming. It is ten years, I think they say, since it was last seen. Poor little Rob! It has frightened him almost out of his wits."

"I should think so," I cried with becoming credulity. "But how came he to see it? I thought you said it only passed at night."

"At midnight," she repeated. "But Rob, you see, is a nervous lad, and night before last he was so restless he could not sleep, so he begged to be put in the window to cool off. This his mother did, and he sat there for a good half-hour alone, looking out at the moonlight. As his mother is an economical woman

45

there was no candle lit in the room, so he got his pleasure out of the shadows which the great trees made on the highroad, when suddenly—you ought to hear the little fellow tell it—he felt the hair rise on his forehead and all his body grow stiff with a terror that made his tongue feel like lead in his mouth. A something he would have called a horse and a carriage in the daytime, but which, in this light and under the influence of the mortal terror he was in, took on a distorted shape which made it unlike any team he was accustomed to, was going by, not as if being driven over the earth and stones of the road,—though there was a driver in front, a driver with an odd three-cornered hat on his head and a cloak about his shoulders, such as the little fellow remembered to have seen hanging in his grandmother's closet,—but as if it floated along without sound or stir; in fact, a spectre team which seemed to find its proper destination when it turned into Lost Man's Lane and was lost among the shadows of that ill-reputed road."

"Pshaw!" was my spirited comment as she paused to take her breath and see how I was affected by this grewsome tale. "A dream of the poor little lad! He had heard stories of this apparition and his imagination supplied the rest."

"No; excuse me, madam, he had been carefully kept from hearing all such tales. You could see this by the way he told his story. He hardly believed what he had himself seen. It was not till some foolish neighbor blurted out, 'Why, that was the phantom coach,' that he had any idea he was not relating a dream."

My second Pshaw! was no less marked than the first.

"He did know about it, notwithstanding," I insisted. "Only he had forgotten the fact. Sleep often supplies us with these lost memories."

"Very true, and your supposition is very plausible, Miss Butterworth, and might be regarded as correct, if he had been the only person to see this apparition. But Mrs. Jenkins saw it too, and she is a woman to be believed."

This was becoming serious.

"Saw it before he did or afterwards?" I asked. "Does she live on the highway or somewhere in Lost Man's Lane?"

"She lives on the highway about a half-mile from the station. She was sitting up with her sick husband and saw it just as it was going down the hill. She said it made no more noise than a cloud slipping by. She expects to lose old Rause. No one could behold such a thing as that and not have some misfortune follow."

I laid all this up in my mind. My hour of waiting was not likely to prove wholly unprofitable.

"You see," the good woman went on, with a relish for the marvellous that stood me in good stead, "there is an old tradition of that road connected with a coach. Years ago, before any of us were born, and the house where you are now staying was a gathering-place for all the gay young bloods of the county, a young man came up from New York to visit Mr. Knollys. I do not mean the father or even the grandfather of the folks you are visiting, ma'am. He was great-grandfather to Lucetta, and a very fine gentleman, if you can trust the pictures that are left of him. But my story has not to do with him. He had a daughter at that time, a widow of great and sparkling attractions, and though she was older than the young man I have mentioned, every one thought he would marry her, she was so handsome and such an heiress.

"But he failed to pay his court to her, and though he was handsome himself and made a fool of more than one girl in the town, every one thought he would return as he had come, a free-hearted bachelor, when suddenly one night the coach was missed from the stables and he from the company, which led to the discovery that the young widow's daughter was gone too, a chit who was barely fifteen, and without a hundredth part of the beauty of her mother. Love only could account for this, for in those days young ladies did not ride with gentlemen in the evening for pleasure, and when it came to the old gentleman's ears, and, what was worse, came to the mother's, there was a commotion in the great house, the echoes of which, some say, have never died out. Though the pipers were playing and the fiddles were squeaking in the great room where they used to dance the night away, Mrs. Knollys, with her white brocade tucked up about her waist, stood with her hand on the great front door, waiting for the horse upon which she was determined to follow the flying lovers. The father, who was a man of eighty years, stood by her side. He was too old to ride himself, but he made no effort to hold her back, though the jewels were tumbling from her hair and the moon had vanished from the highway.

"'I will bring her back or die!' the passionate beauty exclaimed, and not a lip said her nay, for they saw, what neither man nor woman had been able to see up to that moment, that her very life and soul were wrapped up in the man who had stolen away her daughter.

"Shrilly piped the pipes, squeak and hum went the fiddles, but the sound that was sweetest to her was the pound of the horses' hoofs on the road in front. That was music indeed, and as soon as she heard it she bestowed one wild kiss on her father and bounded from the house. An instant later and she was gone. One flash of her white robe at the gate, then all was dark on the highway, and only the old father stood in the wide-open door, waiting, as he vowed he would wait, till his daughter returned.

"She did not go alone. A faithful groom was behind her, and from him was learned the conclusion of that quest. For an hour and a half they rode; then they came upon a chapel in the mountains, in which were burning unwonted lights. At the sight the lady drew rein and almost fell from her horse into the arms of her lackey. 'A marriage!' she murmured; 'a marriage!' and pointed to an empty coach standing in the shadow of a wide-spreading tree. It was their family coach. How well she knew it! Rousing herself, she made for the chapel door. 'I will stop these unhallowed rites!' she cried! 'I am her mother, and she is not of age.' But the lackey drew her back by her rich white dress. 'Look!' he cried, pointing in at one of the windows, and she looked. The man she loved stood before the altar with her daughter. He was smiling in that daughter's face with a look of passionate devotion. It went like a dagger to her heart. Crushing her hands against her face, she wailed out some fearful protest; then she dashed toward the door with 'Stop! stop!' on her lips. But the faithful lackey at her side drew her back once more. 'Listen!' was his word, and she listened. The minister, whose form she had failed to note in her first hurried look, was uttering his benediction. She had come too late. The young couple were married.

"Her servant said, or so the tradition runs, that when she realized this she grew calm as walking death. Making her way into the chapel, she stood ready at the door to greet them as they issued forth, and when they saw her there, with her rich bedraggled robe and the gleam of jewels on a neck she had not even stopped to envelop in more than the veil from her hair, the bridegroom seemed to realize what he had done and stopped the bride, who in her confusion would have fled back to the altar where she had just been made a wife. 'Kneel!' he cried. 'Kneel, Amarynth! Only thus can we ask pardon of our mother.' But at that word, a word which seemed to push her a million miles away from these two beings who but two hours before had been the delight of her life, the unhappy woman gave a cry and fled from their presence. 'Go! go!' were her parting words. 'As you have chosen, you must abide. But let no tongue ever again call me mother.'

"They found her lying on the grass outside. As she could no longer sustain herself on a horse, they put her into the coach, gave the reins to her devoted lackey, and themselves rode off on horseback. One man, the fellow who had driven them to that place, said that the clock struck twelve from the chapel tower as the coach turned away and began its rapid journey home. This may and may not be so. We only know that its apparition always enters Lost Man's Lane a few minutes before one, which is the very hour at which the real coach came back and stopped before Mr. Knollys' gate. And now for the worst, Miss Butterworth. When the old gentleman went down to greet the runaways, he found the lackey on the box and his daughter sitting all alone in the coach. But the soil on the brocaded folds of her white dress was no longer that of mud only. She had stabbed herself to the heart with a bodkin she wore in her hair, and it was a corpse which the faithful negro had been driving down the highway that night."

I am not a sentimental woman, but this story as thus told gave me a thrill I do not know as I really regret experiencing.

"What was this unhappy mother's name?" I asked.

"Lucetta," was the unexpected and none too reassuring answer.

XIII

GOSSIP

This name once mentioned called for more gossip, but of a somewhat different nature.

"The Lucetta of to-day is not like her ancient namesake," observed Mrs. Carter. "She may have the heart to love, but she is not capable of showing that love by any act of daring."

"I don't know about that," I replied, astonished that I felt willing to enter into a discussion with this woman on the very subject I had just shrunk from talking over with the locksmith. "Girls as frail and nervous as she is, sometimes astonish one at a pinch. I do not think Lucetta lacks daring."

"You don't know her. Why, I have seen her jump at the sight of a spider, and heaven knows that they are common enough among the decaying walls in which she lives. A puny chit, Miss Butterworth; pretty enough, but weak. The very kind to draw lovers, but not to hold them. Yet every one pities her, her smile is so heart-broken."

"With ghosts to trouble her and a lover to bemoan, she has surely some excuse for that," said I.

"Yes, I don't deny it. But why has she a lover to bemoan? He seemed a proper man and much beyond the ordinary. Why let him go as she did? Even her sister admits that she loved him."

"I am not acquainted with the circumstances," I suggested.

"Well, there isn't much of a story to it. He is a young man from over the mountains, well educated, and with something of a fortune of his own. He came here to visit the Spears, I believe, and seeing Lucetta leaning one day on the gate in front of her house, he fell in love with her and began to pay her his attentions. That was before the lane got its present bad name, but not before one or two men had vanished from among us. William—that is her brother, you know—has always been anxious to have his sisters marry, so he did not stand in the way, and no more did Miss Knollys, but after two or three weeks of doubtful courtship, the young man went away, and that was the end of it. And a great pity, too, say I, for once clear of that house, Lucetta would grow into another person. Sunshine and love are necessities to most women, Miss Butterworth, especially to such as are weakly and timid."

I thought the qualification excellent.

"You are right," I assented, "and I should like to see the result of them upon Lucetta." Then, with an attempt to still further sound this woman's mind and with it the united mind of the whole village, I remarked: "The young do not usually throw aside such prospects without excellent reasons. Have you never thought that Lucetta was governed by principle in discarding this very excellent young man?"

"Principle? What principle could she have had in letting a desirable husband go?"

"She may have thought the match an undesirable one for him."

"For him? Well, I never thought of that. True, she may. They are known to be poor, but poverty don't count in such old families as theirs. I hardly think she would be influenced by any such consideration. Now, if this had happened since the lane got its bad name and all this stir had been made about the disappearance of certain folks within its precincts, I might have given some weight to your suggestion—women are so queer. But this happened long ago and at a time when the family was highly thought of, leastwise the girls, for William does not go for much, you know—too stupid and too brutal."

William! Would the utterance of that name heighten my suggestion? I surveyed her closely, but could detect no change in her somewhat puzzled countenance.

"My allusions were not in reference to the disappearances," said I. "I was thinking of something else. Lucetta is not well."

"Ah, I know! They say she has some kind of heart complaint, but that was not true then. Why, her cheeks were like roses in those days, and her figure as plump and pretty as any you could see among our village beauties. No, Miss

Butterworth, it was through her weakness she lost him. She probably palled upon his taste. It was noticed that he held his head very high in going out of town."

"Has he married since?" I asked.

"Not to my knowledge, ma'am."

"Then he loved her," I declared.

She looked at me quite curiously. Doubtless that word sounds a little queer on my lips, but that shall not deter me from using it when the circumstances seem to require. Besides, there was once a time—But there, I promised to fall into no digressions.

"You should have been married yourself, Miss Butterworth," said she.

I was amazed, first at her daring, and secondly that I was so little angry at this sudden turning of the tables upon myself. But then the woman meant no offence, rather intended a compliment.

"I am very well contented as I am," I returned. "I am neither sickly nor timid."

She smiled, looked as if she thought it only common politeness to agree with me, and tried to say so, but finding the situation too much for her, coughed and discreetly held her peace. I came to her rescue with a new question:

"Have the women of the Knollys family ever been successful in love? The mother of these girls, say—she who was Miss Althea Burroughs—was her life with her husband happy? I have always been curious to know. She and I were schoolmates."

"You were? You knew Althea Knollys when she was a girl? Wasn't she charming, ma'am? Did you ever see a livelier girl or one with more knack at winning affection? Why, she couldn't sit down with you a half-hour before you felt like sharing everything you had with her. It made no difference whether you were man or woman, it was all the same. She had but to turn those mischievous, pleading eyes upon you for you to become a fool at once. Yet her end was sad, ma'am; too sad, when you remember that she died at the very height of her beauty alone and in a foreign land. But I have not answered your question. Were she and the judge happy together? I have never heard to the contrary, ma'am. I'm sure he mourned her faithfully enough. Some think that her loss killed him. He did not survive her more than three years."

"The children do not favor her much," said I, "but I see an expression now and then in Lucetta which reminds me of her mother."

"They are all Knollys," said she. "Even William has traits which, with a few more brains back of them, would remind you of his grandfather, who was the plainest of his race."

I was glad that the talk had reverted to William.

"He seems to lack heart, as well as brains," I said. "I marvel that his sisters put up with him as well as they do."

"They cannot help it. He is not a fellow to be fooled with. Besides, he holds third share in the house. If they could sell it! But, deary me, who would buy an old tumble-down place like that, on a road you cannot get folks who have any consideration for their lives to enter for love or money? But excuse me, ma'am; I forgot that you are living just now on that very road. I'm sure I beg a thousand pardons."

"I am living there as a guest," I returned. "I have nothing to do with its reputation—except to brave it."

"A courageous thing to do, ma'am, and one that may do the road some good. If you can spend a month with the Knollys girls and come out of their house at the end as hale and hearty as you entered it, it will be the best proof possible that there is less to be feared there than some people think. I shall be glad if you can do it, ma'am, for I like the girls and would be glad to have the reputation of the place restored."

"Pshaw!" was my final comment. "The credulity of the town has had as much to do with its loss as they themselves. That educated people such as I see here should believe in ghosts!"

I say final, for at this moment the good lady, springing up, put an end to our conversation. She had just seen a buggy pass the window.

"It's Mr. Trohm," she exclaimed. "Ma'am, if you wish to return home before Mr. Simsbury comes back you may be able to do so with this gentleman. He's a most obliging man, and lives less than a quarter of a mile from the Misses Knollys."

I did not say I had already met the gentleman. Why, I do not know. I only drew myself up and waited with some small inner perturbation for the result of the inquiry I saw she had gone to make.

<h1 style="text-align:center">XIV</h1>

I FORGET MY AGE, OR, RATHER, REMEMBER IT

Mr. Trohm did not disappoint my expectations. In another moment I perceived him standing in the open doorway with the most genial smile on his lips.

"Miss Butterworth," said he, "I feel too honored. If you will deign to accept a seat in my buggy, I shall only be too happy to drive you home."

I have always liked the manners of country gentlemen. There is just a touch of formality in their bearing which has been quite eliminated from that of their city brothers. I therefore became gracious at once and accepted the seat he offered me without any hesitation.

The heads that showed themselves at the neighboring windows warned us to hasten on our route. Mr. Trohm, with a snap of his whip, touched up his horse, and we rode in dignified calm away from the hotel steps into the wide village street known as the main road. The fact that Mr. Gryce had told me that this was the one man I could trust, joined to my own excellent knowledge of human nature and the persons in whom explicit confidence can be put, made the moment one of great satisfaction to me. I was about to make my appearance at the Knollys mansion two hours before I was expected, and thus outwit Lucetta by means of the one man whose assistance I could conscientiously accept.

We were not slow in beginning conversation. The fine air, the prosperous condition of the town offered themes upon which we found it quite easy to dilate, and so naturally and easily did our acquaintanceship progress that we had turned the corner into Lost Man's Lane before I quite realized it. The entrance from the village offered a sharp contrast to the one I had already traversed. There it was but a narrow opening between sombre and unduly crowding trees. Here it was the gradual melting of a village street into a narrow and less frequented road, which only after passing Deacon Spear's house assumed that aspect of wildness which a quarter of a mile farther on deepened into something positively sombre and repellent.

I speak of Deacon Spear because he was sitting on his front doorstep when we rode by. As he was a resident in the lane, I did not fail to take notice of him, though guardedly and with such restraint as a knowledge of his widowed condition rendered both wise and proper.

He was not an agreeable-looking person, at least to me. His hair was sleek, his beard well cared for, his whole person in good if not prosperous condition, but he had the self-satisfied expression I detest, and looked after us with an aspect of surprise I chose to consider a trifle impertinent. Perhaps he envied Mr. Trohm. If so, he may have had good reason for it—it is not for me to judge.

Up to now I had seen only a few scrub bushes at the side of the road, with here and there a solitary poplar to enliven the dead level on either side of us; but after we had ridden by the fence which sets the boundary to the good deacon's land, I noticed such a change in the appearance of the lane that I could not but exclaim over the natural as well as cultivated beauties which every passing moment was bringing before me.

Mr. Trohm could not conceal his pleasure.

"These are my lands," said he. "I have bestowed unremitting attention upon them for years. It is my hobby, madam. There is not a tree you see that has not received my careful attention. Yonder orchard was set out by me, and the fruit it yields—Madam, I hope you will remain long enough with us to taste a certain rare and luscious peach that I brought from France a few years ago. It gives promise of reaching its full perfection this year, and I shall be gratified indeed if you can give it your approval."

This was politeness indeed, especially as I knew what value men like him set upon each individual fruit they watch ripen under their care. Testifying my appreciation of his kindness, I endeavored to introduce another and less harmless and perhaps less personally interesting topic of conversation. The chimneys of his house were beginning to show over the trees, and I had heard nothing from this man on the subject which should have been the most interesting of all to me at this moment. And he was the only person in town I was at liberty to really confide in, and possibly the only man in town who could give me a reliable statement of the reasons why the family I was visiting was regarded in a doubtful light not only by the credulous villagers, but by the New York police. I began by an allusion to the phantom coach.

"I hear," said I, "that this lane has other claims to attention beyond those afforded by the mysteries connected with it. I hear that it has at times a ghostly visitant in the shape of a spectral horse and carriage."

"Yes," he replied, with a seeming understanding that was very flattering; "do not spare the lane one of its honors. It has its nightly horror as well as its daily fear. I wish the one were as unreal as the other."

"You act as if both were unreal to you," said I. "The contrast between your appearance and that of some other members of the lane is quite marked."

"You refer"—he seemed to hate to speak—"to the Misses Knollys, I presume."

I endeavored to treat the subject lightly.

"To your young enemy, Lucetta," I smilingly replied.

He had been looking at me in a perfectly modest and respectful manner, but he dropped his eyes at this and busied himself abstractedly, and yet I thought with some intention, in removing a fly from the horse's flank with the tip of his whip.

"I will not acknowledge her as an enemy," he quietly returned in strictly modulated tones. "I like the girl too well."

The fly had been by this time dislodged, but he did not look up.

"And William?" I suggested. "What do you think of William?"

Slowly he straightened himself. Slowly he dropped the whip back into its socket. I thought he was going to answer, when suddenly his whole attitude changed and he turned upon me a beaming face full of nothing but pleasure.

"The road takes a turn here. In another moment you will see my house." And even while he spoke it burst upon us, and I instantly forgot that I had just ventured on a somewhat hazardous question.

It was such a pretty place, and it was so beautifully and exquisitely kept. There was a charm about its rose-encircled porch that is only to be found in very old places that have been appreciatively cared for. A high fence painted white inclosed a lawn like velvet, and the house itself, shining with a fresh coat of yellow paint, bore signs of comfort in its white-curtained windows not usually to be found in the solitary dwelling of a bachelor. I found my eyes roving over each detail with delight, and almost blushed, or, rather, had I been twenty years younger might have been thought to blush, as I met his eyes and saw how much my pleasure gratified him.

"You must excuse me if I express too much admiration for what I see before me," I said, with what I have every reason to believe was a highly successful effort to hide my confusion. "I have always had a great leaning towards well-ordered walks and trimly kept flower-beds—a leaning, alas! which I have found myself unable to gratify."

"Do not apologize," he hastened to say. "You but redouble my own pleasure in thus honoring my poor efforts with your regard. I have spared no pains, madam, I have spared no pains to render this place beautiful, and most of what you see, I am proud to say, has been accomplished by my own hands."

"Indeed!" I cried in some surprise, letting my eye rest with satisfaction on the top of a long well-sweep that was one of the picturesque features of the place.

"It may have been folly," he remarked, with a gloating sweep of his eye over the velvet lawn and flowering shrubs—a peculiar look that seemed to express something more than the mere delight of possession, "but I seemed to begrudge any hired assistance in the tending of plants every one of which seems to me like a personal friend."

"I understand," was my somewhat un-Butterworthian reply. I really did not quite know myself. "What a contrast to the dismal grounds at the other end of the lane!"

This was more in my usual vein. He seemed to feel the difference, for his expression changed at my remark.

"Oh, that den!" he exclaimed, bitterly; then, seeing me look a little shocked, he added, with an admirable return to his old manner, "I call any place a den where flowers do not grow." And jumping from the buggy, he gathered an exquisite bunch of heliotrope, which he pressed upon me. "I love sunshine, beds of roses, fountains, and a sweep of lawn like this we see before us. But do not let me bore you. You have probably lingered long enough at the old bachelor's place and now would like to drive on. I will be with you in a moment. Doubtful as it is whether I shall soon again be so fortunate as to be able to offer you any hospitality, I would like to bring you a glass of wine—or, for I see your eyes roaming longingly toward my old-fashioned well, would you like a draft of water fresh from the bucket?"

I assured him I did not drink wine, at which I thought his eyes brightened, but that neither did I indulge in water when in a heat, as at present, at which he looked disappointed and came somewhat reluctantly back to the buggy.

He brightened up, however, the moment he was again at my side.

"Now for the woods," he exclaimed, with what was undoubtedly a forced laugh.

I thought the opportunity one I ought not to slight.

"Do you think," said I, "that it is in those woods the disappearances occur of which Miss Knollys has told me?"

He showed the same hesitancy as before to enter upon this subject.

"I think the less you allow your mind to dwell on this matter the better," said he—"that is, if you are going to remain long in this lane. I do not expend any more thought upon it than is barely necessary, or I should not retain sufficient courage to remain among my roses and my fruits. I wonder—pardon me the indiscretion—that you could bring yourself to enter so ill-reputed a neighborhood. You must be a very brave woman."

"I thought it my duty—" I began. "Althea Knollys was my friend, and I felt I owed a duty toward her children. Besides—" Should I tell Mr. Trohm my real errand in this place? Mr. Gryce had intimated that he was in the confidence of the police, and if so, his assistance in case of necessity might be of inestimable value to me. Yet if no such necessity should arise would I want this man to know that Amelia Butterworth—No, I would not take him into my confidence—not yet. I would only try to get at his idea of where the blame lay—that is, if he had any.

"Besides," he suggested in polite reminder, after waiting a minute or two for me to continue.

"Did I say besides?" was my innocent rejoinder. "I think I meant that after seeing them my sense of the importance of that duty had increased. William especially seems to be a young man of very doubtful amiability."

Immediately the non-commital look returned to Mr. Trohm's face.

"I have no fault to find with William," said he. "He's not the most agreeable companion in the world perhaps, but he has a pretty fancy for fruit—a very pretty fancy."

"One can hardly wonder at that in a neighbor of Mr. Trohm," said I, watching his look, which was fixed somewhat gloomily upon the forest of trees now rapidly closing in around us.

"Perhaps not, perhaps not, madam. The sight of a blossoming honeysuckle hanging from an arbor such as runs along my south walls is a great stimulant to one's taste, madam, I'll not deny that."

"But William?" I repeated, determined not to let the subject go; "have you never thought he was a little indifferent to his sisters?"

"A little, madam."

"And a trifle rough to everything but his dogs?"

"A trifle, madam."

Such reticence seemed unnecessary. I was almost angry, but restrained myself and pursued quietly, "The girls, on the contrary, seem devoted to him?"

"Women have that weakness."

"And act as if they would do—what would they not do for him?"

"Miss Butterworth, I have never seen a more amiable woman than yourself. Will you promise me one thing?"

His manner was respect itself, his smile genial and highly contagious. I could not help responding to it in the way he expected.

"Do not talk to me about this family. It is a painful subject to me. Lucetta— you know the girl, and I shall not be able to prejudice you against her—has conceived the idea that I encourage William in an intimacy of which she does not approve. She does not want him to talk to me. William has a loose tongue in his head and sometimes drops unguarded words about their doings, which if any but William spoke—But there, I am forgetting one of the most important rules of my own life, which is to keep my mouth from babbling and my tongue from guile. Influence of a congenial companion, madam; it is irresistible sometimes, especially to a man living so much alone as myself."

I considered his fault very pardonable, but did not say so lest I should frighten his confidences away.

"I thought there was something wrong between you," I said. "Lucetta acted almost afraid of you this morning. I should think she would be glad of the friendship of so good a neighbor."

His face took on a very sombre look.

"She is afraid of me," he admitted, "afraid of what I have seen or may see of—their poverty," he added, with an odd emphasis. I scarcely think he expected to deceive me.

I did not push the subject an inch farther. I saw it had gone as far as discretion permitted at this time.

We had reached the heart of the forest and were rapidly approaching the Knollys house. As the tops of its great chimneys rose above the foliage, I saw his aspect suddenly change.

"I don't know why I should so hate to leave you here," he remarked.

I myself thought the prospect of re-entering the Knollys mansion somewhat uninviting after the pleasant ride I had had and the glimpse which had been given me of a really cheery home and pleasant surroundings.

"This morning I looked upon you as a somewhat daring woman, the progress of whose stay here would be watched by me with interest, but after the companionship of the last half-hour I am conscious of an anxiety in your regard which makes me doubly wish that Miss Knollys had not shut me out from her home. Are you sure you wish to enter this house again, madam?"

I was surprised—really surprised—at the feeling he showed. If my well-disciplined heart had known how to flutter it would probably have fluttered then, but happily the restraint of years did not fail me in this emergency. Taking advantage of the emotion which had betrayed him into an acknowledgment of his real feelings regarding the dangers lurking in this home, despite the check he had endeavored to put upon his lips, I said, with an attempt at naïveté only to be excused by the exigencies of the occasion:

"Why, I thought you considered this domicile perfectly harmless. You like the girls and have no fault to find with William. Can it be that this great building has another occupant? I do not allude to ghosts. Neither of us are likely to believe in the supernatural."

"Miss Butterworth, you have me at a disadvantage. I do not know of any other occupant which the house can hold save the three young people you have mentioned. If I seem to feel any doubt of them—but I don't feel any doubt. I only dread any place for you which is not watched over by someone interested in your defence. The danger threatening the inhabitants of this lane is such a veiled one. If we knew where it lurked, we would no longer call it danger. Sometimes I think the ghosts you allude to are not as innocent as mere spectres usually are. But don't let me frighten you. Don't—" How quick his voice changed! "Ah, William, I have brought back your guest, you see! I couldn't let her sit out the noon hour in old Carter's parlor. That would be too much for even so amiable a person as Miss Butterworth to endure."

I had hardly realized we were so near the gate and certainly was surprised to find William anywhere within hearing. That his appearance at this moment was anything but welcome, must be evident to every one. The sentence which it interrupted might have contained the most important advice, or at the least a warning I could ill afford to lose. But destiny was against me, and being one who accepts the inevitable with good grace, I prepared to alight, with Mr. Trohm's assistance.

The bunch of heliotrope I held was a little in my way or I should have managed the jump with confidence and dignified agility. As it was, I tripped slightly, which brought out a chuckle from William that at the moment seemed more wicked to me than any crime. Meanwhile he had not let matters proceed thus far without putting more than one question.

"And where's Simsbury? And why did Miss Butterworth think she had got to sit in Carter's parlor?"

"Mr. Simsbury," said I as soon as I could recover from the mingled exertion and embarrassment of my descent to terra firma, "felt it necessary to take the horse to the shoer's. That is a half-day's work, as you know, and I felt confident that he and especially you would be glad to have me accept any means for escaping so dreary a waiting."

The grunt he uttered was eloquent of anything but satisfaction.

"I'll go tell the girls," he said. But he didn't go till he had seen Mr. Trohm enter his buggy and drive slowly off.

That all this did not add to my liking for William goes without saying.

BOOK II

THE FLOWER PARLOR

XV

LUCETTA FULFILS MY EXPECTATION OF HER

It was not till Mr. Trohm had driven away that I noticed, in the shadow of the trees on the opposite side of the road, a horse tied up, whose empty saddle bespoke a visitor within. At any other gate and on any other road this would not have struck me as worthy of notice, much less of comment. But here, and after all that I had heard during the morning, the circumstance was so unexpected I could not help showing my astonishment.

"A visitor?" I asked.

"Some one to see Lucetta."

William had no sooner said this than I saw he was in a state of high excitement. He had probably been in this condition when we drove up, but my attention being directed elsewhere I had not noticed it. Now, however, it was perfectly plain to me, and it did not seem quite the excitement of displeasure, though hardly that of joy.

"She doesn't expect you yet," he pursued, as I turned sharply toward the house, "and if you interrupt her—D—n it, if I thought you would interrupt her——"

I thought it time to teach him a lesson in manners.

"Mr. Knollys," I interposed somewhat severely, "I am a lady. Why should I interrupt your sister or give her or you a moment of pain?"

"I don't know," he muttered. "You are so very quick I was afraid you might think it necessary to join her in the parlor. She is perfectly able to take care of herself, Miss Butterworth, and if she don't do it—" The rest was lost in indistinct guttural sounds.

I made no effort to answer this tirade. I took my usual course in quite my usual way to the front steps and proceeded to mount them without so much as looking behind me to see whether or not this uncouth representative of the Knollys name had kept at my heels or not.

Entering the door, which was open, I came without any effort on my part upon Lucetta and her visitor, who proved to be a young gentleman. They were standing together in the middle of the hall and were so absorbed in what they were saying that they neither saw nor heard me. I was therefore enabled to catch the following sentences, which struck me as of some moment. The first was uttered by her, and in very pleading tones:

"A week—I only ask a week. Then perhaps I can give you an answer which will satisfy you."

His reply, in manner if not in matter, proclaimed him the lover of whom I had so lately heard.

"I cannot, dear girl; indeed, I cannot. My whole future depends upon my immediately making the move in which I have asked you to join me. If I wait a week, my opportunity will be gone, Lucetta. You know me and you know how I love you. Then come——"

A rude hand on my shoulder distracted my attention. William stood lowering behind me and, as I turned, whispered in my ear:

"You must come round the other way. Lucetta is so touchy, the sight of you will drive every sensible idea out of her head."

His blundering whisper did what my presence and by no means light footsteps had failed to do. With a start Lucetta turned and, meeting my eye, drew back in visible confusion. The young man followed her hastily.

"Is it good-by, Lucetta?" he pleaded, with a fine, manly ignoring of our presence that roused my admiration.

She did not answer. Her look was enough. William, seeing it, turned furious at once, and, bounding by me, faced the young man with an oath.

"You're a fool to take no from a silly chit like that," he vociferated. "If I loved a girl as you say you love Lucetta, I'd have her if I had to carry her away by force. She'd stop screaming before she was well out of the lane. I know women. While you listen to them they'll talk and talk; but once let a man take matters into his own hands and—" A snap of his fingers finished the sentence. I thought the fellow brutal, but scarcely so stupid as I had heretofore considered him.

His words, however, might just as well have been uttered into empty air. The young man he so violently addressed appeared hardly to have heard him, and as for Lucetta, she was so nearly insensible from misery that she had sufficient ado to keep herself from falling at her lover's feet.

"Lucetta, Lucetta, is it then good-by? You will not go with me?"

"I cannot. William, here, knows that I cannot. I must wait till——"

But here her brother seized her so violently by the wrist that she stopped from sheer pain, I fear. However that was, she turned pale as death under his clutch, and, when he tried to utter some hot, passionate words into her ear, shook her head, but did not speak, though her lover was gazing with a last, final appeal into her eyes. The delicate girl was bearing out my estimate of her.

Seeing her thus unresponsive, William flung her hand from him and turned upon me.

"It's your fault," he cried. "You would come in——"

But, at this, Lucetta, recovering her poise in a moment, cried out shrilly:

"For shame, William! What has Miss Butterworth to do with this? You are not helping me with your roughness. God knows I find this hour hard enough, without this show of anxiety on your part to be rid of me."

"There's woman's gratitude for you," was his snarling reply. "I offer to take all the responsibilities on my own shoulders and make it right with—with her sister, and all that, and she calls it desire to get rid of her. Well, have your own way," he growled, storming down the hall; "I'm done with it for one."

The young man, whose attitude of reserve, mixed with a strange and lingering tenderness for this girl, whom he evidently loved without fully understanding her, was every minute winning more and more of my admiration, had meanwhile raised her trembling hand to his lips in what was, as we all could see, a last farewell.

In another moment he was walking by us, giving me as he passed a low bow that for all its grace did not succeed in hiding from me the deep and heartfelt disappointment with which he quitted this house. As his figure passed through the door, hiding for one moment the sunshine, I felt an oppression such as has not often visited my healthy nature, and when it passed and disappeared, something like the good spirit of the place seemed to go with it, leaving in its place doubt, gloom, and a morbid apprehension of that unknown something which in Lucetta's eyes had rendered his dismissal necessary.

"Where's Saracen? I declare I'm nothing but a fool without that dog," shouted William. "If he has to be tied up another day—" But shame was not entirely eliminated from his breast, for at Lucetta's reproachful "William!" he sheepishly dropped his head and strode out, muttering some words I was fain to accept as an apology.

I had expected to encounter a wreck in Lucetta, as, this episode in her life closed, she turned toward me. But I did not yet know this girl, whose frailty seemed to lie mostly in her physique. Though she was suffering far more than her defence of me to her brother would seem to denote, there was a spirit in her approach and a steady look in her dark eye which assured me that I could not calculate upon any loss in Lucetta's keenness, in case we came to an issue over the mystery that was eating into the happiness as well as the honor of this household.

"I am glad to see you," were her unexpected words. "The gentleman who has just gone out was a lover of mine; at least he once professed to care for me very much, and I should have been glad to have married him, but there were reasons which I once thought most excellent why this seemed anything but expedient, and so I sent him away. To-day he came without warning to ask me to go away with him, after the hastiest of ceremonies, to South America, where a splendid prospect has suddenly opened for him. You see, don't you, that I could not do that; that it would be the height of selfishness in me to leave Loreen—to leave William——"

"Who seems only too anxious to be left," I put in, as her voice trailed off in the first evidence of embarrassment she had shown since she faced me.

"William is a difficult man to understand," was her firm but quiet retort. "From his talk you would judge him to be morose, if not positively unkind, but in action—" She did not tell me how he was in action. Perhaps her truthfulness got the better of her, or perhaps she saw it would be hard work to prejudice me now in his favor.

XVI

LOREEN

Lucetta had said to her departing lover, that in a week she might be able (were he willing or in a position to wait) to give him a more satisfactory answer. Why in a week?

That her hesitation sprang from the mere dislike of leaving her sister so suddenly, or that she had sacrificed her life's happiness to any childish idea of decorum, I did not think probable. The spirit she had shown, her immovable attitude under a temptation which had not only romance to recommend it, but everything else which could affect a young and sensitive woman, argued in my mind the existence of some uncompleted duty of so exacting and imperative a nature that she could not even consider the greatest interests of her own life until this one thing was out of her way. William's rude question of the morning, "What shall we do with the old girl till it is all over?" recurred to me in support of this theory, making me feel that I needed no further confirmation, to be quite certain that a crisis was approaching in this house which would tax my powers to the utmost and call perhaps for the use of the whistle which I had received from Mr. Gryce, and which, following his instructions, I had tied carefully about my neck. Yet how could I associate Lucetta with crime, or dream of the police in connection with the serene Loreen, whose every look was a rebuke to all that was false, vile, or even common? Easily, my readers, easily, with that great, hulking William in my remembrance. To shield him, to hide perhaps his deformity of soul from the world, even such gentle and gracious women as these have been known to enter into acts which to an unprejudiced eye and an unbiased conscience would seem little short of fiendish. Love for an unworthy relative, or rather the sense of duty toward those of one's own blood, has driven many a clear-minded woman to her ruin, as may be seen any day in the police annals.

I am quite aware that I have not as yet put into definite words the suspicion upon which I was now prepared to work. Up to this time it had been too vague, or rather of too monstrous a character for me not to consider other theories, such as, for instance, the possible connection of old Mother Jane with the unaccountable disappearances which had taken place in this lane. But after this scene, the increased assurance I was hourly receiving that something extraordinary and out of keeping with the customary appearances of the household was secretly going on in some one of the various chambers of that long corridor I had been prevented from entering, forced me to accept and act upon the belief that these young women held in charge a prisoner of some kind, of whose presence in the house they dreaded the discovery.

Now, who could this prisoner be?

Common sense supplied me with but one answer; Silly Rufus, the boy who within a few days had vanished from among the good people of this seemingly guileless community.

This theory once established in my mind, I applied myself to a consideration of the means at my disposal for determining its validity. The simplest, surest, but least satisfactory to one of my nature was to summon the police and have the house thoroughly searched, but this involved, in case I had been deceived by appearances—as was possible even to a woman of my experience and discrimination,—a scandal and an opprobrium which I would be the last to inflict upon Althea's children, unless justice to the rest of the world demanded it.

It was in consideration of this very fact, perhaps, that I had been chosen for this duty instead of some regular police spy. Mr. Gryce, as I very well knew, has made it his rule of life never to risk the reputation of any man or woman without reasons so excellent as to carry their own exoneration with them, and should I, a woman, with full as much heart as himself, if not quite as much brain (at least in the estimation of people in general), by any premature exposure of my suspicions, subject these young friends of mine to humiliations they are far too weak and too poor to rise above?

No, rather would I trust a little longer to my own perspicacity and make sure by the use of my own eyes that the situation called for the interference I had, as you may say, at the end of the cord I wore about my neck.

Lucetta had not asked me how I came to be back so much sooner than she had reason to expect me. The unlooked-for arrival of her lover had probably put all idea of her former plans out of her head. I therefore gave her the shortest of explanations when we met at the dinner table. Nothing further seemed to be necessary, for the girls were even more abstracted than before, and William positively boorish till a warning glance from Loreen recalled him to his better self, which meant silence.

The afternoon was spent in very much the same way as the evening before. Neither sister remained an instant with me after the other entered my company, and though the alternations were less frequent than at that time, their peculiarities were more marked and less naturally accounted for. It was while Loreen was with me that I made the suggestion which had been hovering on my lips ever since the noon.

"I consider this," I observed, in one of the pauses of our more than fitful conversation, "one of the most interesting houses it has ever been my good fortune to enter. Would you mind my roaming about a bit just to enjoy the old-time flavor of its great empty rooms? I know they are mostly closed and possibly unfurnished, but to a connoisseur like myself in colonial architecture, this rather adds to, than detracts from, their interest."

"Impossible," she was going to say, but caught herself back in time and changed the imperative word to one more conciliatory if equally unyielding.

"I am sorry, Miss Butterworth, to deny you this gratification, but the condition of the rooms and the unhappy excitement into which we have been thrown by the unfortunate visit paid to Lucetta by a gentleman to whom she is only too much attached, make it quite impossible for me to consider any such undertaking to-day. To-morrow I may find it easier; but, if not, be assured you shall see every nook and corner of this house before you finally leave it."

"Thank you. I will remember that. To one of my tastes an ancient room in a time-honored mansion like this, affords a delight not to be understood by one who knows less of the last century's life. The legends connected with your great drawing-room below [we were sitting in my room, I having refused to be cooped up in their dreary side parlor, and she not having offered me any other spot more cheerful] are sufficient in themselves to hold me entranced for an hour. I heard one of them to-day."

"Which?"

She spoke more quickly than usual, and for her quite sharply.

"That of Lucetta's namesake," I explained. "She who rode through the night after a daughter who had won her lover's heart away from her.

"Ah, it is a well-known tale, but I think Mrs. Carter might have left its relation to us. Did she tell you anything else?"

"No other tradition of this place," I assured her.

"I am glad she was so considerate. But why—if you will pardon me—did she happen to light upon that story? We have not heard those incidents spoken of for years."

"Not since the phantom coach flew through this road the last time," I ventured, with a smile that should have disarmed her from suspecting any ulterior motive on my part in thus introducing a subject which could not be altogether pleasing to her.

"The phantom coach! Have you heard of that?"

I wish it had been Lucetta who had said this and to whom my reply was due. The opportunities would have been much greater for an injudicious display of feeling on her part and for a suitable conclusion on mine.

But it was Loreen, and she never forgot herself. So I had to content myself with the persuasion that her voice was just a whit less clear than usual and her serenity enough impaired for her to look out of my one high and dismal window instead of into my face.

"My dear,"—I had not called her this before, though the term had frequently risen to my lips in answer to Lucetta—"you should have gone with me into the village to-day. Then you would not need to ask if I had heard of the phantom coach."

The probe had reached the quick at last. She looked quite startled.

"You amaze me," she said. "What do you mean, Miss Butterworth? Why should I not have needed to ask?"

"Because you would have heard it whispered about in every lane and corner. It is common talk in town to-day. You must know why, Miss Knollys."

She was not looking out of the window now. She was looking at me.

"I assure you," she murmured, "I do not know at all. Nothing could be more incomprehensible to me. Explain yourself, I entreat you. The phantom coach is but a myth to me, interesting only as involving certain long-vanished ancestors of mine."

"Of course," I assented. "No one of real sense could regard it in any other light. But villagers will talk, and they say—you will soon know what, if I do not tell you myself—that it passed through the lane on Tuesday night."

"Tuesday night!" Her composure had been regained, but not so entirely but that her voice slightly trembled. "That was before you came. I hope it was not an omen."

I was in no mood for pleasantry.

"They say that the passing of this apparition denotes misfortune to those who see it. I am therefore obviously exempt. But you—did you see it? I am just curious to know if it is visible to those who live in the lane. It ought to have turned in here. Were you fortunate enough to have been awake at that moment and to have seen this spectral appearance?"

She shuddered. I was not mistaken in believing I saw this sign of emotion, for I was watching her very closely, and the movement was unmistakable.

"I have never seen anything ghostly in my life," said she. "I am not at all superstitious."

If I had been ill-natured or if I had thought it wise to press her too closely, I might have inquired why she looked so pale and trembled so visibly.

But my natural kindness, together with an instinct of caution, restrained me, and I only remarked:

"There you are sensible, Miss Knollys—doubly so as a denizen of this house, which, Mrs. Carter was obliging enough to suggest to me, is considered by many as haunted."

The straightening of Miss Knollys' lips augured no good to Mrs. Carter.

"Now I only wish it was," I laughed dryly. "I should really like to meet a ghost, say, in your great drawing-room, which I am forbidden to enter."

"You are not forbidden," she hastily returned. "You may explore it now if you will excuse me from accompanying you; but you will meet no ghosts. The hour is not propitious."

Taken aback by her sudden amenity, I hesitated for a moment. Would it be worth while for me to search a room she was willing to have me enter? No, and yet any knowledge which could be obtained in regard to this house might be of use to me or to Mr. Gryce. I decided to embrace her offer, after first testing her with one other question.

"Would you prefer to have me steal down these corridors at night and dare their dusky recesses at a time when spectres are supposed to walk the halls they once flitted through in happy consciousness?"

"Hardly." She made the greatest effort to sustain the jest, but her concern and dread were manifest. "I think I had better give you the keys now, than subject you to the drafts and chilling discomforts of this old place at midnight."

I rose with a semblance of eager anticipation.

"I will take you at your word," said I. "The keys, my dear. I am going to visit a haunted room for the first time in my life."

I do not think she was deceived by this feigned ebullition. Perhaps it was too much out of keeping with my ordinary manner, but she gave no sign of surprise and rose in her turn with an air suggestive of relief.

"Excuse me, if I precede you," she begged. "I will meet you at the head of the corridor with the keys."

I was in hopes she would be long enough in obtaining them to allow me to stroll along the front hall to the opening into the corridor I was so anxious to enter. But the spryness I showed, seemed to have a corresponding effect upon her, for she almost flew down the passageway before me and was back at my side before I could take a step in the coveted direction.

"These will take you into any room on the first floor," said she. "You will meet with dust and Lucetta's abhorrence, spiders, but for these I shall make no apologies. Girls who cannot provide comforts for the few rooms they utilize, cannot be expected to keep in order the large and disused apartments of a former generation."

"I hate dirt and despise spiders," was my dry retort, "but I am willing to brave both for the pleasure of satisfying my love for the antique." At which she handed me the keys, with a calm smile which was not without its element of sadness.

"I will be here on your return," she said, leaning over the banisters to speak to me as I took my first steps down. "I shall want to hear whether you are repaid for your trouble."

I thanked her and proceeded on my way, somewhat doubtful whether by so doing I was making the best possible use of my opportunities.

XVII

THE FLOWER PARLOR

The lower hall did not correspond exactly with the one above. It was larger, and through its connection with the front door, presented the shape of a letter T—that is, to the superficial observer who was not acquainted with the size of the house and had not had the opportunity of remarking that at the extremities of the upper hall making this T, were two imposing doors usually found shut except at meal-times, when the left-hand one was thrown open, disclosing a long and dismal corridor similar to the ones above. Half-way down this corridor was the dining-room, into which I had now been taken three times.

The right-hand one, I had no doubt, led the way into the great drawing-room or dancing-hall which I had started out to see.

Proceeding first to the front of the house, where some glimmer of light penetrated from the open sitting-room door, I looked the keys over and read what was written on the several tags attached to them. They were seven in number, and bore some such names as these: "Blue Chamber," "Library," "Flower Parlor," "Shell Cabinet," "Dark Parlor"—all of which was very suggestive, and, to an antiquarian like myself, most alluring.

But it was upon a key marked "A" I first fixed my attention. This, I had been told, would open the large door at the extremity of the upper hall, and when I made a trial with it I found it to move easily, though somewhat gratingly, in the lock, releasing the great doors, which in another moment swung inward with a growling sound which might have been startling to a nervous person filled with the legends of the place.

But in me the only emotion awakened was one of disgust at the nauseous character of the air which instantly enveloped me. Had I wished for any further proof than was afforded by the warning given me by the condition of the hinges, that the foot of man had not lately invaded these precincts, I would have had it in the mouldy atmosphere and smell of dust that greeted me on the threshold. Neither human breath nor a ray of outdoor sunshine seemed to have disturbed its gloomy quiet for years, and when I moved, as I presently did, to open one of the windows I dimly discerned at my right, I felt such a movement of something foul and noisome amid the decaying rags of the carpet through which I was stumbling that I had to call into use the stronger elements of my character not to back out of a place so given over to rot and the creatures that infest it.

"What a spot," thought I, "for Amelia Butterworth to find herself in!" and wondered if I could ever wear again the three-dollar-a-yard silk dress in which I was then enveloped. Of my shoes I took no account. They were ruined, of course.

I reached the window in safety, but could not open it; neither could I move the adjoining one. There were sixteen in all, or so I afterwards found, and not till I reached the last (you see, I am very persistent) did I succeed in loosening the bar that held its inner shutter in place. This done, I was able to lift the window, and for the first time in years, perhaps, let in a ray of light into this desolated apartment.

The result was disappointing. Mouldy walls, worm-eaten hangings, two very ancient and quaint fireplaces, met my eyes, and nothing more. The room was absolutely empty. For a few minutes I allowed my eyes to roam over the great rectangular space in which so much that was curious and interesting had once taken place, and then, with a vague sense of defeat, turned my eyes outward, anxious to see what view could be obtained from the window I had opened. To my astonishment, I saw before me a high wall with here and there a window in it, all tightly barred and closed, till by a careful inspection about me I realized that I was looking upon the other wing of the building, and that between these wings extended a court so narrow and long that it gave to the building the shape, as I have before said, of the letter U. A dreary prospect, reminding one of the view from a prison, but it had its point of interest, for in the court below me, the brick pavement of which was half obliterated by grass, I caught sight of William in an attitude so different from any I had hitherto seen him assume that I found it difficult to account for it till I caught sight of the jaws of a dog protruding from under his arms, and then I realized he was hugging Saracen.

The dog was tied, but the comfort which William seemed to take in just this physical contact with his rough skin was something worth seeing. It made me quite thoughtful for a moment.

I detest dogs, and it gives me a creepy sensation to see them fondled, but sincerity of feeling appeals to me, and no one could watch William Knollys with his dogs without seeing that he really loved the brutes. Thus in one day I had witnessed the best and worst side of this man. But wait! Had I seen the worst? I was not so sure that I had.

He had not noticed my peering, for which I was duly thankful, and after another fruitless survey of the windows in the wall before me, I drew back and prepared to leave the place. This was by no means a pleasant undertaking. I could now see what I had only felt before, and to traverse the space before me amid beetles and spiders required a determination of no ordinary nature. I was glad when I reached the great doors and more than glad when they closed behind me.

"So much for Room A," thought I.

The next most promising apartment was in the same corridor as the dining-room. It was called the Dark Parlor. Entering it, I found it dark indeed, but not because of lack of light, but because its hangings were all of a dismal red and its furniture of the blackest ebony. As this mainly consisted of shelves and cabinets placed against three of its four walls, the effect was gloomy indeed, and fully accounted for the name which the room had received. I lingered in it, however, longer than I had in the big drawing-room, chiefly because the shelves contained books.

Had anything better offered I might not have continued my explorations, but not seeing exactly how I could pass away the time more profitably, I chose out another key and began to search for the Flower Parlor. I found it beyond the dining-room in the same hall as the Dark Parlor.

It was, as I might have expected from the name, the brightest and most cheerful spot I had yet found in the whole house. The air in it was even good, as if sunshine and breeze had not been altogether shut out of it, yet I had no sooner taken one look at its flower-painted walls and pretty furniture than I felt an oppression difficult to account for. Something was wrong about this room. I am not superstitious and have no faith in premonitions, but once seized by a conviction, I have never known myself to be mistaken as to its import. Something was wrong about this room—what, it was my business to discover.

Letting in more light, I took a closer survey of the objects I had hitherto seen but dimly. They were many and somewhat contradictory in character. The floor was bare—the first bare floor I had come upon—but the shades in the windows, the chintz-covered lounges drawn up beside tables bestrewn with books and other objects of comfort and luxury, bespoke a place in common if not every-day use.

A faint smell of tobacco assured me in whose use, and from the minute I recognized that this was William's sanctum, my curiosity grew unbounded and I neglected nothing which would be likely to attract the keenest-eyed detective in Mr. Gryce's force. There were several things to be noted there: First, that this lumbering lout of a man read, but only on one topic—vivisection; secondly, that he was not a reader merely, for there were instruments in the cases heaped up on the tables about me, and in one corner—it made me a little sick, but I persevered in searching out the corners—a glass case with certain horrors in it which I took care to note, but which it is not necessary for me to describe. Another corner was blocked up by a closet which stood out in the room in a way to convince me it had been built in after the room was otherwise finished. As I crossed over to examine the door, which did not appear to me to be quite closed, I noticed on the floor at my feet a huge discoloration. This was the worst thing I had yet encountered, and while I did not feel quite justified in giving it a name, I could not but feel some regret for the worm-eaten rags of the drawing-room, which, after all, are more comfortable underfoot than bare boards with such suggestive marks upon them as these.

The door to the closet was, as I had expected, slightly ajar, a fact for which I was profoundly grateful, for, set it down to breeding or a natural recognition of other people's rights, I would have found it most difficult to turn the knob of a closet door, inspection of which had not been offered me.

But finding it open, I gave it just a little pull and found—well, it was a surprise, much more so than the sight of a skeleton would have been—that the whole interior was taken up by a small circular staircase such as you find in public libraries where the books are piled up in tiers. It stretched from the floor to the ceiling, and dark as it was I thought I detected the outlines of a trap-door by means of which communication was established with the room above. Anxious to be convinced of this, I consulted with myself as to what a detective would do in my place. The answer came readily enough: "Mount the stairs and feel for yourself whether there is a lock there." But my delicacy or—shall I acknowledge it for once?—an instinct of timidity seemed to restrain me, till a remembrance of Mr. Gryce's sarcastic look which I had seen honoring lesser occasions than these, came to nerve me, and I put foot on the stairs which had last been trod—by whom, shall I say? William? Let us hope by William, and William only.

Being tall, I had to mount but a few steps before reaching the ceiling.

Pausing for breath, the air being close and the stairs steep, I reached up and felt for the hinge or clasp I had every reason to expect to encounter. I found it almost immediately, and, satisfied now that nothing but a board separated me from the room above, I tried that board with my finger and was astonished to feel it yield. As this was a wholly unexpected discovery I drew back and asked myself if it would be wise to pursue it to the point of raising this door, and had hardly settled the question in my own mind, when the sound of a voice raised in a soothing murmur, revealed the fact that the room above was not empty, and that I would be committing a grave indiscretion in thus tampering with a means of entrance possibly under the very eye of the person speaking.

If the voice I had heard had been all that had come to my ears, I might have ventured after a moment of hesitation to brave the displeasure of Miss Knollys by an attempt which would have at once satisfied me as to the correctness of the suspicions which were congealing my blood as I stood there, but another voice—the heavy and threatening voice of William—had broken into this murmur, and I knew that if I so much as awakened in him the least suspicion of my whereabouts, I would have to dread an anger that might not know where to stop.

I therefore rested from further efforts in this direction, and fearing he might bethink him of some errand which would bring him to the trap-door himself, I began a retreat which I made slow only from my desire not to make any noise. I succeeded as well as if my feet had been shod in velvet and my dress had been made of wool instead of a rustling silk, and when once again I found myself planted in the centre of the Flower Parlor, the closet door closed, and no evidence remaining of my late attempt to probe this family secret, I drew a deep breath of relief that was but a symbol of my devout thankfulness.

I did not mean to remain much longer in this spot of evil suggestions, but spying the corner of a book protruding from under a cushion of one of the lounges, I had a curiosity to see if it were similar to the others I had handled. Drawing it out, I took one look at it.

I need not tell what it was, but after a hasty glance here and there through its pages, I put it back, shuddering. If any doubt remained in my breast that William was one of those monsters who feed their morbid cravings by experiments upon the weak and defenceless, it had been dispelled by what I had just seen in this book.

However, I did not leave the room immediately. As it was of the greatest importance that I should be able to locate in which of the many apartments on the floor above, the supposed prisoner was lodged, I cast about me for the means of doing this through the location of the room in which I then was. As this could only be done by affixing some token to the window, which could be recognized from without, I thought, first, of thrusting the end of my handkerchief through one of the slats of the outside blinds; secondly, of simply leaving one of these blinds ajar; and finally, of chipping off a piece with the penknife I always carry with innumerable other small things in the bag I invariably wear at my side. (Fashion, I hold, counts for nothing against convenience.)

This last seemed by much the best device. A handkerchief could be discovered and pulled out, an open blind could be shut, but a sliver once separated from the wood of the casement, nothing could replace it or even cover it up without itself attracting attention.

Taking out my knife, I glanced at the door leading into the hall, found it still shut and everything quiet behind it. Then I took a look into the shrubs and bushes of the yard outside, and, observing nothing to disturb me, snipped off a bit from one of the outer edges of the slats and then carefully reclosed the blinds and the window.

I was crossing the threshold when I heard a rapid footstep in the hall. Miss Knollys was hastening down the hall to my side.

"Oh, Miss Butterworth," she exclaimed, with one quick look into the room I was leaving, "this is William's den, the one spot he never allows any of us to enter. I don't know how the key came to be upon the string. It never was before, and I am afraid he never will forgive me."

"He need never know that I have been the victim of such a mistake," said I. "My feet leave no trail, and as I use no perfumes he will never suspect that I have enjoyed a glimpse of these old-fashioned walls and ancient cabinets."

"The slats of the blinds are a little open," she remarked, her eyes searching my face for some sign that I am sure she did not find there. "Were they so when you came in?"

"I hardly think so; it was very dark. Shall I put them as I found them?"

"No. He will not notice." And she hurried me out, still eying me breathlessly as if she half distrusted my composure.

"Come, Amelia," I now whispered in self-admonition, "the time for exertion has come. Show this young woman, who is not much behind you in self-control, some of the lighter phases of your character. Charm her, Amelia, charm her, or you may live to rue this invasion into family secrets more than you may like to acknowledge at the present moment."

A task of some difficulty, but I rejoice in difficult tasks, and before another half-hour had passed, I had the satisfaction of seeing Miss Knollys entirely restored to that state of placid melancholy which was the natural expression of her calm but unhappy nature.

We visited the Shell Cabinet, the Blue Parlor, and another room, the peculiarities of which I have forgotten. Frightened by the result of leaving me to my own devices, she did not quit me for an instant, and when, my curiosity quite satisfied, I hinted that a short nap in my own room would rest me for the evening, she proceeded with me to the door of my apartment.

"The locksmith whom I saw this morning has not kept his word," I remarked as she was turning away.

"None of the tradesmen here do that," was her cold answer. "I have given up expecting having any attention paid to my wants."

"Humph," thought I. "Another pleasant admission. Amelia Butterworth, this has not been a cheerful day."

XVIII

THE SECOND NIGHT

I cannot say that I looked forward to the night with any very cheerful anticipations. The locksmith having failed to keep his appointment, I was likely to have no more protection against intrusion than I had had the night before, and while I cannot say that I especially feared any unwelcome entrance into my apartment, I should have gone to my rest with a greater sense of satisfaction if a key had been in the lock and that key had been turned by my own hand on my own side of the door.

The atmosphere of gloom which settled down over the household after the evening meal, seemed like the warning note of something strange and evil awaiting us. So marked was this, that many in my situation would have further disturbed these girls by some allusion to the fact. But that was not the rôle I had set myself to play at this crisis. I remembered what Mr. Gryce had said about winning their confidence, and though the turmoil evident in Lucetta's mind and the distraction visible even in the careful Miss Knollys led me to expect a culmination of some kind before the night was over, I not only hid my recognition of this fact, but succeeded in sufficiently impressing them with the contentment which my own petty employments afforded me (I am never idle even in other persons' houses) for them to spare me the harassment of their alternate visits, which, in their present mood and mine promised little in the way of increased knowledge of their purposes and much in the way of distraction and the loss of that nerve upon which I calculated for a successful issue out of the possible difficulties of this night.

Had I been a woman of ordinary courage, I would have sounded three premonitory notes upon my whistle before blowing out my candle, but while I am not lacking, I hope, in many of the finer feminine qualities which link me to my sex, I have but few of that sex's weaknesses and none of its instinctive reliance upon others which leads it so often to neglect its own resources. Till I saw good reasons for summoning the police, I proposed to preserve a discreet silence, a premature alarm being in their eyes, as I knew from many talks with Mr. Gryce, the one thing suggestive of a timid and inexperienced mind.

Hannah had brought me a delicious cup of tea at ten, the influence of which was to make me very drowsy at eleven, but I shook this weakness off and began my night's watch in a state of stern composure which I verily believe would have awakened Mr. Gryce's admiration had it been consonant with the proprieties for him to have seen it. Indeed the very seriousness of the occasion was such that I could not have trembled if I would, every nerve and faculty being strained to their utmost to make the most of every sound which might arise in the now silent and discreetly darkened house.

I had purposely omitted the precaution of pushing my bed against the door of my room, as I had done the night before, being anxious to find myself in a position to cross its threshold at the least alarm. That this would come, I felt positive, for Hannah in leaving my room had taken pains to say, in unconscious imitation of what Miss Knollys had remarked the night before:

"Don't let any queer sounds you may hear disturb you, Miss Butterworth. There's nothing to hurt you in this house; nothing at all." An admonition which I am sure her young mistresses would not have allowed her to utter if they had been made acquainted with her intention.

But though in a state of high expectation, and listening, as I supposed, with every faculty alert, the sounds I apprehended delayed so long that I began after an hour or two unaccountably to nod in my chair, and before I knew it I was asleep, with the whistle in my hand and my feet pressed against the panels of the door I had set myself to guard. How deep that sleep was or how long I indulged in it, I can only judge from the state of emotion in which I found myself when I suddenly woke. I was sitting there still, but my usually calm frame was in a violent tremble, and I found it difficult to stir, much more to speak. Some one or something was at my door.

An instant and my powerful nature would have asserted itself, but before this could happen the stealthy step drew nearer, and I heard the quiet, almost noiseless, insertion of a key into the lock, and the quick turn which made me a prisoner.

This, with the indignation it caused, brought me quickly to myself. So the door had a key after all, and this was the use it was reserved for. Rising quickly to my feet, I shouted out the names of Loreen, Lucetta, and William, but received no other response than the rapid withdrawal of feet down the corridor. Then I felt for the whistle, which had somehow slipped from my hand, but failed to find it in the darkness, nor when I went to search for the matches to relight the candle I had left standing on a table near by, could I by any means succeed in igniting one, so that I presently had the pleasure of finding myself shut up in my room, with no means of communicating with the world outside and with no light to render the situation tolerable. This was having the tables turned upon me with a vengeance and in a way for which I could not account. I could understand why they had locked me in the room and why they had not heeded my cry of indignant appeal, but I could not comprehend how my whistle came to be gone, nor why the matches, which were sufficiently plentiful in the safe, refused one and all to perform their office.

On these points I felt it necessary to come to some sort of conclusion before I proceeded to invent some way out of my difficulties. So, dropping on my knees by the chair in which I had been sitting, I began a quiet search for the petty object upon which, nevertheless, hung not my safety perhaps, but all chances of success in an undertaking which was every moment growing more serious. I did not find it, but I did find where it had gone. In the floor near the door, my hand encountered a hole which had been covered up by a rug early in the evening, but which I now distinctly remembered having pushed aside with my feet when I took my seat there. This aperture was not large, but it was so deep that my hand failed to reach to the bottom of it; and into this hole by some freak of chance had slipped the small whistle I had so indiscreetly taken into my hand. The mystery of the matches was less easy of solution; so I let it go after a moment of indecisive thought and bent my energies once again to listen, when suddenly and without the least warning there rose from somewhere in the house a cry so wild and unearthly that I started up appalled, and for a moment could not tell whether I was laboring under some fearful dream or a still more fearful reality.

A rushing of feet in the distance and an involuntary murmur of voices soon satisfied me, however, on this score, and drawing upon every energy I possessed, I listened for a renewal of the cry which was yet curdling my blood. But none came, and presently all was as still as if no sound had arisen to disturb the midnight, though every fibre in my body told me that the event I had feared—the event of which I hardly dared mention the character even to myself—had taken place, and that I, who was sent there to forestall it, was not only a prisoner in my room, but a prisoner through my own folly and my inordinate love of tea.

The anger with which I contemplated this fact, and the remorse I felt at the consequences which had befallen the innocent victim whose scream I had just heard, made me very wide-awake indeed, and after an ineffectual effort to make my voice heard from the window, I called my usual philosophy to my aid and decided that since the worst had happened and I, a prisoner, had to await events like any other weak and defenceless woman, I might as well do it with calmness and in a way to win my own approval at least. The dupe of William and his sisters, I would not be the dupe of my own fears or even of my own regrets.

The consequence was a renewed equanimity and a gentle brooding over the one event of the day which brought no regret in its train. The ride with Mr. Trohm, and the acquaintanceship to which it had led, were topics upon which I could rest with great soothing effect through the weary hours stretching between me and daylight. Consequently of Mr. Trohm I thought.

Whether the almost deathly quiet into which the house had now fallen, or the comforting nature of my meditations held inexorably to the topic I had chosen, acted as a soporific upon me I cannot tell, but greatly as I dislike to admit it, feeling sure that you will expect to hear I kept myself awake all that night, I insensibly sank from great alertness to an easy indifference to my surroundings, and from that to vague dreams in which beds of lilies and trellises covered with roses mingled strangely with narrow, winding staircases whose tops ended in the swaying branches of great trees; and so, into quiet and a nothingness that were only broken into by a rap at my door and a cheerful:

"Eight o'clock, ma'am. The young ladies are waiting."

I bounded, literally bounded from my chair. Such a summons, after such a night! What did it mean? I was sitting half dressed in my chair before my door in a straightened and uncomfortable attitude, and therefore had not dreamed that I had been upon the watch all night, yet the sunshine in the room, the cheery tones such as I had not heard even from this woman before, seemed to argue that my imagination had played me false and that no horrors had come to disturb my rest or render my waking distressing.

Stretching out my hand toward the door, I was about to open it, when I bethought me.

"Turn the key in the lock," said I. "Somebody was careful enough of my safety to fasten me in last night."

An exclamation of astonishment came from outside the door.

"There is no key here, ma'am. The door is not locked. Shall I open it and come in?"

I was about to say yes in my anxiety to talk to the woman, but remembering that nothing was to be gained by letting it be seen to what an extent I had carried my suspicions, I hastily disrobed and crept into bed. Pulling the coverings about me, I assumed a comfortable attitude and then cried:

"Come in."

The door immediately opened.

"There, ma'am! What did I tell you? Locked?—this door? Why, the key has been lost for months."

"I cannot help it," I protested, but with little if any asperity, for it did not suit me that she should see I was moved by any extraordinary feeling. "A key was put in that lock about midnight, and I was locked in. It was about the time some one screamed in your own part of the house."

"Screamed?" Her brows took a fine pucker of perplexity. "Oh, that must have been Miss Lucetta."

"Lucetta?"

"Yes, ma'am; she had an attack, I believe. Poor Miss Lucetta! She often has attacks like that."

Confounded, for the woman spoke so naturally that only a suspicious nature like mine would fail to have been deceived by it, I raised myself on my elbow and gave her an indignant look.

"Yet you said just now that the young ladies were expecting me to breakfast."

"Yes, and why not?" Her look was absolutely guileless. "Miss Lucetta sometimes keeps us up half the night, but she does not miss breakfast on that account. When the turn is over, she is as well as ever she was. A fine young lady, Miss Lucetta. I'd lose my two hands for her any day."

"She certainly is a remarkable girl," I declared, not, however, as dryly as I felt. "I can hardly believe I dreamed about the key. Let me feel of your pocket," I laughed.

She, without the smallest hesitancy, pulled aside her apron.

"I am sorry you put so little confidence in my word, ma'am, but Lor' me, what you heard is nothing to what some of our guests have complained of—in the days, I mean, when we did have guests. I have known them to scream out themselves in the middle of the night and vow they saw white figures creeping up and down the halls—all nonsense, ma'am, but believed in by some folks. You don't look as if you believed in ghosts."

"And I don't," I said, "not a whit. It would be a poor way to try to frighten me. How is Mr. William this morning?"

"Oh, he's well and feeding the dogs, ma'am. What made you think of him?"

"Politeness, Hannah," I found myself forced to say. "He's the only man in the house. Why shouldn't I think of him?"

She fingered her apron a minute and laughed.

"I didn't know you liked him. He's so rough, it isn't everybody who understands him," she said.

"Must one understand a person to like him?" I queried good-humoredly. I was beginning to think I might have dreamed about that key.

"I don't know," she said, "I don't always understand Miss Lucetta, but I like

73

her through and through, ma'am, as I like this little finger," and holding up this member to my inspection, she crossed the room for my water-pitcher, which she proposed to fill with hot water.

I followed her closely with my eyes. When she came back, I saw her attention caught by the break in the flooring, which she had not noticed on entering.

"Oh," she exclaimed, "what a shame!" her honest face coloring as she drew the rug back over the small black gap. "I am sure, ma'am," she cried, "you must think very poorly of us. But I assure you, ma'am, it's honest poverty, nothing but honest poverty as makes them so neglectful," and with an air as far removed from mystery as her frank, good-natured manner seemed to be from falsehood, she slid from the room with a kind:

"Don't hurry, ma'am. It is Miss Knollys' turn in the kitchen, and she isn't as quick as Miss Lucetta."

"Humph," thought I, "supposing I had called in the police."

But by the time she had returned with the water, my doubts had reawakened. She was not changed in manner, though I have no doubt she had recounted all that I had said, below, but I was, for I remembered the matches and thought I saw a way of tripping her up in her self-complacency.

Just as she was leaving me for the second time I called her back.

"What is the matter with your matches?" I asked. "I couldn't make them light last night."

With a wholly undisturbed countenance she turned toward the bureau and took up the china trinket that held the few remaining matches I had not scraped on the piece of sandpaper I myself had fastened up alongside the door. A sheepish cry of dismay at once escaped her.

"Why, these are old matches!" she declared, showing me the box in which a half-dozen or so burned matches stood with their burned tops all turned down.

"I thought they were all right. I'm afraid we are a little short of matches."

I did not like to tell her what I thought about it, but it made me doubly anxious to join the young ladies at breakfast and judge for myself from their conduct and expression if I had been deceived by my own fears into taking for realities the phantasies of a nightmare, or whether I was correct in ascribing to fact that episode of the key with all the possibilities that lay behind it.

I did not let my anxiety, however, stand in the way of my duty. Mr. Gryce had bid me carry the whistle he had sent me constantly about my person, and I felt that he would have the right to reproach me if I left my room without making some endeavor to recover this lost article. How to do this without aid or appliances of any kind was a problem. I knew where it was, but I could not see it, much less reach it. Besides, they were waiting for me—never a pleasant thought. It occurred to me that I might lower into the hole a lighted candle hung by a string.

Looking over my effects, I chose out a hairpin, a candle, and two corset laces, (Pardon me. I am as modest as most of my sex, but I am not squeamish. Corset laces are strings, and as such only I present them to your notice.) I should like to have added a button-hook to my collection, but not having as yet discarded the neatly laced boot of my ancestor, I could only produce a small article from my toilet-service which shall remain unmentioned, as I presently discarded it and turned my whole attention to the other objects I have named. A poor array, but out of them I hoped to find the means of fishing up my lost whistle.

My intention was to lower first a lighted candle into the hole by means of a string tied about its middle, then to drop a line on the whistle thus discovered and draw it up with the point of a bent hairpin, which I fondly hoped I could make do the service of a hook. To think was to try. The candle was soon down in the hole, and by its light the whistle was easily seen. The string and bent hairpin went down next. I was successful in hooking the prize and proceeded to pull it up with great care. For an instant I realized what a ridiculous figure I was cutting, stooping over a hole in the floor on both knees, a string in each hand, leading apparently to nowhere, and I at work cautiously steadying one and as carefully pulling on the other. Having hooked the string holding the whistle over the first finger of the hand holding the candle, I may have become too self-conscious to notice the slight release of weight on the whistle hand. Whatever the reason, when the end of the string came in sight there was no whistle on it. The charred end showed me that the candle had burned the cord, letting the whistle fall again out of reach. Down went the candle again. It touched bottom, but no whistle was to be seen. After a long and fruitless search, I concluded to abandon my whistle-fishing excursion, and, rising from my cramped and undignified position, I proceeded to pull up the candle. To my surprise and delight, I found the whistle firmly stuck to the lower side of it. Some drops of candle grease had fallen upon the whistle where it lay. The candle coming in contact with it, the two had adhered, and I became indebted to accident rather than to acumen for the restoration of the precious article.

XIX

A KNOT OF CRAPE

I was prepared for some change in the appearance of my young hostesses, but not for so great a one as I saw on entering the dining-room that memorable morning. The blinds, which were always half closed, were now wide open, and under the cheerful influence of the light which was thus allowed to enter, the table and all its appointments had a much less dreary look than before. Behind the urn sat Miss Knollys, with a smile on her lips, and in the window William stood whistling a cheerful air, unrebuked. Lucetta was not present, but to my great astonishment she presently walked in with her hands laden with sprays of morning-glory, which she flung down in the centre of the board. It was the first time I had seen any attempt made by any of them to lighten the sombreness of their surroundings, and it was also the first time I had seen the three together.

I was more disconcerted by this simple show of improved spirits than I like to acknowledge. In the first place, they were natural and not forced; and, secondly, they were to all appearance unconscious.

They were not marked enough to show relief, and in Lucetta especially did not serve to hide the underlying melancholy of a disappointed girl, yet it was not what I expected from my supposed experiences of the night, and led me to answer a little warily when, with a frank laugh, Loreen exclaimed:

"So you have lost your character as a practical woman, Miss Butterworth? Hannah tells me you were the victim of a ghostly visit last night."

"Hannah gossips unmercifully," was my cautious and somewhat peevish reply. "If I chose to dream that I was locked into my room by some erratic spectre, I cannot see why she should take the confession of my folly out of my mouth. I was going to relate the fact myself, with all the accompaniments of rushing steps and wild and unearthly cries which are expected by the listeners to a veritable ghost story. But now I have simply to defend myself from a charge of credulity. It's too bad, Miss Knollys, much too bad. I did not come to a haunted house for this."

My manner, rather than my words, seemed to completely deceive them. Perhaps it deceived myself, for I began to feel a loss of the depression which had weighed upon me ever since that scream rang in my ears at midnight. It disappeared still further when Lucetta said:

"If your ramblings through the old rooms on this floor were the occasion of this nightmare, you must be prepared for a recurrence of the same to-night, for I am going to take you through the upper rooms myself this morning. Isn't that the programme, Loreen? Or have you changed your mind and planned a drive for Miss Butterworth?"

"She shall do both," Loreen answered. "When she is tired of tramping through dusty chambers and examining the decayed remnants of old furniture which encumber them, William stands ready to drive her over the hills, where she will find views well worth her attention."

"Thank you," said I. "It is a pleasant prospect." But inwardly I uttered anything but thanks; rather asked myself if I had not played the part of a fool in ascribing so much importance to the events of the past night, and decided almost without an argument that I had.

However, beliefs die hard in a mind like mine, and though I was ready to consider that an inflamed imagination may often carry us beyond the bounds of fact and even into the realm of fancy and misconception, I yet was not ready to give up my suspicions altogether, or to acknowledge that I had no foundation for the fear that something uncanny if not awful had taken place under this roof the night before. The very naturalness I observed in this hitherto restrained trio might be the result of the removal of some great strain, and if that was the case—Ah, well, alertness is the motto of the truly wise. It is when vigilance sleeps that the enemy gains the victory. I would not let myself be deceived even at the cost of a little ridicule. Amelia Butterworth was still awake, even under a semblance of well-laid suspicion.

My footsteps were not dogged after this as they had hitherto been in my movements about the house. I was allowed to go and come and even to stray into the second long corridor, without any other let than my own discretion and good breeding. Lucetta joined me, to be sure, after a while, but only as guide and companion. She took me into rooms I forgot the next minute, and into others I remember to this day as quaint memorials of a past ever and always interesting to me. We ransacked the house, yet after all was over and I sat down to rest in my own room, two formidable questions rose in my mind for which I found no satisfactory answer. Why, with so many more or less attractive bedchambers at their command, had they chosen to put me into a hole, where the very flooring was unsafe, and the outlook the most dismal that could be imagined? and why, in all our peregrinations in and out of rooms, had we always passed one door without entering? She had said that it was William's—a sufficient explanation, if true, and I have no doubt it was,—but the change of countenance with which she passed it and the sudden lightening of her tread (so instinctive that she was totally unconscious of it) marked that door as one it would be my duty to enter if fate should yet give me the opportunity. That it was the one in communication with the Flower Parlor I felt satisfied, but in order to make assurance doubly sure I resolved upon a tour through the shrubbery outside, that I might compare the location of the window having the chipped blind with that of this room, which was, as well as I could calculate, the third from the rear on the left-hand side.

When, therefore, William called up to know if I was ready for my drive, I answered back that I found myself very tired and would be glad to exchange the pleasure he offered, for a visit to the stables.

This, as I expected, caused considerable comment and some disturbance. They wanted me to repeat my experience of the day before and spend two if not more hours of the morning out of the house. But I did not mean to gratify them. Indeed I felt that my duty held me to the house, and was so persistent in my wishes, or rather in my declaration of them, that all opposition had to give way, even in the stubborn William.

"I thought you had a dread of dogs," was the final remark with which he endeavored to turn me aside from my purpose. "I have three in the barn and two in the stable, and they make a great fuss when I come around, I assure you."

"Then they will have enough to do without noticing me," said I, with a brazen assumption of courage sufficiently surprising if I had had any real intention of invading a place so guarded. But I had not. I no more meant to enter the stables than to jump off the housetop, but it was necessary that I should start for them and make the start from the left wing of the house.

How I managed the intractable William and led him as I did from bush to bush and shrub to shrub, up and down the length of that interminable façade of the left wing, would make an interesting story in itself. The curiosity I showed in plants, even such plants as had survived the neglect that had made a wilderness of this old-time garden; the indifference which, contrary to all my habits, I persisted in manifesting to every inconvenience I encountered in the way of straightforward walking to any object I set my fancy upon examining; the knowledge I exhibited, and the interest which I took it for granted he felt in all I discovered and all I imparted to him, would form the basis of a farce of no ordinary merit had it not had its birth in interests and intents bordering on the tragic.

A row of bushes of various species ran along the wall and covered in some instances the lower ledges of the first row of windows. As I made for a certain shrub which I had observed growing near what I supposed to be the casement from whose blind I had chipped a small sliver, I allowed my enthusiasm to bubble over, in my evident desire to display my erudition.

"This," said I, "is, without any doubt at all, a stunted but undoubted specimen of that rare tree found seldom north of the thirtieth degree, the Magnolia grandiflora. I have never seen it but once before, and that was in the botanical gardens in Washington. Note its leaves. You have noted its flowers, smaller undoubtedly than they should be—but then you must acknowledge it has been in a measure neglected—are they not fine?"

Here I pulled a branch down which interfered with my view of the window. There was no chip visible in the blinds thus discovered. Seeing this, I let the branch go. "But the oddest feature of this tree and one with which you are perhaps not acquainted" (I wonder if anybody is?) "is that it will not grow within twenty feet of any plant which scatters pollen. See for yourself. This next shrub bears no flower" (I was moving along the wall), "nor this." I drew down a branch as I spoke, caught sight of the mark I was looking for, and let the bough spring back. I had found the window I wanted.

His grunts and groans during all this formed a running accompaniment which would have afforded me great secret amusement had my purpose been less serious. As it was, I could pay but little attention to him, especially after I had stepped back far enough to take a glance at the window over the one I had just located as that of the Flower Parlor. It was, as I expected, the third one from the rear corner; but it was not this fact which gave me a thrill of feeling so strong that I have never had harder work to preserve my equanimity. It was the knot of black crape with which the shutters were tied together.

XX

QUESTIONS

I kept the promise I had made to myself and did not go to the stables. Had I intended to go there, I could not have done so after the discovery I have just mentioned. It awakened too many thoughts and contradictory surmises. If this knot was a signal, for whom was this signal meant? If it was a mere acknowledgment of death, how reconcile the sentimentality which prompted such an acknowledgment with the monstrous and diseased passions lying at the base of the whole dreadful occurrence? Lastly, if it was the result of pure carelessness, a bit of crape having been caught up and used for a purpose for which any ordinary string would have answered, what a wonderful coincidence between it and my thoughts,—a coincidence, indeed, amounting almost to miracle!

Marvelling at the whole affair and deciding nothing, I allowed myself to stroll down alone to the gate, William having left me at my peremptory refusal to drag my skirts any longer through the briers. The day being bright and the sunshine warm, the road looked less gloomy than usual, especially in the direction of the village and Deacon Spear's cottage. The fact is, that anything seemed better than the grim and lowering walls of the house behind me. If my home was there, so was my dread, and I welcomed the sight of Mother Jane's heavy figure bent over her herbs at the door of her hut, a few paces to my left, where the road turned.

Had she not been deaf, I believed I would have called her. As it was, I contented myself with watching the awkward swayings of her body as she pottered to and fro among her turnips and carrots. My eyes were still on her when I suddenly heard the clatter of a horse's hoofs on the highway. Looking up, I encountered the trim figure of Mr. Trohm, bending to me from a fine sorrel.

"Good morning, Miss Butterworth. It's a great relief to me to see you in such good health and spirits this morning," were the pleasant words with which he endeavored, perhaps, to explain his presence in a spot more or less under a ban.

It was certainly a surprise. What right had I to look for such attentions from a man whose acquaintance I had made only the day before? It touched me, little as I am in the habit of allowing myself to be ruled by trivial sentimentalities, and though I was discreet enough to avoid any further recognition of his kindness than was his due from a lady of great self-respect, he was evidently sufficiently gratified by my response to draw rein and pause for a moment's conversation under the pine trees. This for the moment seemed so natural that I forgot that more than one pair of eyes might be watching me from the windows behind us—eyes which might wonder at a meeting which to the foolish understandings of the young might have the look of premeditation. But, pshaw! I am talking as if I were twenty instead of— Well, I will leave you to consult our family record on that point. There are certain secrets which even the wisest among us cannot be blamed for preserving.

"How did you pass the night?" was Mr. Trohm's first question. "I hope in all due peace and quiet."

"Thank you," I returned, not seeing why I should increase his anxiety in my regard. "I have nothing to complain of. I had a dream; but dreams are to be expected where one has to pass a half-dozen empty rooms to one's apartment."

He could not restrain his curiosity.

"A dream!" he repeated. "I do not believe in sleep that is broken by dreams, unless they are of the most cheerful sort possible. And I judge from what you say that yours were not cheerful."

I wanted to confide in him. I felt that in a way he had a right to know what had happened to me, or what I thought had happened to me, under this roof. And yet I did not speak. What I could tell would sound so puerile in the broad sunshine that enveloped us. I merely remarked that cheerfulness was not to be expected in a domicile so given over to the ravages of time, and then with that lightness and versatility which characterize me under certain exigencies, I introduced a topic we could discuss without any embarrassment to himself or me.

"Do you see Mother Jane over there?" I asked. "I had some talk with her yesterday. She seems like a harmless imbecile."

"Very harmless," he acquiesced; "her only fault is greed; that is insatiable. Yet it is not strong enough to take her a quarter of a mile from this place. Nothing could do that, I think. She believes that her daughter Lizzie is still alive and will come back to the hut some day. It's very sad when you think that the girl's dead, and has been dead nearly forty years."

"Why does she harp on numbers?" I asked. "I heard her mutter certain ones over and over."

"That is a mystery none of us have ever been able to solve," said he. "Possibly she has no reason for it. The vagaries of the witless are often quite unaccountable."

He remained looking at me long after he had finished speaking, not, I felt sure, from any connection he found between what he had just said and anything to be observed in me, but from—Well, I was glad that I had been carefully trained in my youth to pay the greatest attention to my morning toilets. Any woman can look well at night and many women in the flush of a bright afternoon, but the woman who looks well in the morning needs not always to be young to attract the appreciative gaze of a man of real penetration. Mr. Trohm was such a man, and I did not begrudge him the pleasure he showed in my neat gray silk and carefully adjusted collar. But he said nothing, and a short silence ensued, which was perhaps more of a compliment than otherwise. Then he uttered a short sigh and lifted the reins.

"If only I were not debarred from entering," he smiled, with a short gesture toward the house.

I did not answer. Even I understand that on occasion the tongue plays but a sorry part in interviews of this nature.

He sighed again and uttered some short encouragement to his horse, which started that animal up and sent him slowly pacing down the road toward the cheerful clearing whither my own eyes were looking with what I was determined should not be construed even by the most sanguine into a glance of anything like wistfulness. As he went he made a bow I have never seen surpassed in my own parlor in Gramercy Park, and upon my bestowing upon him a return nod, glanced up at the house with an intentness which seemed to increase as some object, invisible to me at that moment, caught his eye. As that eye was directed toward the left wing, and lifted as far as the second row of windows, I could not help asking myself if he had seen the knot of crape which had produced upon me so lugubrious an impression. Before I could make sure of this he had passed from sight, and the highway fell again into shadow—why, I hardly knew, for the sun certainly had been shining a few minutes before.

XXI

MOTHER JANE

"Well, well, what did Trohm want here this morning?" cried a harsh voice from amid the tangled walks behind me. "Seems to me he finds this place pretty interesting all of a sudden."

I turned upon the intruder with a look that should have daunted him. I had recognized William's courteous tones and was in no mood to endure a questioning so unbecoming in one of his age to one of mine. But as I met his eye, which had something in it besides anger and suspicion—something that was quizzical if not impertinent—I changed my intention and bestowed upon him a conciliatory smile, which I hope escaped the eye of the good angel who records against man all his small hypocrisies and petty deceits.

"Mr. Trohm rides for his health," said I. "Seeing me looking up the road at Mother Jane, he stopped to tell me some of the idiosyncrasies of that old woman. A very harmless courtesy, Mr. Knollys."

"Very," he echoed, not without a touch of sarcasm. "I only hope that is all," he muttered, with a sidelong look back at the house. "Lucetta hasn't a particle of belief in that man's friendship, or, rather, she believes he never goes anywhere without a particular intention, and I do believe she's right, or why should he come spying around here just at a time when"—he caught himself up with almost a look of terror—"when—when you are here?" he completed lamely.

"I do not think," I retorted, more angrily than the occasion perhaps warranted, "that the word spying applies to Mr. Trohm. But if it does, what has he to gain from a pause at the gate and a word to such a new acquaintance as I am?"

"I don't know," William persisted suspiciously. "Trohm's a sharp fellow. If there was anything to see, he would see it without half looking. But there isn't. You don't know of anything wrong here, do you, which such a man as that, hand in glove with the police as we know him to be, might consider himself interested in?"

Astonished both at this blundering committal of himself and at the certain sort of anxious confidence he showed in me, I hesitated for a moment, but only for a moment, since, if half my suspicions were true, this man must not know that my perspicacity was more to be feared than even Mr. Trohm's was.

"If Mr. Trohm shows an increased interest in this household during the last two days," said I, with a heroic defiance of ridicule which I hope Mr. Gryce has duly appreciated, "I beg leave to call your attention to the fact that on yesterday morning he came to deliver a letter addressed to me which had inadvertently been left at his house, and that this morning he called to inquire how I had spent the night, which, in consideration of the ghosts which are said to haunt this house and the strange and uncanny apparitions which only three nights ago made the entrance to this lane hideous to one pair of eyes at least, should not cause a gentleman's son like yourself any astonishment. It does not seem odd to me, I assure you."

He laughed. I meant he should, and, losing almost instantly his air of doubt and suspicion, turned toward the gate from which I had just moved away, muttering:

"Well, it's a small matter to me anyway. It's only the girls that are afraid of Mr. Trohm. I am not afraid of anything but losing Saracen, who has pined like the deuce at his long confinement in the court. Hear him now; just hear him."

And I could hear the low and unhappy moaning of the hound distinctly. It was not a pleasant sound, and I was almost tempted to bid William unloose the dog, but thought better of it.

"By the way," said he, "speaking of Mother Jane, I have a message to her from the girls. You will excuse me if I speak to the poor woman."

Alarmed by his politeness more than I ever have been by his roughness and inconsiderate sarcasms, I surveyed him inquiringly as he left the gate, and did not know whether to stand my ground or retreat to the house. I decided to stand my ground; a message to this woman seeming to me a matter of some interest.

I was glad I did, for after some five minutes' absence, during which he had followed her into the house, I saw him come back again in a state of sullen displeasure, which, however, partially disappeared when he saw me still standing by the gate.

"Ah, Miss Butterworth, you can do me a favor. The old creature is in one of her stubborn fits to-day, and won't give me a hearing. She may not be so deaf to you; she isn't apt to be to women. Will you cross the road and speak to her? I will go with you. You needn't be afraid."

The way he said this, the confidence he expected to inspire, had almost a ghastly effect upon me. Did he know or suspect that the only thing I feared in this lane was he? Evidently not, for he met my eye quite confidently.

It would not do to shake his faith at such a moment as this, so calling upon Providence to see me safely through this adventure, I stepped into the highway and went with him into Mother Jane's cottage.

Had I been favored with any other companion than himself, I should have been glad of this opportunity. As it was, I found myself ignoring any possible danger I might be running, in my interest in the remarkable interior to which I was thus introduced.

Having been told that Mother Jane was poor, I had expected to confront squalor and possibly filth, but I never have entered a cleaner place or one in which order made the poorest belongings look more decent. The four walls were unfinished, and so were the rafters which formed the ceiling, but the floor, neatly laid in brick, was spotless, and the fireplace, also of brick, was as deftly swept as one could expect from the little scrub I saw hanging by its side. Crouched within this fireplace sat the old woman we had come to interview. Her back was to us, and she looked helplessly and hopelessly deaf.

"Ask her," said William, pointing towards her with a rude gesture, "if she will come to the house at sunset. My sisters have some work for her to do. They will pay her well."

Advancing at his bidding, I passed a rocking-chair, in the cushion of which a dozen patches met my eye. This drew my eyes toward a bed, over which a counterpane was drawn, made up of a thousand or more pieces of colored calico, and noticing their varied shapes and the intricacy with which they were put together, I wondered whether she ever counted them. The next moment I was at her back.

"Seventy," burst from her lips as I leaned over her shoulder and showed her the coin which I had taken pains to have in my hand.

"Yours," I announced, pointing in the direction of the house, "if you will do some work for Miss Knollys to-night."

Slowly she shook her head before burying it deeper in the shawl she wore wrapped about her shoulders. Listening a minute, I thought I heard her mutter: "Twenty-eight, ten, but no more. I can count no more. Go away!"

But I'm nothing if not persistent. Feeling for her hands, which were hidden away somewhere under her shawl, I touched them with the coin and cried again:

"This and more for a small piece of work to-night. Come, you are strong; earn it."

"What kind of work is it?" I asked innocently, or it must have appeared innocently, of Mr. Knollys, who was standing at my back.

He frowned, all the black devils in his heart coming into his look at once.

"How do I know! Ask Loreen; she's the one who sent me. I don't take account of what goes on in the kitchen."

I begged his pardon, somewhat sarcastically I own, and made another attempt to attract the attention of the old crone, who had remained perfectly callous to my allurements.

"I thought you liked money," I said. "For Lizzie, you know, for Lizzie."

But she only muttered in lower and lower gutturals, "I can count no more"; and, disgusted at my failure, being one who accounts failure as little short of disgrace, I drew back and made my way toward the door, saying: "She's in a different mood from what she was yesterday when she snatched a quarter from me at the first intimation it was hers. I don't think you can get her to do any work to-night. Innocents take these freaks. Isn't there some one else you can call in?"

The scowl that disfigured his none too handsome features was a fitting prelude to his words.

"You talk," said he, "as if we had the whole village at our command. How did you succeed with the locksmith yesterday? Came, didn't he? Well, that's what we have to expect whenever we want any help."

Whirling on his heel, he led the way out of the hut, whither I would have immediately followed him if I had not stopped to take another look at the room, which struck me, even upon a second scrutiny, as one of the best ordered and best kept I had ever entered. Even the strings and strings of dried fruits and vegetables, which hung in festoons from every beam of the roof, were free from dust and cobwebs, and though the dishes were few and the pans scarce, they were bright and speckless, giving to the shelf along which they were ranged a semblance of ornament.

"Wise enough to keep her house in order," thought I, and actually found it hard to leave, so attractive to my eyes are absolute neatness and order.

William was pushing at his own gate when I joined him. He looked as if he wished I had spent the morning with Mother Jane, and was barely civil in our walk up to the house. I was not, therefore, surprised when he burst into a volley of oaths at the doorway and turned upon me almost as if he would forbid me the house, for tap, tap, tap, from some distant quarter came a distinct sound like that of nails being driven into a plank.

XXII

THE THIRD NIGHT

Mother Jane must have changed her mind after we left her. For late in the evening I caught a glimpse of her burly figure in the kitchen as I went to give Hannah some instructions concerning certain little changes in the housekeeping arrangements which the girls and I had agreed were necessary to our mutual comfort.

I wished to address the old crone, but warned, by the ill-concealed defiance with which Hannah met my advances, that any such attempt on my part would be met by anything but her accustomed good-nature, I refrained from showing my interest in her strange visitor, or from even appearing conscious of her own secret anxieties and evident preoccupation.

Loreen and Lucetta exchanged a meaning look as I rejoined them in the sitting-room; but my volubility in regard to the domestic affair which had just taken me to the kitchen seemed to speedily reassure them, and when a few minutes later I said good-night and prepared to leave the room, it was with the conviction that I had relieved their mind at the expense of my own. Mother Jane in the kitchen at this late hour meant business. What that business was, I seemed to know only too well.

I had formed a plan for the night which required some courage. Recalling Lucetta's expression of the morning, that I might expect a repetition of the former night's experiences, I prepared to profit by the warning in a way she little meant. Satisfied that if there was any truth in the suspicions I had formed, there would be an act performed in this house to-night which, if seen by me, would forever settle the question agitating the whole countryside, I made up my mind that no locked door should interfere with my opportunity of doing so. How I effected this result I will presently relate.

Lucetta had accompanied me to my door with a lighted candle.

"I hear you had some trouble with matches last night," said she. "You will find them all right now. Hannah must be blamed for some of this carelessness." Then as I began some reassuring reply, she turned upon me with a look that was almost fond, and, throwing out her arms, cried entreatingly: "Won't you give me a little kiss, Miss Butterworth? We have not given you the best of welcomes, but you are my mother's old friend, and sometimes I feel a little lonely."

I could easily believe that, and yet I found it hard to embrace her. Too many shadows swam between Althea's children and myself. She saw my hesitancy (a hesitancy I could not but have shown even at the risk of losing her confidence), and, paling slightly, dropped her hands with a pitiful smile.

"You don't like me," she said. "I do not wonder, but I was in hopes you would for my mother's sake. I have no claims myself."

"You are an interesting girl, and you have, what your mother had not, a serious side to your nature that is anything but displeasing to me. But my kisses, Lucetta, are as rare as my tears. I had rather give you good advice, and that is a fact. Perhaps it is as strong a proof of affection as any ordinary caress would be."

"Perhaps," she assented, but she did not encourage me to give it to her notwithstanding. Instead of that, she drew back and bade me a gentle good-night, which for some reason made me sadder than I wished to be at a crisis demanding so much nerve. Then she walked quickly away, and I was left to face the night alone.

Knowing that I should be rather weakened than helped by the omission of any of the little acts of preparation with which I am accustomed to calm my spirits for the night, I went through them all, with just as much precision as if I had expected to spend the ensuing hours in rest. When all was done and only my cup of tea remained to be quaffed, I had a little struggle with myself, which ended in my not drinking it at all. Nothing, not even this comfortable solace for an unsatisfactory day, should stand in the way of my being the complete mistress of my wits this night. Had I known that this tea contained a soporific in the shape of a little harmless morphine, I would have found this act of self-denial much easier.

It was now eleven. Confident that nothing would be done while my light was burning, I blew it out, and, taking a candle and some matches in my hand, softly opened my door and, after a moment of intense listening, stepped out and closed it carefully behind me. Nothing could be stiller than the house or darker than the corridor.

"Am I watched or am I not watched?" I queried, and for an instant stood undecided. Then, seeing nothing and hearing nothing, I slipped down the hall to the door beyond mine and, opening it with all the care possible, stepped inside.

I knew the room. I had taken especial note of it in my visit of the morning. I knew that it was nearly empty and that there was a key in the lock which I could turn. I therefore felt more or less safe in it, especially as its window was undarkened by the branches that hung so thickly across my own casement, shutting me in, or seeming to shut me in, from all communication with the outside world and the unknown guardian which I had been assured constantly attended my summons.

That I might strengthen my spirits by one glimpse of this same outside world, before settling down for the watch I had set for myself, I stepped softly to the window and took one lingering look without. A belt of forest illumined by a gibbous moon met my eyes; nothing else. Yet this sight was welcome, and it was only after I had been struck by the possibility of my own figure being seen at the casement by some possible watcher in the shadows below, that I found the hardihood necessary to withdraw into the darker precincts of the room, and begin that lonely watch which my doubts and expectations rendered necessary.

This was the third I had been forced to keep, and it was by far the most dismal; for though the bolted door between me and the hall promised me personal safety, there presently rose in some far-off place a smothered repetition of that same tap, tap, tap which had sent the shudders over me upon my sudden entrance into the house early in the morning. Heard now, it caused me to tremble in a way I had not supposed possible to one of my hardy nature, and while with this recognition of my feminine susceptibility to impressions there came a certain pride in the stanchness of purpose which led me to restrain all acknowledgment of fear, by any recourse to my whistle, I was more than glad when even this sound ceased, and I had only to expect the swishing noise of a skirt down the hall, and that stealthy locking of the door of the room I had taken the precaution of leaving.

It came sooner than I expected, came just in the way it had previously done, only that the person paused a moment to listen before hastening back. The silence within must have satisfied her, for I heard a low sigh like that of relief, before the steps took themselves back. That they would turn my way gave me a momentary concern, but I had too completely lulled my young hostesses' suspicions, or (let me be faithful to all the possibilities of the case) they had put too much confidence in the powder with which they had seasoned my nightly cup of tea, for them to doubt that I was soundly asleep in my own quarters.

Three minutes later I followed those steps as far down the corridor as I dared to go. For, since my last appearance in it, a candle had been lit in the main hall, and faint as was its glimmer, it was still a glimmer into the circle of which I felt it would be foolhardiness for me to step. At some twenty paces, then, from the opening, I paused and gave myself up to listening. Alas, there was plenty now for me to hear.

You have heard the sound; we all have heard the sound, but few of us in such a desolate structure and at the hour and under the influences of midnight! The measured tread of men struggling under a heavy weight, and that weight—how well I knew it! as well as if I had seen it, as I really did in my imagination.

They advanced from the adjoining corridor, from the room I had as yet found no opportunity of entering, and they approached surely and slowly the main hall near which I was standing in such a position as rendered it impossible for me to see anything if they took the direct course to the head of the stairs and so down, as there was every reason to expect they would. I did not dare to draw nearer, however, so concentrated my faculties anew upon listening, when suddenly I perceived on the great white wall in front of me— the wall of the main hall, I mean, toward which the opening looked—the shapeless outline of a drooping head, and realized that the candle had been placed in such a position that the wall must receive the full shadow of the passing cortège.

And thus it was I saw it, huge, distorted, and suggestive beyond any picture I ever beheld,—the passing of a body to its long home, carried by six anxious figures, four of which seemed to be those of women.

But that long home! Where was it located—in the house or in the grounds? It was a question so important that for a moment I could think of nothing but how I could follow the small procession, without running the risk of discovery.

It had reached the head of the stairs by this time, and I heard Miss Knollys' low, firm voice enjoining silence. Then the six bearers began to descend with their burden.

Ere they reached the foot, a doubt struck me. Would it be better to follow them or to take the opportunity afforded by every member of the household being engaged in this task, to take a peep into the room where the death had occurred? I had not decided, when I heard them take the forward course from the foot of the stairs to what, to my straining ear, seemed to be the entrance to the dining-room corridor. But as in my anxiety to determine this fact I slipped far enough forward to make sure that their destination lay somewhere within reach of the Flower Parlor, I was so struck by the advantages to be gained by a cautious use of the trap-door in William's room, that I hesitated no longer, but sped with what swiftness I could toward the spot from which I had so lately heard this strange procession advance.

A narrow band of light lying across the upper end of the long corridor, proved that the door was not only ajar, but that a second candle was burning in the room I was about to invade; but this was scarcely to be regretted, since there could be no question of the emptiness of the room. The six figures I had seen go by embraced every one who by any possibility could be considered as having part in this transaction—William, Mr. Simsbury, Miss Knollys, Lucetta, Hannah, and Mother Jane. No one else was left to guard this room, so I pushed the door open quite boldly and entered.

What I saw there I will relate later, or, rather, I will but hint at now. A bed with a sheet thrown back, a stand covered with vials, a bureau with a man's shaving paraphernalia upon it, and on the wall such pictures as only sporting gentlemen delight in. The candle was guttering on a small table upon which, to my astonishment, a Bible lay open. Not having my glasses with me, I could not see what portion of the sacred word was thus disclosed, but I took the precaution to indent the upper leaf with my thumb-nail, so that I might find it again in case of future opportunity. My attention was attracted by other small matters that would be food for thought at a more propitious moment, but at that instant the sound of voices coming distinctly to my ear from below, warned me that a halt had been made at the Flower Parlor, and that the duty of the moment was to locate the trap-door and if possible determine the means of raising it.

This was less difficult than I anticipated. Either this room was regarded as so safe from intrusion that a secret like this could be safely left unguarded, or the door which was plainly to be seen in one corner had been so lately lifted, that it had hardly sunk back into its place. I found it, if the expression may be used of a horizontal object, slightly ajar and needing but the slightest pull to make it spring upright.

The hole thus disclosed was filled with the little staircase up which I had partly mounted in my daring explorations of the day before. It was dark now, darker than it was then, but I felt that I must descend by it, for plainly to be heard now through the crack in the closet door, which seemed to have a knack of standing partly open, I could hear the heavy tread of the six bearers as they entered the parlor below, still carrying their burden, concerning the destination of which I was so anxious to be informed.

That it could be in the room itself was too improbable for consideration. Yet if they took up their stand in this room it was for a purpose, and what that purpose was I was determined to know. The noise their feet made on the bare boards of the floor and the few words I now heard uttered in William's stolid tones and Lucetta's musical treble assured me that my own light steps would no more be heard, than my dark gown of quiet wool would be seen through the narrow slit through which I was preparing to peer. Yet it took no small degree of what my father used to call pluck, for me to put foot on this winding staircase and descend almost, as it were, into the midst of what I must regard as the last wicked act of a most cowardly and brutal murder.

I did it, however, and after a short but grim communion with my own heart, which would persist in beating somewhat noisily, I leaned forward with all the precaution possible and let my gaze traverse the chamber in which I had previously seen such horrors as should have prepared me for this last and greatest one.

In a moment I understood the whole. A long square hole in the floor, lately sawed, provided an opening through which the plain plank coffin, of which I now caught sight, was to be lowered into the cellar and so into the grave which had doubtless been dug there. The ropes in the hands of the six persons, in whose identity I had made no mistake, was proof enough of their intention; and, satisfied as I now was of the means and mode of the interment which had been such a boundless mystery to me, I shrank a step upward, fearing lest my indignation and the horror I could not but feel, from this moment on, of Althea's children, would betray me into some exclamation which might lead to my discovery and a similar fate.

One other short glance, in which I saw them all ranged around the dark opening, and I was up out of their reach, Lucetta's face and Lucetta's one sob as the ropes began to creak, being the one memory which followed me the most persistently. She, at least, was overwhelmed with remorse for a deed she was perhaps only answerable for in that she failed to make known to the world her brother's madness and the horrible crimes to which it gave rise.

I took one other look around his room before I fled to my own, or rather, to the one in which I had taken refuge while my own was under lock and key. That I spent the next two hours on my knees no one can wonder. When my own room was unlocked, as it was before the day broke, I hastened to enter it and lay my head with all its unhappy knowledge on my pillow. But I did not sleep; and, what was stranger still, never once thought of sounding a single note on the whistle which would have brought the police into this abode of crime. Perhaps it was a wise omission. I had seen enough that was horrible that night without beholding Althea's children arrested before my eyes.

BOOK III
FORWARD AND BACK

XXIII

ROOM 3, HOTEL CARTER

I rose at my usual hour. I dressed myself with my usual care. I was, to a superficial observer at least, in all respects my usual self when Hannah came to my door to ask what she could do for me. As there was nothing I wanted but to get out of this house, which had become unbearable to me, I replied with the utmost cheerfulness that my wants were all supplied and that I would soon be down, at which she answered that in that case she must bestir herself or the breakfast would not be ready, and hurried away.

There was no one in the dining-room when I entered, and judging from appearances that several minutes must elapse before breakfast would be ready, I took occasion to stroll through the grounds and glance up at the window of William's room. The knot of crape was gone.

I would have gone farther, but just then I heard a great rushing and scampering, and, looking up, saw an enormous dog approaching at full gallop from the stables. Saracen was loose.

I did not scream or give way to other feminine expressions of fear, but I did return as quickly as possible to the house, where I now saw I must remain till William chose to take me into town.

This I was determined should take place as soon after breakfast as practicable. The knowledge which I now possessed warranted, nay, demanded, instant consultation with the police, and as this could best be effected by following out the orders I had received from Mr. Gryce, I did not consider any other plan than that of meeting the man on duty in Room No. 3 at the hotel.

Loreen, Lucetta, and William were awaiting me in the hall, and made no apology for the flurry into which I had been thrown by my rapid escape from Saracen. Indeed I doubt if they noticed it, for with all the attempt they made to seem gay and at ease, the anxieties and fatigue of the foregoing nights were telling upon them, and from Miss Knollys down, they looked physically exhausted. But they also looked mentally relieved. In the clear depths of Lucetta's eye there was now no wavering, and the head which was always turning in anxious anticipation over her shoulder rested firm, though not as erect as her sister's, who had less cause perhaps for regret and sorrow.

William was joyful to a degree, but it was a forced joviality which only became real when he heard a sudden, quick bark under the window and the sound of scraping paws against the mastic coating of the wall outside. Then he broke out into a loud laugh of unrestrained pleasure, crying out thoughtlessly:

"There's Saracen. How quick he knows——"

A warning look from Lucetta stopped him.

"I mean," he stammered, "it's a dull dog that cannot find his master. Miss Butterworth, you will have to overcome your fear of dogs if you stay with us long. Saracen is unbound this morning, and"—he used a great oath—"he's going to remain so."

By which I came to understand that it was not out of consideration for me he had been tied up in the court till now, but for reasons connected with their own safety and the preservation of the secret which they so evidently believed had been buried with the body, which I did not like to remember lay at that very minute too nearly under our feet for my own individual comfort.

However, this has nothing to do with the reply I made to William.

"I hope he does not run with the buggy," I objected. "I want to take a ride very much this morning and could get small pleasure out of it if that dog must be our companion."

"I cannot go out this morning," William began, but changed his sentence, possibly at the touch of his sister's foot under the table, into: "But if you say I must, why, I must. You women folks are so plagued unreasonable."

Had he been ten years younger I would have boxed his ears; had he been that much older I would have taken cue and packed my trunk before he could have finished the cup of coffee he was drinking. But he was just too old to reprimand in the way just mentioned, and not old enough to appreciate any display of personal dignity or self-respect on the part of the person he had offended. Besides, he was a knave; so I just let his impertinence pass with the remark:

"I have purchases to make in the village": and so that matter ended, manifestly to the two girls' relief, who naturally did not like to see me insulted, even if they did not possess sufficient power over their brother to prevent it.

One other small episode and then I will take you with me to the village. As we were leaving the table, where I ate less than common, notwithstanding all my efforts to seem perfectly unconcerned, Lucetta, who had waited for her brother to go out, took me gently by the arm, and, eying me closely, said:

"Did you have any dreams last night, Miss Butterworth? You know I promised you some."

The question disconcerted me, and for a moment I felt like taking the two girls into my confidence and bidding them fly from the shame and doom so soon to fall upon their brother; but the real principle underlying all such momentary impulses on my part deterred me, and in as light a tone as I could command and not be an absolute hypocrite, I replied that I was sorry to disappoint her, but I had had no dreams, which seemed to please her more than it should, for if I had had no dreams I certainly had suffered from the most frightful realities.

I will not describe our ride into town. Saracen did go with us, and indignation not only rendered me speechless, but gave to my thoughts a turn which made that half-hour of very little value to me. Mother Jane's burly figure crouching in her doorway might otherwise have given me opportunity for remark, and so might the dubious looks of people we met on the highroad—looks to which I am so wholly unaccustomed that I had difficulty in recognizing myself as the butt of so much doubt and possibly dislike. I attributed this, however, all to the ill repute under which William so deservedly labored, and did not allow myself to more than notice it. Indeed, I could only be sorry for people who did not know in what consideration I was held at home, and who, either through ignorance or prejudice, allowed themselves privileges they would be the first to regret did they know the heart and mind of Amelia Butterworth.

Once in the village, I took the direction of affairs.

"Set me down at the hotel," I commanded, "and then go about such business as you may have here in town. I am not going to allow myself to be tracked all over by that dog."

"I have no business," was the surly reply.

"Then make some," was my sharp retort. "I want to see the locksmith—that locksmith who wouldn't come to do an honest piece of work for me in your house; and I want to buy dimities and wools and sewing silks at the dry-goods store over there. Indeed I have a thousand things to do, and expect to spend half the morning before the counters. Why, man, I haven't done any shopping for a week."

He gaped at me perfectly aghast (as I meant he should), and, having but little experience of city ladies, took me at my word and prepared to beat an honorable retreat. As a result, I found myself ten minutes later standing on the top step of the hotel porch, watching William driving away with Saracen perched on the seat beside him. Then I realized that the village held no companions for him, and did not know whether I felt glad or sorry.

To the clerk who came to meet me, I said quietly, "Room No. 3, if you please," at which he gave a nod of intelligence and led me as unostentatiously as possible into a small hall, at the end of which I saw a door with the aforesaid number on it.

"If you will take a seat inside," said he, "I will send you whatever you may desire for your comfort."

"I think you know what that is," I rejoined, at which he nodded again and left me, closing the door carefully behind him as he went.

The few minutes which elapsed before my quiet was disturbed were spent by me in thinking. There were many little questions to settle in my own mind, for which a spell of uninterrupted contemplation was necessary. One of these was whether, in the event of finding the police amenable, I should reveal or hide from these children of my old friend, the fact that it was through my instrumentality that their nefarious secret had been discovered. I wished—nay, I hoped—that the affair might be so concluded, but the possibility of doing so seemed so problematical, especially since Mr. Gryce was not on hand to direct matters, that I spent very little time on the subject, deep and important as it was to all concerned.

What most occupied me was the necessity of telling my story in such a way as to exonerate the girls as much as possible. They were mistaken in their devotion and most unhappy in the exercise of it, but they were not innately wicked and should not be made to appear so. Perhaps the one thing for which I should yet have the best cause to congratulate myself, would be the opportunity I had gained of giving to their connection with this affair its true and proper coloring.

I was still dwelling on this thought when there came a knock at my door which advised me that the visitor I expected had arrived. To open and admit him was the work of a moment, but it took more than a moment for me to overcome my surprise at seeing in my visitor no lesser person than Mr. Gryce himself, who in our parting interview had assured me he was too old and too feeble for further detective work and must therefore delegate it to me.

"Ah!" I ejaculated slowly. "It is you, is it? Well, I am not surprised." (I shouldn't have been.) "When you say you are old, you mean old enough to pull the wool over other people's eyes, and when you say you are lame, you mean that you only halt long enough to let others get far enough ahead for them not to see how fast you hobble up behind them. But do not think I am not happy to see you. I am, Mr. Gryce, for I have discovered the secret of Lost Man's Lane, and find it somewhat too heavy a one for my own handling."

To my surprise he showed this was more than he expected.

"You have?" he asked, with just that shade of incredulity which it is so tantalizing to encounter. "Then I suppose congratulations are in order. But are you sure, Miss Butterworth, that you really have obtained a clue to the many strange and fearful disappearances which have given to this lane its name?"

"Quite sure," I returned, nettled. "Why do you doubt it? Because I have kept so quiet and not sounded one note of alarm from my whistle?"

"No," said he. "Knowing your self-restraint so well, I cannot say that that is my reason."

"What is it, then?" I urged.

"Well," said he, "my real reason for doubting if you have been quite as successful as you think, is that we ourselves have come upon a clue about which there can be no question. Can you say the same of yours?"

You will expect my answer to have been a decided "Yes," uttered with all the positiveness of which you know me capable. But for some reason, perhaps because of the strange influence this man's personality exercises upon all—yes, all—who do not absolutely steel themselves against him, I faltered just long enough for him to cry:

"I thought not. The clue is outside the Knollys house, not in it, Miss Butterworth, for which, of course, you are not to be blamed or your services scorned. I have no doubt they have been invaluable in unearthing a secret, if not the secret."

"Thank you," was my quiet retort. I thought his presumption beyond all bounds, and would at that moment have felt justified in snapping my fingers at the clue he boasted of, had it not been for one thing. What that thing is I am not ready yet to state.

"You and I have come to issue over such matters before," said he, "and therefore need not take too much account of the feelings it is likely to engender. I will merely state that my clue points to Mother Jane, and ask if you have found in the visit she paid at the house last night anything which would go to strengthen the suspicion against her."

"Perhaps," said I, in a state of disdain that was more or less unpardonable, considering that my own suspicions previous to my discovery of the real tragedy enacted under my eyes at the Knollys mansion had played more or less about this old crone.

"Only perhaps?" He smiled, with a playful forbearance for which I should have been truly grateful to him.

"She was there for no good purpose," said I, "and yet if you had not characterized her as the person most responsible for the crimes we are here to investigate, I should have said from all that I then saw of her conduct that she acted as a supernumerary rather than principal, and that it is to me you should look for the correct clue to the criminal, notwithstanding your confidence in your own theories and my momentary hesitation to assert that there was no possible defect in mine."

"Miss Butterworth,"—I thought he looked a trifle shaken,—"what did Mother Jane do in that closely shuttered house last night?"

Mother Jane? Well! Did he think I was going to introduce my tragic story by telling what Mother Jane did? I must have looked irritated, and indeed I think I had cause.

"Mother Jane ate her supper," I snapped out angrily. "Miss Knollys gave it to her. Then she helped a little with a piece of work they had on hand. It will not interest you to know what. It has nothing to do with your clue, I warrant."

He did not get angry. He has an admirable temper, has Mr. Gryce, but he did stop a minute to consider.

"Miss Butterworth," he said at last, "most detectives would have held their peace and let you go on with what you have to tell without a hint that it was either unwelcome or unnecessary, but I have consideration for persons' feelings and for persons' secrets so long as they do not come in collision with the law, and my opinion is, or was when I entered this room, that such discoveries as you have made at your old friend's house" (Why need he emphasize friend—did he think I forgot for a moment that Althea was my friend?) "were connected rather with some family difficulty than with the dreadful affair we are considering. That is why I hastened to tell you that we had found a clue to the disappearances in Mother Jane's cottage. I wished to save the Misses Knollys."

If he had thought to mollify me by this assertion, he did not succeed. He saw it and made haste to say:

"Not that I doubt your consideration for them, only the justness of your conclusions."

"You have doubted those before and with more reason," I replied, "yet they were not altogether false."

"That I am willing to acknowledge, so willing that if you still think after I have told my story that yours is apropos, then I will listen to it only too eagerly. My object is to find the real criminal in this matter. I say at the present moment it is Mother Jane."

"God grant you are right," I said, influenced in spite of myself by the calm assurance of his manner. "If she was at the house night before last between eleven and twelve, then perhaps she is all you think her. But I see no reason to believe it—not yet, Mr. Gryce. Supposing you give me one. It would be better than all this controversy. One small reason, Mr. Gryce, as good as"—I did not say what, but the fillip it gave to his intention stood me in good stead, for he launched immediately into the matter with no further play upon my curiosity, which was now, as you can believe, thoroughly aroused, though I could not believe that anything he had to bring up against Mother Jane could for a moment stand against the death and the burial I had witnessed in Miss Knollys' house during the two previous nights.

XXIV

THE ENIGMA OF NUMBERS

"When in our first conversation on this topic I told you that Mother Jane was not to be considered in this matter, I meant she was not to be considered by you. She was a subject to be handled by the police, and we have handled her. Yesterday afternoon I made a search of her cabin." Here Mr. Gryce paused and eyed me quizzically. He sometimes does eye me, which same I cannot regard as a compliment, considering how fond he is of concentrating all his wisdom upon small and insignificant objects.

"I wonder," said he, "what you would have done in such a search as that. It was no common one, I assure you. There are not many hiding-places between Mother Jane's four walls."

I felt myself begin to tremble, with eagerness, of course.

"I wish I had been given the opportunity," said I—"that is, if anything was to be found there."

He seemed to be in a sympathetic mood toward me, or perhaps—and this is the likelier supposition—he had a minute of leisure and thought he could afford to give himself a little quiet amusement. However that was, he answered me by saying:

"The opportunity is not lost. You have been in her cabin and have noted, I have no doubt, its extreme simplicity. Yet it contains, or rather did contain up till last night, distinct evidences of more than one of the crimes which have been perpetrated in this lane."

"Good! And you want me to guess where you found them? Well, it's not fair."

"Ah, and why not?"

"Because you probably did not find them on your first attempt. You had time to look about. I am asked to guess at once and without second trial what I warrant it took you several trials to determine."

He could not help but laugh. "And why do you think it took me several trials?"

"Because there is more than one thing in that room made up of parts."

"Parts?" He attempted to look puzzled, but I would not have it.

"You know what I mean," I declared; "seventy parts, twenty-eight, or whatever the numbers are she so constantly mutters."

His admiration was unqualified and sincere.

"Miss Butterworth," said he, "you are a woman after my own heart. How came you to think that her mutterings had anything to do with a hiding-place?"

"Because it did not have anything to do with the amount of money I gave her. When I handed her twenty-five cents, she cried, 'Seventy, twenty-eight, and now ten!' Ten what? Not ten cents or ten dollars, but ten——"

"Why do you stop?"

"I do not want to risk my reputation on a guess. There is a quilt on the bed made up of innumerable pieces. There is a floor of neatly laid brick——"

"And there is a Bible on the stand whose leaves number many over seventy."

"Ah, it was in the Bible you found——"

His smile put mine quite to shame.

"I must acknowledge," he cried, "that I looked in the Bible, but I found nothing there beyond what we all seek when we open its sacred covers. Shall I tell my story?"

He was evidently bursting with pride. You would think that after a half-century of just such successes, a man would take his honors more quietly. But pshaw! Human nature is just the same in the old as in the young. He was no more tired of compliment or of awakening the astonishment of those he confided in, than when he aroused the admiration of the force by his triumphant handling of the Leavenworth Case. Of course in presence of such weakness I could do nothing less than give him a sympathetic ear. I may be old myself some day. Besides, his story was likely to prove more or less interesting.

"Tell your story?" I repeated. "Don't you see that I am"—I was going to say "on pins and needles till I hear it," but the expression is too vulgar for a woman of my breeding; so I altered the words, happily before they were spoken, into "that I am in a state of the liveliest curiosity concerning the whole matter? Tell your story, of course."

"Well, Miss Butterworth, if I do, it is because I know you will appreciate it. You, like myself, placed weight upon the numbers she is forever running over, and you, like myself, have conceived the possibility of these numbers having reference to something in the one room she inhabits. At first glance the extreme bareness of the spot seemed to promise nothing to my curiosity. I looked at the floor and detected no signs of any disturbance having taken place in its symmetrically laid bricks for years. Yet I counted up to seventy one way and twenty-eight the other, and marking the brick thus selected, began to pry it out. It came with difficulty and showed me nothing underneath but green mold and innumerable frightened insects. Then I counted the bricks the other way, but nothing came of it. The floor does not appear to have been disturbed for years. Turning my attention away from the floor, I began upon the quilt. This was a worse job than the other, and it took me an hour to rip apart the block I settled upon as the suspicious one, but my labor was entirely wasted. There was no hidden treasure in the quilt. Then I searched the walls, using the measurements seventy by twenty-eight, but no result followed these endeavors, and—well, what do you think I did then?"

"You will tell me," I said, "if I give you one more minute to do it in."

"Very well," said he. "I see you do not know, madam. Having searched below and around me, I next turned my attention overhead. Do you remember the strings and strings of dried vegetables that decorate the beams above?"

"I do," I replied, not stinting any of the astonishment I really felt.

"Well, I began to count them next, and when I reached the seventieth onion from the open doorway, I crushed it between my fingers and—these fell out, madam—worthless trinkets, as you will immediately see, but——"

"Well, well," I urged.

"They have been identified as belonging to the peddler who was one of the victims in whose fate we are interested."

"Ah, ah!" I ejaculated, somewhat amazed, I own. "And number twenty-eight?"

"That was a carrot, and it held a really valuable ring—a ruby surrounded by diamonds. If you remember, I once spoke to you of this ring. It was the property of young Mr. Chittenden and worn by him while he was in this village. He disappeared on his way to the railway station, having taken, as many can vouch, the short detour by Lost Man's Lane, which would lead him directly by Mother Jane's cottage."

"You thrill me," said I, keeping down with admirable self-possession my own thoughts in regard to this matter. "And what of No. ten, beyond which she said she could not count?"

"In ten was your twenty-five-cent piece, and in various other vegetables, small coins, whose value taken collectively would not amount to a dollar. The only numbers which seemed to make any impression on her mind were those connected with these crimes. Very good evidence, Miss Butterworth, that Mother Jane holds the clue to this matter, even if she is not responsible for the death of the individuals represented by this property."

"Certainly," I acquiesced, "and if you examined her after her return from the Knollys mansion last night you would probably have found upon her some similar evidence of her complicity in the last crime of this terrible series. It would needs have been small, as Silly Rufus neither indulged in the brass trinkets sold by the old peddler nor the real jewelry of a well-to-do man like Mr. Chittenden."

"Silly Rufus?"

"He was the last to disappear from these parts, was he not?"

"Yes, madam."

"And as such, should have left some clue to his fate in the hands of this old crone, if her motive in removing him was, as you seem to think, entirely that of gain."

"I did not say it was entirely so. Silly Rufus would be the last person any one, even such a non compos mentis as Mother Jane, would destroy for hope of gain."

"But what other motive could she have? And, Mr. Gryce, where could she bestow the bodies of so many unfortunate victims, even if by her great strength she could succeed in killing them?"

"There you have me," said he. "We have not been able as yet to unearth any bodies. Have you?"

"No," said I, with some little show of triumph showing through my disdain, "but I can show you where to unearth one."

He should have been startled, profoundly startled. Why wasn't he? I asked this of myself over and over in the one instant he weighed his words before answering.

"You have made some definite discoveries, then," he declared. "You have come across a grave or a mound which you have taken for a grave."

I shook my head.

"No mound," said I. Why should I not play for an instant or more with his curiosity? He had with mine.

"Ah, then, why do you talk of unearthing? No one has told you where you can lay hand on Silly Rufus' body, I take it."

"No," said I. "The Knollys house is not inclined to give up its secrets."

He started, glancing almost remorsefully first at the tip, then at the head of the cane he was balancing in his hand.

"It's too bad," he muttered, "but you've been led astray, Miss Butterworth,—excusably, I acknowledge, quite excusably, but yet in a way to give you quite wrong conclusions. The secret of the Knollys house—But wait a moment. Then you were not locked up in your room last night?"

"Scarcely," I returned, wavering between the doubts he had awakened by his first sentence and the surprise which his last could not fail to give me.

"I might have known they would not be likely to catch you in a trap," he remarked. "So you were up and in the halls?"

"I was up," I acknowledged, "and in the halls. May I ask where you were?"

He paid no heed to the last sentence. "This complicates matters," said he, "and yet perhaps it is as well. I understand you now, and in a few minutes you will understand me. You thought it was Silly Rufus who was buried last night. That was rather an awful thought, Miss Butterworth. I wonder, with that in your mind, you look as well as you do this morning, madam. Truly you are a wonderful woman—a very wonderful woman."

"A truce to compliments," I begged. "If you know as much as your words imply of what went on in that ill-omened house last night, you ought to show some degree of emotion yourself, for if it was not Silly Rufus who was laid away under the Flower Parlor, who, then, was it? No one for whom tears could openly be shed or of whose death public acknowledgment could be made, or we would not be sitting here talking away at cross purposes the morning after his burial."

"Tears are not shed or public acknowledgment made for the subject of a half-crazy man's love for scientific investigation. It was no human being whom you saw buried, madam, but a victim of Mr. Knollys' passion for vivisection."

"You are playing with me," was my indignant answer; "outrageously and inexcusably playing with me. Only a human being would be laid away in such secrecy and with such manifestations of feeling as I was witness to. You must think me in my dotage, or else——"

"We will take the rest of the sentence for granted," he dryly interpolated. "You know that I can have no wish to insult your intelligence, Miss Butterworth, and that if I advance a theory on my own account I must have ample reasons for it. Now can you say the same for yours? Can you adduce irrefutable proof that the body we buried last night was that of a man? If you can, there is no more to be said, or, rather, there is everything to be said, for this would give to the transaction a very dreadful and tragic significance which at present I am not disposed to ascribe to it."

Taken aback by his persistence, but determined not to acknowledge defeat until forced to it, I stolidly replied: "You have made an assertion, and it is for you to adduce proof. It will be time enough for me to talk when your own theory is proved untenable."

He was not angry: fellow-feeling for my disappointment made him unusually gentle. His voice was therefore very kind when he said:

"Madam, if you know it to have been a man, say so. I do not wish to waste my time."

"I do not know it."

"Very well, then, I will tell you why I think my supposition true. Mr. Knollys, as you probably have already discovered, is a man with a secret passion for vivisection."

"Yes, I have discovered that."

"It is known to his family, and it is known to a very few others, but it is not known to the world at large, not even to his fellow-villagers.'

"I can believe it," said I.

"His sisters, who are gentle girls, regard the matter as the gentle-hearted usually do. They have tried in every way to influence him to abandon it, but unsuccessfully so far, for he is not only entirely unamenable to persuasion, but has a nature of such brutality he could not live without some such excitement to help away his life in this dreary house. All they can do, then, is to conceal these cruelties from the eyes of the people who already execrate him for his many roughnesses and the undoubted shadow under which he lives. Time was when I thought this shadow had a substance worth our investigation, but a further knowledge of his real fault and a completer knowledge of his sisters' virtues turned my inquiries in a new direction, where I have found, as I have told you, actual reason for arresting Mother Jane. Have you anything to say against these conclusions? Cannot you see that all your suspicions can be explained by the brother's cruel impulses and the sisters' horror of having those impulses known?"

I thought a moment; then I cried out boldly: "No, I cannot, Mr. Gryce. The anxiety, the fear, which I have seen depicted on these sisters' faces for days might be explained perhaps by this theory; but the knot of crape on the window-shutter, the open Bible in the room of death—William's room, Mr. Gryce,—proclaim that it was a human being, and nothing less, for whom Lucetta's sobs went up."

"I do not follow you," he said, moved for the first time from his composure. "What do you mean by a knot of crape, and when was it you obtained entrance into William's room?"

"Ah," I exclaimed in dry retort; "you are beginning to see that I have something as interesting to report as yourself. Did you think me a superficial egotist, without facts to back my assertions?"

"I should not have done you that injustice."

"I have penetrated, I think, deeper than even yourself, into William's character. I think him capable—But do satisfy my curiosity on one point first, Mr. Gryce. How came you to know as much as you do about last night's proceedings? You could not have been in the house. Did Mother Jane talk after she got back?"

The tip of his cane was up, and he frowned at it. Then the handle took its place, and he gave it a good-natured smile.

"Miss Butterworth," said he, "I have not succeeded in making Mother Jane at any time go beyond her numerical monologue. But you have been more successful." And with a sudden marvellous change of expression, pose, and manner he threw over his head my shawl, which had fallen to the floor in my astonishment, and, rocking himself to and fro before me, muttered grimly:

"Seventy! Twenty-eight! Ten! No more! I can count no more! Go."

"Mr. Gryce, it was you——"

"Whom you interviewed in Mother Jane's cottage with Mr. Knollys," he finished. "And it was I who helped to bury what you now declare, to my real terror and astonishment, to have been a human being. Miss Butterworth, what about the knot of crape? Tell me."

<h1 style="text-align:center">XXV</h1>

<h1 style="text-align:center">TRIFLES, BUT NOT TRIFLING</h1>

I was so astounded I hardly took in this final question.

He had been the sixth party in the funeral cortège I had seen pause in the Flower Parlor. Well, what might I not expect from this man next!

But I am methodical even under the greatest excitement and at the most critical instants, as those who have read That Affair Next Door have had ample opportunity to know. Once having taken in the startling fact he mentioned, I found it impossible to proceed to establish my standpoint till I knew a little more about his.

"Wait," I said; "tell me first if I have ever seen the real Mother Jane; or were you the person I saw stooping in the road, and of whom I bought the pennyroyal?"

"No," he replied; "that was the old woman herself. My appearance in the cottage dates from yesterday noon. I felt the need of being secretly near you, and I also wished for an opportunity to examine this humble interior unsuspected and unobserved. So I prevailed upon the old woman to exchange places with me; she taking up her abode in the woods for the night and I her old stool on the hearthstone. She was the more willing to do this from the promise I gave her to watch out for Lizzie. That I would don her own Sunday suit and personate her in her own home she evidently did not suspect. Had not wit enough, I suppose. At the present moment she is back in her old place."

I nodded my thanks for this explanation, but was not deterred from pressing the point I was anxious to have elucidated.

"If," I went on to urge, "you took advantage of your disguise to act as assistant in the burial which took place last night, you are in a much better situation than myself to decide the question we are at present considering. Was it because of any secret knowledge thus gained you declare so positively that it was not a human being you helped lower in its grave?"

"Partially. Having some skill in these disguises, especially where my own infirmities can have full play, as in the case of this strong but half-bent woman, I had no reason to think my own identity was suspected, much less discovered. Therefore I could trust to what I saw and heard as being just what Mother Jane herself would be allowed to see or hear under the same circumstances. If, therefore, these young people and this old crone had been,

100

as you seem to think they are, in league for murder, Lucetta would hardly have greeted me as she did when she came down to meet me in the kitchen."

"And how was that? What did she say?"

"She said: 'Ah, Mother Jane, we have a piece of work for you. You are strong, are you not?'"

"Humph!"

"And then she commiserated me a bit and gave me food which, upon my word, I found hard to eat, though I had saved my appetite for the occasion. Before she left me she bade me sit in the inglenook till she wanted me, adding in Hannah's ear as she passed her: 'There is no use trying to explain anything to her. Show her when the time comes what there is to do and trust to her short memory to forget it before she leaves the house. She could not understand my brother's propensity or our shame in pandering to it. So attempt nothing, Hannah. Only keep the money in her view.'"

"So, and that gave you no idea?"

"It gave me the idea I have imparted to you, or, rather, added to the idea which had been instilled in me by others."

"And this idea was not affected by what you saw afterwards?"

"Not in the least—rather strengthened. Of the few words I overheard, one was uttered in reference to yourself by Miss Knollys. She said: 'I have locked Miss Butterworth again into her room. If she accuses me of having done so, I shall tell her our whole story. Better she should know the family's disgrace than imagine us guilty of crimes of which we are utterly incapable.'"

"So! so!" I cried, "you heard that?"

"Yes, madam, I heard that, and I do not think she knew she was dropping that word into the ear of a detective, but on this point you are, of course, at liberty to differ with me."

"I am not yet ready to avail myself of the privilege," I retorted. "What else did these girls let fall in your hearing?"

"Not much. It was Hannah who led me into the upper hall, and Hannah who by signs and signals rather than words showed me what was expected of me. However, when, after the box was lowered into the cellar, Hannah was drawing me away, Lucetta stepped up and whispered in her ear: 'Don't give her the biggest coin. Give her the little one, or she may mistake our reasons for secrecy. I wouldn't like even a fool to do that even for the moment it would remain lodged in Mother Jane's mind.'"

"Well, well," I again cried, certainly puzzled, for these stray expressions of the sisters were in a measure contradictory not only of the suspicions I entertained, but of the facts which had seemingly come to my attention.

Mr. Gryce, who was probably watching my face more closely than he did the cane with whose movements he was apparently engrossed, stopped to give a caressing rub to the knob of that same cane before remarking:

"One such peep behind the scenes is worth any amount of surmise expended on the wrong side of the curtain. I let you share my knowledge because it is your due. Now if you feel willing to explain what you mean by a knot of crape on the shutter, I am at your service, madam."

I felt that it would be cruel to delay my story longer, and so I began it. It was evidently more interesting than he expected, and as I dilated upon the special features which had led me to believe that it was a thinking, suffering mortal like ourselves who had been shut up in William's room and afterwards buried in the cellar under the Flower Parlor, I saw his face lengthen and doubt take the place of the quiet assurance with which he had received my various intimations up to this time. The cane was laid aside, and from the action of his right forefinger on the palm of his left hand I judged that I was making no small impression on his mind. When I had finished, he sat for a minute silent; then he said:

"Thanks, Miss Butterworth; you have more than fulfilled my hopes. What we buried was undoubtedly human, and the question now is, Who was it, and of what death did he die?" Then, after a meaning pause: "You think it was Silly Rufus."

I will astonish you with my reply. "No," said I, "I do not. That is where you make a mistake, Mr. Gryce."

XXVI

A POINT GAINED

He was surprised, for all his attempts to conceal it.

"No?" said he. "Who, then? You are becoming interesting, Miss Butterworth."

This I thought I could afford to ignore.

"Yesterday," I proceeded, "I would have declared it to be Silly Rufus, in the face of God and man, but after what I saw in William's room during the hurried survey I gave it, I am inclined to doubt if the explanation we have to give to this affair is so simple as that would make it. Mr. Gryce, in one corner of that room, from which the victim had so lately been carried, was a pair of shoes that could never have been worn by any boy-tramp I have ever seen or known of."

"They were Loreen's, or possibly Lucetta's."

"No, Loreen and Lucetta both have trim feet, but these were the shoes of a child of ten, very dainty at that, and of a cut and make worn by women, or rather, I should say, by girls. Now, what do you make of that?"

He did not seem to know what to make of it. Tap, tap went his finger on his seasoned palm, and as I watched the slowness with which it fell, I said to myself, "I have proposed a problem this time that will tax even Mr. Gryce's powers of deduction."

And I had. It was minutes before he ventured an opinion, and then it was with a shade of doubt in his tone that I acknowledge to have felt some pride in producing.

"They were Lucetta's shoes. The emotions under which you labored—very pardonable emotions, madam, considering the circumstances and the hour—"

"Excuse me," said I. "We do not want to waste a moment. I was excited,

102

suitably and duly excited, or I would have been a stone. But I never lose my head under excitement, nor do I part with my sense of proportion. The shoes were not Lucetta's. She never wore any approaching them in smallness since her tenth year."

"Has Simsbury a daughter? Has there not been a child about the house some time to assist the cook in errands and so on?"

"No, or I should have seen her. Besides, how would the shoes of such a person come into William's room?"

"Easily. Secrecy was required. You were not to be disturbed; so shoes were taken off that quiet might result."

"Was Lucetta shoeless or William or even Mother Jane? You have not told me that you were requested to walk in stocking feet up the hall. No, Mr. Gryce, the shoes were the shoes of a girl. I know it because it was matched by a dress I saw hanging up in a sort of wardrobe."

"Ah! You looked into the wardrobe?"

"I did and felt justified in doing so. It was after I had spied the shoes."

"Very good. And you saw a dress?"

"A little dress; a dress with a short skirt. It was of silk too; another anomaly—and the color, I think, was blue, but I cannot swear to that point. I was in great haste and took the briefest glance. But my brief glances can be trusted, Mr. Gryce. That, I think, you are beginning to know."

"Certainly," said he, "and as proof of it we will now act upon these two premises—that the victim in whose burial I was an innocent partaker was a human being and that this human being was a girl-child who came into the house well dressed. Now where does that lead us? Into a maze, I fear."

"We are accustomed to mazes," I observed.

"Yes," he answered somewhat gloomily, "but they are not exactly desirable in this case. I want to find the Knollys family innocent."

"And I. But William's character, I fear, will make that impossible."

"But this girl? Who is she, and where did she come from? No girl has been reported to us as missing from this neighborhood."

"I supposed not."

"A visitor—But no visitor could enter this house without it being known far and wide. Why, I heard of your arrival here before I left the train on which I followed you. Had we allowed ourselves to be influenced by what the people about here say, we would have turned the Knollys house inside out a week ago. But I don't believe in putting too much confidence in the prejudice of country people. The idea they suggested, and which you suggest without putting it too clearly into words, is much too horrible to be acted upon without the best of reasons. Perhaps we have found those reasons, yet I still feel like asking, Where did this girl come from and how could she have become a prisoner in the Knollys house without the knowledge of—Madam, have you met Mr. Trohm?"

The question was so sudden I had not time to collect myself. But perhaps it was not necessary that I should, for the simple affirmation I used seemed to satisfy Mr. Gryce, who went on to say:

"It is he who first summoned us here, and it is he who has the greatest interest in locating the source of these disappearances, yet he has seen no child come here."

"Mr. Trohm is not a spy," said I, but the remark, happily, fell unheeded.

"No one has," he pursued. "We must give another turn to our suppositions."

Suddenly a silence fell upon us both. His finger ceased to lay down the law, and my gaze, which had been searching his face inquiringly, became fixed. At the same moment and in much the same tone of voice we both spoke, he saying, "Humph!" and I, "Ah!" as a prelude to the simultaneous exclamation:

"The phantom coach!"

We were so pleased with this discovery that we allowed a moment to pass in silent contemplation of each other's satisfaction. Then he quietly added:

"Which on the evening preceding your arrival came from the mountains and passed into Lost Man's Lane, from which no one ever saw it emerge."

"It was no phantom," I put in.

"It was their own old coach bringing to the house a fresh victim."

This sounded so startling we both sat still for a moment, lost in the horror of it, then I spoke:

"People living in remote and isolated quarters like this are naturally superstitious. The Knollys family know this, and, remembering the old legend, forbore to contradict the conclusions of their neighbors. Loreen's emotion when the topic was broached to her is explained by this theory."

"It is not a pleasant one, but we cannot be wrong in contemplating it."

"Not at all. This apparition, as they call it, was seen by two persons; therefore it was no apparition but a real coach. It came from the mountains, that is, from the Mountain Station, and it glided—ah!"

"Well?"

"Mr. Gryce, it was its noiselessness that gave it its spectral appearance. Now I remember a petty circumstance which I dare you to match, in corroboration of our suspicions."

"You do?"

I could not repress a slight toss of my head. "Yes, I do," I repeated.

He smiled and made the slightest of deprecatory gestures.

"You have had advantages——" he began.

"And disadvantages," I finished, determined that he should award me my full meed of praise. "You are probably not afraid of dogs. I am. You could visit the stables."

"And did; but I found nothing there."

"I thought not!" I could not help the exclamation. It is so seldom one can really triumph over this man. "Not having the cue, you would not be apt to see what gives this whole thing away. I would never have thought of it again if we had not had this talk. Is Mr. Simsbury a neat man?"

"A neat man? Madam, what do you mean?"

"Something important, Mr. Gryce. If Mr. Simsbury is a neat man, he will have thrown away the old rags which, I dare promise you, cumbered his stable floor the morning after the phantom coach was seen to enter the lane. If he is not, you may still find them there. One of them, I know, you will not find. He pulled it off of his wheel with his whip the afternoon he drove me down from the station. I can see the sly look he gave me as he did it. It made no impression on me then, but now——"

"Madam, you have supplied the one link necessary to the establishment of this theory. Allow me to felicitate you upon it. But whatever our satisfaction may be from a professional standpoint, we cannot but feel the unhappy nature of the responsibility incurred by these discoveries. If this seemingly respectable family stooped to such subterfuge, going to the length of winding rags around the wheels of their lumbering old coach to make it noiseless, and even tying up their horse's feet for this same purpose, they must have had a motive dark enough to warrant your worst suspicions. And William was not the only one involved. Simsbury, at least, had a hand in it, nor does it look as if the girls were as innocent as we would like to consider them."

"I cannot stop to consider the girls," I declared. "I can no longer consider the girls."

"Nor I," he gloomily assented. "Our duty requires us to sift this matter, and it shall be sifted. We must first find if any child alighted from the cars at the Mountain Station on that especial night, or, what is more probable, from the little station at C., five miles farther back in the mountains."

"And—" I urged, seeing that he had still something to say.

"We must make sure who lies buried under the floor of the room you call the Flower Parlor. You may expect me at the Knollys house some time to-day. I shall come quietly, but in my own proper person. You are not to know me, and, unless you desire it, need not appear in the matter."

"I do not desire it."

"Then good-morning, Miss Butterworth. My respect for your abilities has risen even higher than before. We part in a similar frame of mind for once."

And this he expected me to regard as a compliment.

XXVII

THE TEXT WITNESSETH

I have a grim will when I choose to exert it. After Mr. Gryce left the hotel, I took a cup of tea with the landlady and then made a round of the stores. I bought dimity, sewing silk, and what not, as I said I would, but this did not occupy me long (to the regret probably of the country merchants, who expected to make a fool of me and found it a by no means easy task), and was quite ready for William when he finally drove up.

The ride home was a more or less silent one. I had conceived such a horror of the man beside me, that talking for talk's sake was impossible, while he was in a mood which it would be charity to call non-communicative. It may be that my own reticence was at the bottom of this, but I rather think not. The remark he made in passing Deacon Spear's house showed that something more than spite was working in his slow but vindictive brain.

"There's a man of your own sort," he cried. "You won't find him doing anything out of the way; oh, no. Pity your visit wasn't paid there. You'd have got a better impression of the lane."

To this I made no reply.

At Mr. Trohm's he spoke again:

"I suppose that you and Trohm had the devil of a say about Lucetta and the rest of us. I don't know why, but the whole neighborhood seems to feel they've a right to use our name as they choose. But it isn't going to be so, long. We have played poor and pinched and starved all I'm going to. I'm going to have a new horse, and Lucetta shall have a dress, and that mighty quick too. I'm tired of all this shabbiness, and mean to have a change."

I wanted to say, "No change yet; change under the present circumstances would be the worst thing possible for you all," but I felt that this would be treason to Mr. Gryce, and refrained, saying simply, as he looked sideways at me for a word:

"Lucetta needs a new dress. That no one can deny. But you had better let me get it for her, or perhaps that is what you mean."

The grunt which was my only answer might be interpreted in any way. I took it, however, for assent.

As soon as I was relieved of his presence and found myself again with the girls, I altered my whole manner and cried out in querulous tones:

"Mrs. Carter and I have had a difference." (This was true. We did have a difference over our cup of tea. I did not think it necessary to say this difference was a forced one. Some things we are perfectly justified in keeping to ourselves.) "She remembers a certain verse in the New Testament one way and I in another. We had not time to settle it by a consultation with the sacred word, but I cannot rest till it is settled, so will you bring your Bible to me, my dear, that I may look that verse up?"

We were in the upper hall, where I had taken a seat on the old-fashioned sofa there. Lucetta, who was standing before me, started immediately to do my bidding, without stopping to think, poor child, that it was very strange I did not go to my own room and consult my own Bible as any good Presbyterian would be expected to do. As she was turning toward the large front room I stopped her with the quiet injunction:

"Get me one with good print, Lucetta. My eyes won't bear much straining."

At which she turned and to my great relief hurried down the corridor toward William's room, from which she presently returned, bringing the very volume I was anxious to consult.

Meanwhile I had laid aside my hat. I felt flurried and unhappy, and showed it. Lucetta's pitiful face had a strange sweetness in it this morning, and I felt sure as I took the sacred book from her hand that her thoughts were all with the lover she had sent from her side and not at all with me or with what at the moment occupied me. Yet my thoughts at this moment involved, without doubt, the very deepest interests of her life, if not that very lover she was brooding over in her darkened and resigned mind. As I realized this I heaved an involuntary sigh, which seemed to startle her, for she turned and gave me a quick look as she was slipping away to join her sister, who was busy at the other end of the hall.

The Bible I held was an old one, of medium size and most excellent print. I had no difficulty in finding the text and settling the question which had been my ostensible reason for wanting the book, but it took me longer to discover the indentation which I had made in one of its pages; but when I did, you may imagine my awe and the turmoil into which my mind was cast, when I found that it marked those great verses in Corinthians which are so universally read at funerals:

"Behold I shew you a mystery. We shall not all sleep, but we shall all be changed."

"In a moment, in the twinkling of an eye——"

XXVIII

AN INTRUSION

I was so moved by this discovery that I was not myself for several moments.

The reading of these words over the body which had been laid away under the Flower Parlor was in keeping with the knot of crape on the window-shutter and argued something more than remorse on the part of some one of the Knollys family. Who was this one, and why, with such feelings in the breast of any of the three, had the deceit and crime to which I had been witness succeeded to such a point as to demand the attention of the police? An impossible problem of which I dared seek no solution, even in the faces of these seemingly innocent girls.

I was, of course, in no position to determine what plan Mr. Gryce intended to pursue. I only knew what course I myself meant to follow, which was to remain quiet and sustain the part I had already played in this house as visitor and friend. It was therefore as such both in heart and manner that I hastened from my room late in the afternoon to inquire the meaning of the cry I had just heard issue from Lucetta's lips. It had come from the front of the house, and, as I hastened thither, I met the two Misses Knollys, looking more openly anxious and distraught than at any former time of anxiety and trouble.

As they looked up and saw my face, Loreen paused and laid her hand on Lucetta's arm. But Lucetta was not to be restrained.

"He has dared to enter our gates, bringing a police officer with him," was her hoarse and almost unintelligible cry. "We know that the man with him is a police officer because he was here once before, and though he was kind enough then, he cannot have come the second time except to——"

Here the pressure of Loreen's hand was so strong as to make the feeble Lucetta quiver. She stopped, and Miss Knollys took up her words:

"Except to make us talk on subjects much better buried in oblivion. Miss Butterworth, will you go down with us? Your presence may act as a restraint. Mr. Trohm seems to have some respect for you."

"Mr. Trohm?"

"Yes. It is his coming which has so agitated Lucetta. He and a man named Gryce are just coming up the walk. There goes the knocker. Lucetta, you must control yourself or leave me to face these unwelcome visitors alone."

Lucetta, with a sudden fierce effort, subdued her trembling.

"If he must be met," said she, "my anger and disdain may give some weight to your quiet acceptance of the family's disgrace. I shall not accept his denunciations quietly, Loreen. You must expect me to show some of the feelings that I have held in check all these years." And without waiting for reply, without waiting even to see what effect these strange words might have upon me, she dashed down the stairs and pulled open the front door.

We had followed rapidly, too rapidly for speech ourselves, and were therefore in the hall when the door swung back, revealing the two persons I had been led to expect. Mr. Trohm spoke first, evidently in answer to the defiance to be seen in Lucetta's face.

"Miss Knollys, a thousand pardons. I know I am transgressing, but, I assure you, the occasion warrants it. I am certain you will acknowledge this when you hear what my errand is."

"Your errand? What can your errand be but to——"

Why did she pause? Mr. Gryce had not looked at her. Yet that it was under his influence she ceased to commit herself I am as convinced as we can be of anything in a world which is half deceit.

"Let us hear your errand," put in Loreen, with that gentle emphasis which is no sign of weakness.

"I will let this gentleman speak for me," returned Mr. Trohm. "You have seen him before—a New York detective of whose business in this town you cannot be ignorant."

Lucetta turned a cold eye upon Mr. Gryce and quietly remarked:

"When he visited this lane a few days ago, he professed to be seeking a clue to the many disappearances which have unfortunately taken place within its precincts."

Mr. Trohm's nod was one of acquiescence. But Lucetta was still looking at the detective.

"Is that your business now?" she asked, appealing directly to Mr. Gryce.

His fatherly accents when he answered her were a great relief after the alternate iciness and fire with which she had addressed his companion and himself.

"I hardly know how to reply without arousing your just anger. If your brother is in——"

"My brother would face you with less patience than we. Tell us your errand, Mr. Gryce, and do not think of calling in my brother till we have failed to answer your questions or satisfy your demands."

"Very well," said he. "The quickest explanation is the kindest in these cases. I merely wish, as a police officer whose business it is to locate the disappearances which have made this lane notorious, and who believes the surest way to do this is to find out once and for all where they did not and could not have taken place, to make an official search of these premises as I already have those of Mother Jane and of Deacon Spear."

"And my errand here," interposed Mr. Trohm, "is to make everything easier by the assurance that my house will be the next to undergo a complete investigation. As all the houses in the lane will be visited alike, none of us need complain or feel our good name attacked."

This was certainly thoughtful of him, but knowing how much they had to fear, I could not expect Loreen or Lucetta to show any great sense either of his kindness or Mr. Gryce's consideration. They were in no position to have a search made of their premises, and, serene as was Loreen's nature and powerful as was Lucetta's will, the apprehension under which they labored was evident to us all, though neither of them attempted either subterfuge or evasion.

"If the police wish to search this house, it is open to them," said Loreen.

"But not to Mr. Trohm," quoth Lucetta, quickly. "Our poverty should be our protection from the curiosity of neighbors."

"Mr. Trohm has no wish to intrude," was Mr. Gryce's conciliatory remark; but Mr. Trohm said nothing. He probably understood why Lucetta wished to curtail his stay in this house better than Mr. Gryce did.

XXIX

IN THE CELLAR

I had meanwhile stood silent. There was no reason for me to obtrude myself, and I was happy not to do so. This does not mean, however, that my presence was not noticed. Mr. Trohm honored me with more than one glance during these trying moments, in which I read the anxiety he felt lest my peace of mind should be too much disturbed, and when, in response to the undoubted dismissal he had received from Lucetta, he prepared to take his leave, it was upon me he bestowed his final look and most deferential bow. It was a tribute to my position and character which all seemed to feel, and I was not at all surprised when Lucetta, after carefully watching his departure, turned to me with childlike impetuosity, saying:

"This must be very unpleasant for you, Miss Butterworth, yet must we ask you to stand our friend. God knows we need one."

"I shall never forget I occupied that position toward your mother," was my straightforward reply, and I did not forget it, not for a moment.

"I shall begin with the cellar," Mr. Gryce announced.

Both girls quivered. Then Loreen lifted her proud head and said quietly:

"The whole house is at your disposal. Only I pray you to be as expeditious as possible. My sister is not well, and the sooner our humiliation is over, the better it will be for her."

And, indeed, Lucetta was in a state that aroused even Mr. Gryce's anxiety. But when she saw us all hovering over her she roused herself with an extraordinary effort, and, waving us aside, led the way to the kitchen, from which, as I gathered, the only direct access could be had to the cellar. Mr. Gryce immediately followed, and behind him came Loreen and myself, both too much agitated to speak. At the Flower Parlor Mr. Gryce paused as if he had forgotten something, but Lucetta urged him feverishly on, and before long we were all standing in the kitchen. Here a surprise awaited us. Two men were sitting there who appeared to be strangers to Hannah, from the lowering looks she cast them as she pretended to be busy over her stove. This was so out of keeping with her usual good humor as to attract the attention even of her young mistress.

"What is the matter, Hannah?" asked Lucetta. "And who are these men?"

"They are my men," said Mr. Gryce. "The job I have undertaken cannot be carried on alone."

The quick look the two sisters interchanged did not escape me, or the quiet air of resignation which was settling slowly over Loreen.

"Must they go into the cellar too?" she asked.

Mr. Gryce smiled his most fatherly smile as he said:

"My dear young ladies, these men are interested in but one thing; they are searching for a clue to the disappearances that have occurred in this lane. As they will not find this in your cellar, nothing else that they may see there will remain in their minds for a moment."

Lucetta said no more. Even her indomitable spirit was giving way before the inevitable discovery that threatened them.

"Do not let William know," were the low words with which she passed Hannah; but from the short glimpse I caught of William's burly figure standing in the stable door, under the guardianship of two detectives, I felt this injunction to be quite superfluous. William evidently did know.

I was not going to descend the cellar stairs, but the girls made me.

"We want you with us," Loreen declared in no ordinary tones, while Lucetta paused and would not go on till I followed. This surprised me. I no longer seemed to have any clue to their motives; but I was glad to be one of the party.

Hannah, under Loreen's orders, had furnished one of the men with a lighted lantern, and upon our descent into the dark labyrinth below, it became his duty to lead the way, which he did with due circumspection. What all this underground space into which we were thus introduced had ever been used for, it would be difficult to tell. At present it was mostly empty. After passing a small collection of stores, a wine-cellar, the very door of which was unhinged and lay across the cellar bottom, we struck into a hollow void, in which there was nothing worth an instant's investigation save the earth under our feet.

This the two foremost detectives examined very carefully, detaining us often longer, I thought, than Mr. Gryce desired or Lucetta had patience for. But nothing was said in protest nor did the older detective give an order or manifest any special interest in the investigation till he saw the men in front stoop and throw out of the way a coil of rope, when he immediately hurried forward and called upon the party to stop.

The girls, who were on either side of me, crossed glances at this command, and Lucetta, who had been tottering for the last few minutes, fell upon her knees and hid her face in the hollow of her two hands. Loreen came around and stood by her, and I do not know which of them presented the most striking picture of despair, the shrinking Lucetta or Loreen with her quivering form uplifted to meet the shafts of fate without a droop of her eyelids or a murmur from her lips. The light of the one lantern which, intentionally or unintentionally, was concentrated on this pathetic group, made it stand out from the midst of the surrounding darkness in a way to draw the gaze of Mr.

Gryce upon them. He looked, and his own brow became overcast. Evidently we were not far from the cause of their fears.

Ordering the candle lifted, he surveyed the ceiling above, at which Loreen's lips opened slightly in secret dread and amazement. Then he commanded the men to move on slowly, while he himself looked overhead rather than underneath, which seemed to astonish his associates, who evidently had heard nothing of the hole which had been cut in the floor of the Flower Parlor.

Suddenly I heard a slight gasp from Lucetta, who had not moved forward with the rest of us. Then her rushing figure flew by us and took up its stand by Mr. Gryce, who had himself paused and was pointing with an imperious forefinger to the ground under his feet.

"You will dig here," said he, not heeding her, though I am sure he was as well acquainted with her proximity as we.

"Dig?" repeated Loreen, in what we all saw was a final effort to stave off disgrace and misery.

"My duty demands it," said he. "Some one else has been digging here within a very few days, Miss Knollys. That is as evident as is the fact that a communication has been made with this place through an opening into the room above. See!" And taking the lantern from the man at his side, he held it up toward the ceiling.

There was no hole there now, but there were ample evidences of there having been one, and that within a very short time. Loreen made no further attempt to stay him.

"The house is at your disposal," she reiterated, but I do not think she knew what she said. The man with the bundle in his arms was already unrolling it on the cellar bottom. A spade came to light, together with some other tools. Lifting the spade, he thrust it smartly into the ground toward which Mr. Gryce's inexorable finger still pointed. At the sight and the sound it made, a thrill passed through Lucetta which made her another creature. Dashing forward, she flung herself down upon the spot with lifted head and outstretched arms.

"Stop your desecrating hand!" she cried. "This is a grave—the grave, sirs, of our mother!"

XXX

INVESTIGATION

The shock of these words—if false, most horrible; if true, still more horrible—threw us all aback and made even Mr. Gryce's features assume an aspect quite uncommon to them.

"Your mother's grave?" said he, looking from her to Loreen with very

111

evident doubt. "I thought your mother died seven or more years ago, and this grave has been dug within three days."

"I know," she whispered. "To the world my mother has been dead many, many years, but not to us. We closed her eyes night before last, and it was to preserve this secret, which involves others affecting our family honor, that we resorted to expedients which have perhaps attracted the notice of the police and drawn this humiliation down upon us. I can conceive no other reason for this visit, ushered in as it was by Mr. Trohm."

"Miss Lucetta"—Mr. Gryce spoke quickly; if he had not I certainly could not have restrained some expression of the emotions awakened in my own breast by this astounding revelation—"Miss Lucetta, it is not necessary to bring Mr. Trohm's name into this matter or that of any other person than myself. I saw the coffin lowered here, which you say contained the body of your mother. Thinking this a strange place of burial and not knowing it was your mother to whom you were paying these last dutiful rites, I took advantage of my position as detective to satisfy myself that nothing wrong lay behind so mysterious a death and burial. Can you blame me, Miss? Would I have been a man to trust if I had let such an event as this go by unchallenged?"

She did not answer. She had heard but one sentence of all this long speech.

"You saw my mother's coffin lowered? Where were you that you should see that? In some of these dark passages, let in by I know not what traitor to our peace of mind." And her eyes, which seemed to have grown almost supernaturally large and bright under her emotions, turned slowly in their sockets till they rested with something like doubtful accusation upon mine. But not to remain there, for Mr. Gryce recalled them almost instantly by this short, sharp negative.

"No, I was nearer than that. I lent my strength to this burial. If you had thought to look under Mother Jane's hood, you would have seen what would have forced these explanations then and there."

"And you——"

"I was Mother Jane for the nonce. Not from choice, Miss, but from necessity. I was impersonating the old woman when your brother came to the cottage. I could not give away my plans by refusing the task your brother offered me."

"It is well." Lucetta had risen and was now standing by the side of Loreen. "Such a secret as ours defies concealment. Even Providence takes part against us. What you want to know we must tell, but I assure you it has nothing to do with the business you profess to be chiefly interested in—nothing at all."

"Then perhaps you and your sister will retire," said he. "Distracted as you are by family griefs, I would not wish to add one iota to your distress. This lady, whom you seem to regard with more or less favor as friend or relative, will stay to see that no dishonor is paid to your mother's remains. But your mother's face we must see, Miss Lucetta, if only to lighten the explanations you will doubtless feel called upon to make."

It was Loreen who answered this.

"If it must be," said she, "remember your own mother and deal reverently with ours." Which entreaty and the way it was uttered, gave me my first distinct conviction that these girls were speaking the truth, and that the diminutive body we had come to unearth was that of Althea Knollys, whose fairy-like form I had so long supposed commingled with foreign soil.

The thought was almost too much for my self-possession, and I advanced upon Loreen with a dozen burning questions on my lips when the voice of Mr. Gryce stopped me.

"Explanations later," said he. "For the present we want you here."

It was no easy task for me to linger there with all my doubts unsolved, waiting for the decisive moment when Mr. Gryce should say: "Come! Look! Is it she?" But the will that had already sustained me through so many trying experiences did not fail me now, and, grievous as was the ordeal, I passed steadily through it, being able to say, though not without some emotion, I own: "It is Althea Knollys! Changed almost beyond conception, but still these girls' mother!" which was a happier end to this adventure than that we had first feared, mysterious as the event was, not only to myself, but, as I could see, to the acute detective as well.

The girls had withdrawn long before this, just as Mr. Gryce had desired, and I now expected to be allowed to join them, but Mr. Gryce detained me till the grave was refilled and made decent again, when he turned and to my intense astonishment—for I had thought the matter was all over and the exoneration of this household complete—said softly and with telling emphasis in my ear:

"Our work is not done yet. They who make graves so readily in cellars must have been more or less accustomed to the work. We have still some digging to do."

XXXI

STRATEGY

I was overwhelmed.

"What," said I, "you still doubt?"

"I always doubt," he gravely replied. "This cellar bottom offers a wide field for speculation. Too wide, perhaps, but, then, I have a plan."

Here he leaned over and whispered a few concise sentences into my ear in a tone so low I should feel that I was betraying his confidence in repeating them. But their import will soon become apparent from what presently occurred.

"Light Miss Butterworth to the stairway," Mr. Gryce now commanded one of the men, and thus accompanied I found my way back to the kitchen, where Hannah was bemoaning uncomforted the shame which had come upon the house.

I did not stop to soothe her. That was not my cue, nor would it have answered my purpose. On the contrary, I broke into angry ejaculations as I passed her:

"What a shame! Those wretches cannot be got away from the cellar. What do you suppose they expect to find there? I left them poking hither and thither in a way that will be very irritating to Miss Knollys when she finds it out. I wonder William stands it."

What she said in reply I do not know. I was half way down the hall before my own words were finished.

My next move was to go to my room and take from my trunk a tiny hammer and some very small, sharp-pointed tacks. Curious articles, you will think, for a woman to carry on her travels, but I am a woman of experience, and have known only too often what it was to want these petty conveniences and not be able to get them. They were to serve me an odd turn now. Taking a half-dozen tacks in one hand and concealing the hammer in my bag, I started boldly for William's room. I knew that the girls were not there, for I had heard them talking together in the sitting-room as I came up. Besides, if they were, I had a ready answer for any demand they might make.

Searching out his boots, I turned them over, and into the sole of each I drove one of my small tacks. Then I put them back in the same place and position in which I found them. Task number one was accomplished.

When I issued from the room, I went as quickly as I could below. I was now ready for a talk with the girls, whom I found as I had anticipated, talking and weeping together in the sitting-room.

They rose as I came in, awaiting my first words in evident anxiety. They had not heard me go up-stairs. I immediately allowed my anxiety and profound interest in this matter to have full play.

"My poor girls! What is the meaning of this? Your mother just dead, and the matter kept from me, her friend! It is astounding—incomprehensible! I do not know what to make of it or of you."

"It has a strange look," Loreen gravely admitted; "but we had reasons for this deception, Miss Butterworth. Our mother, charming and sweet as you remember her, has not always done right, or, what you will better understand, she committed a criminal act against a person in this town, the penalty of which is state's prison."

With difficulty the words came out. With difficulty she kept down the flush of shame which threatened to overwhelm her and did overwhelm her more sensitive sister. But her self-control was great, and she went bravely on, while I, in faint imitation of her courage, restrained my own surprise and intolerable sense of shock and bitter sorrow under a guise of simple sympathy.

"It was forgery," she explained. "This has never before passed our lips. Though a cherished wife and a beloved mother, she longed for many things my father could not give her, and in an evil hour she imitated the name of a rich man here and took the check thus signed to New York. The fraud was not detected, and she received the money, but ultimately the rich man whose money she had spent, discovered the use she had made of his name, and, if she had not escaped, would have had her arrested. But she left the country, and the only revenge he took, was to swear that if she ever set foot again in X., he would call the police down upon her. Yes, if she were dying, and they had to drag her from the brink of the grave. And he would have done it; and knowing this, we have lived under the shadow of this fear for eleven years. My father died under it, and my mother—ah, she spent all the remaining years of her life under foreign skies, but when she felt the hand of death upon her, her affection for her own flesh and blood triumphed over her discretion, and she came, secretly, I own, but still with that horror menacing her, to these doors, and begging our forgiveness, lay down under the roof where we were born, and died with the halo of our love about her."

"Ah," said I, thinking of all that had happened since I had come into this house and finding nothing but confirmation of what she was saying, "I begin to understand."

But Lucetta shook her head.

"No," said she, "you cannot understand yet. We who had worn mourning for her because my father wished to make this very return impossible, knew nothing of what was in store for us till a letter came saying she would be at the C. station on the very night we received it. To acknowledge our deception, to seek and bring her home openly to this house, could not be thought of for a moment. How, then, could we satisfy her dying wishes without compromising her memory and ourselves? Perhaps you have guessed, Miss Butterworth. You have had time since we revealed the unhappy secret of this household."

"Yes," said I. "I have guessed."

Lucetta, with her hand laid on mine, looked wistfully into my face.

"Don't blame us!" she cried. "Our mother's good name is everything to us, and we knew no other way to preserve it than by making use of the one superstition of this place. Alas! our efforts were in vain. The phantom coach brought our mother safely to us, but the circumstances which led to our doors being opened to outsiders, rendered it impossible for us to carry out our plans unsuspected. Her grave has been discovered and desecrated, and we——"

She stopped, choked. Loreen took advantage of her silence to pursue the explanations she seemed to think necessary.

"It was Simsbury who undertook to bring our dying mother from C. station to our door. He has a crafty spirit under his meek ways, and dressed himself in a way to lend color to the superstition he hoped to awaken. William, who did not dare to accompany him for fear of arousing gossip, was at the gate when the coach drove in. It was he who lifted our mother out, and it was while she still clung to him with her face pressed close to his breast that we saw her first. Ah! what a pitiable sight it was! She was so wan, so feeble, and yet so radiantly happy.

"She looked up at Lucetta, and her face grew wonderful in its unearthly beauty. She was not the mother we remembered, but a mother whose life had culminated in the one desire to see and clasp her children again. When she could tear her eyes away from Lucetta, she looked at me, and then the tears came, and we all wept together, even William; and thus weeping and murmuring words of welcome and cheer, we carried her up-stairs and laid her in the great front chamber. Alas! we did not foresee what would happen the very next morning—I mean the arrival of your telegram, to be followed so soon by yourself."

"Poor girls! Poor girls!" It was all I could say. I was completely overwhelmed.

"The first night after your arrival we moved her into William's room as being more remote and thus a safer refuge for her. The next night she died. The dream which you had of being locked in your room was no dream. Lucetta did that in foolish precaution against your trying to search us out in the night. It would have been better if we had taken you into our confidence."

"Yes," I assented, "that would have been better." But I did not say how much better. That would have been giving away my secret.

Lucetta had now recovered sufficiently to go on with the story.

"William, who is naturally colder than we and less sensitive in regard to our mother's good name, has shown some little impatience at the restraint imposed upon him by her presence, and this was an extra burden, Miss Butterworth, but that and all the others we have been forced to bear" (the generous girl did not speak of her own special grief and loss) "have all been rendered useless by the unhappy chance which has brought into our midst this agent of the police. Ah, if I only knew whether this was the providence of God rebuking us for years of deception, or just the malice of man seeking to rob us of our one best treasure, a mother's untarnished name!"

"Mr. Gryce acts from no malice—" I began, but I saw they were not listening.

"Have they finished down below?" asked Lucetta.

"Does the man you call Gryce seem satisfied?" asked Loreen.

I drew myself up physically and mentally. My second task was about to begin.

"I do not understand those men," said I. "They seem to want to look farther than the sacred spot where we left them. If they are going through a form, they are doing it very thoroughly."

"That is their duty," observed Loreen, but Lucetta took it less calmly.

"It is an unhappy day for us!" cried she. "Shame after shame, disgrace upon disgrace! I wish we had all died in our childhood. Loreen, I must see William. He will be doing some foolish thing, swearing or——"

"My dear, let me go to William," I urgently put in. "He may not like me overmuch, but I will at least prove a restraint to him. You are too feeble. See, you ought to be lying on the couch instead of trying to drag yourself out to the stables."

And indeed at that moment Lucetta's strength gave suddenly out, and she sank into Loreen's arms insensible.

When she was restored, I hurried away to the stables, still in pursuit of the task which I had not yet completed. I found William sitting doggedly on a stool in the open doorway, grunting out short sentences to the two men who lounged in his vicinity on either side. He was angry, but not as angry as I had seen him many times before. The men were townsfolk and listened eagerly to his broken sentences. One or two of these reached my ears.

"Let 'em go it. It won't be now or to-day they'll settle this business. It's the devil's work, and devils are sly. My house won't give up that secret, or any other house they'll be likely to visit. The place I would ransack—But Loreen would say I was babbling. Goodness knows a fellow's got to talk about something when his fellow-townsfolk come to see him." And here his laugh broke in, harsh, cruel, and insulting. I felt it did him no good, and made haste to show myself.

Immediately his whole appearance changed. He was so astonished to see me there that for a moment he was absolutely silent; then he broke out again into another loud guffaw, but this time in a different tone.

"Why, it's Miss Butterworth," he laughed. "Here, Saracen! Come, pay your respects to the lady who likes you so well."

And Saracen came, but I did not forsake my ground. I had espied in one corner just what I had hoped to see there, and Saracen's presence afforded me the opportunity of indulging in one or two rather curious antics.

"I am not afraid of the dog," I declared, with marked loftiness, shrinking toward the pail of water I had already marked with my eye. "Not at all afraid," I continued, catching up the pail and putting it before me as the dog made a wild rush in my direction. "These gentlemen will not see me hurt." And though they all laughed—they would have been fools if they had not—and the dog jumped the pail and I jumped—not a pail, but a broom-handle that was lying amid all the rest of the disorder on the floor—they did not see that I had succeeded in doing what I wished, which was to place that pail so near to William's feet that—But wait a moment; everything in its own time. I escaped the dog, and next moment had my eye on him. He did not move after that, which rather put a stop to the laughter, which observing, I drew very near to William, and with a sly gesture to the two men, which for some reason they seemed to understand, whispered in the rude fellow's ear:

"They've found your mother's grave under the Flower Parlor. Your sisters told me to tell you. But that is not all. They're trampling hither and yon through all the secret places in the cellar, turning up the earth with their spades. I know they won't find anything, but we thought you ought to know—"

Here I made a feint of being startled, and ceased. My second task was done. The third only remained. Fortunately at that moment Mr. Gryce and his followers showed themselves in the garden. They had just come from the cellar and played their part in the same spirit I had mine. Though they were too far off for their words to be heard, the air of secrecy they maintained and the dubious looks they cast towards the stable, could not but evince even to William's dull understanding that their investigations had resulted in a doubt which left them far from satisfied; but, once this impression made, they did not linger long together. The man with the lantern moved off, and Mr. Gryce turned towards us, changing his whole appearance as he advanced, till no one could look more cheerful and good-humored.

"Well, that is over," he sighed, with a forced air of infinite relief. "Mere form, Mr. Knollys—mere form. We have to go through these pretended investigations at times, and good people like yourself have to submit; but I assure you it is not pleasant, and under the present circumstances—I am sure you understand me, Mr. Knollys—the task has occasioned me a feeling almost of remorse; but that is inseparable from a detective's life. He is obliged every day of his life to ride over the tenderest emotions. Forgive me! And now, boys, scatter till I call you together again. I hope our next search will be without such sorrowful accompaniments."

It succeeded. William stared at him and stared at the men slowly filing off down the yard, but was not for a moment deceived by these overflowing expressions. On the contrary, he looked more concerned than he had while seated between the two men manifestly set to guard him.

"The deuce!" he cried, with a shrug of his shoulders that expressed anything but satisfaction. "Lucetta always said—" But even he knew enough not to finish that sentence, low as he had mumbled it. Watching him and watching

Mr. Gryce, who at that moment turned to follow his men, I thought the time had come for action. Making another spring as if in fresh terror of Saracen, who, by the way, was eying me with the meekness of a lamb, I tipped over that pail with such suddenness and with such dexterity that its whole contents poured in one flood over William's feet. My third task was accomplished.

The oath he uttered and the excuses which I volubly poured forth could not have reached Mr. Gryce's ears, for he did not return. And yet from the way his shoulders shook as he disappeared around the corner of the house, I judge that he was not entirely ignorant of the subterfuge by which I hoped to force this blundering booby of ours to change the boots he wore for one of the pairs into which I had driven those little tacks.

XXXII

RELIEF

The plan succeeded. Mr. Gryce's plans usually do. William went immediately to his room, and in a little while came down and hastened into the cellar.

"I want to see what mischief they have done," said he.

When he came back, his face was beaming.

"All right," he shouted to his sisters, who had come into the hall to meet him. "Your secret's out, but mine——"

"There, there!" interposed Loreen, "you had better go up-stairs and prepare for supper. We must eat, William, or rather, Miss Butterworth must eat, whatever our sorrows or disappointments."

He took the rebuke with a grunt and relieved us of his company. Little did he think as he went whistling up the stairs that he had just shown Mr. Gryce where to search for whatever might be lying under the broad sweep of that cellar-bottom.

That night—it was after supper, which I did not eat for all my natural stoicism—Hannah came rushing in where we all sat silent, for the girls showed no disposition to enlarge their confidences in regard to their mother, and no other topic seemed possible, and, closing the door behind her, said quickly and with evident chagrin:

"Those men are here again. They say they forgot something. What do you think it means, Miss Loreen? They have spades and lanterns and——"

"They are the police, Hannah. If they forgot something, they have the right to return. Don't work yourself up about that. The secret they have already found out was our worst. There is nothing to fear after that." And she dismissed Hannah, merely bidding her let us know when the house was quite clear.

Was she right? Was there nothing worse for them to fear? I longed to leave these trembling sisters, longed to join the party below and follow in the track of the tiny impressions made by the tacks I had driven into William's soles. If there was anything hidden under the cellar-bottom, natural anxiety would carry him to the spot he had most to fear; so they would only have to dig at the places where these impressions took a sharp turn.

But was there anything hidden there? From the sisters' words and actions I judged there was nothing serious, but would they know? William was quite capable of deceiving them. Had he done so? It was a question.

It was solved for us by Mr. Gryce's reappearance in the room an hour or so later. From the moment the light fell upon his kindly features I knew that I might breathe again freely. It was not the face he showed in the house of a criminal, nor did his bow contain any of the false deference with which he sometimes tries to hide his secret doubt or contempt.

"I have come to trouble you for the last time, ladies. We have made a double search through this house and through the stables, and feel perfectly justified in saying that our duty henceforth will lead us elsewhere. The secrets we have surprised are your own, and if possible shall remain so. Your brother's propensity for vivisection and the return and death of your mother bear so little on the real question which interests this community that we may be able to prevent their spread as gossip through the town. That this may be done conscientiously, however, I ought to know something more of the latter circumstance. If Miss Butterworth will then be good enough to grant me a few minutes' conference with these ladies, I may be able to satisfy myself to such an extent as to let this matter rest where it is."

I rose with right good will. A mountain weight had been lifted from me, proof positive that I had really come to love these girls.

What they told him, whether it was less or more than they told me, I cannot say, and for the moment did not know. That it had not shaken his faith in them was evident, for when he came out to where I was waiting in the hall his aspect was even more encouraging than it had been before.

"No guile in those girls," he whispered as he passed me. "The clue given by what seemed mysterious in this house has come to naught. To-morrow we take up another. The trinkets found in Mother Jane's cottage are something real. You may sleep soundly to-night, Miss Butterworth. Your part has been well played, but I know you are glad that it has failed."

And I knew that I was glad, too, which is the best proof that there is something in me besides the detective instinct.

The front door had scarcely closed behind him when William came storming in. He had been gossiping over the fence with Mr. Trohm, and had been beguiled into taking a glass of wine in his house. This was evident without his speaking of it.

"Those sneaks!" cried he. "I hear they've been back again, digging and stirring up our cellar-bottom like mad. That's because you're so dreadful shy, you girls. You're afraid of this, you're afraid of that. You don't want folks to know that mother once—Well, well, there it is now! If you had not tried to keep this wretched secret, it would have been an old matter by this time, and my affairs would have been left untouched. But now every fool will cry out at me in this staid, puritanical old town, and all because a few bones have been found of animals which have died in the cause of science. I say it's all your fault! Not that I have anything to be ashamed of, because I haven't, but because this other thing, this d—d wicked series of disappearances, taking place, for aught we know, a dozen rods from our gates (though I think—but no matter what I think—you all like, or say you like, old Deacon Spear), has made every one so touchy in this pharisaical town that to kill a fly has become a crime even if it is to save oneself from poison. I'm going to see if I cannot make folks blink askance at some other man than me. I'm going to find out who or what causes these disappearances."

This was a declaration to make us all stare and look a little bit foolish. William playing the detective! Well, what might I not live to see next! But the next moment an overpowering thought struck me. Might this Deacon Spear by any chance be the rich man whose animosity Althea Knollys had awakened?

BOOK IV

THE BIRDS OF THE AIR

XXXIII

LUCETTA

The next morning I rose with the lark. I had slept well, and all my old vigor had returned. A new problem was before me; a problem of surpassing interest, now that the Knollys family had been eliminated from the list of persons regarded with suspicion by the police. Mother Jane and the jewels were to be Mr. Gryce's starting-point for future investigation. Should they be mine? My decision on this point halted, and thinking it might be helped by a breath of fresh air, I decided upon an early stroll as a means of settling this momentous question.

There was silence in the house when I passed through it on my way to the front door. But that silence had lost its terrors and the old house its absorbing mystery. Yet it was not robbed of its interest. When I realized that Althea Knollys, the Althea of my youth, had just died within its walls as ignorant of my proximity as I of hers, I felt that no old-time romance, nor any terror brought by flitting ghost or stalking apparition, could compare with the wonder of this return and the strange and thrilling circumstances which had attended it. And the end was not yet. Peaceful as everything now looked, I still felt that the end had not come.

The fact that Saracen was loose in the yard gave me some slight concern as I opened the great front door and looked out. But the control under which I had held him the day before encouraged me in my venture, and after a few words with Hannah, who was careful not to let me slip away unnoticed, I boldly stepped forth and took my solitary way down to the gate.

It was not yet eight, and the grass was still heavy with dew. At the gate I paused. I wished to go farther, but Mr. Gryce's injunction had been imperative about venturing into the lane alone. Besides—No, that was not a horse's hoof. There could be no one on the road so early as this. I was alarming myself unnecessarily, yet—Well, I held my place, a little awkwardly, perhaps. Self-consciousness is always awkward, and I could not help being a trifle self-conscious at a meeting so unexpected and—But the more I attempt to explain, the more confused my expressions become, so I will just say that, by this very strange chance, I was leaning over the gate when Mr. Trohm rode up for the second time and found me there.

I did not attempt any excuses. He is gentleman enough to understand that a woman of my temperament rises early and must have the morning air. That he should feel the same necessity is a coincidence, natural perhaps, but still a coincidence. So there was nothing to be said about it.

But had there been, I would not have spoken, for he seemed so gratified at finding me enjoying nature at this early hour that any words from me would have been quite superfluous. He did not dismount—that would have shown intention—but he stopped, and—well, we have both passed the age of romance, and what he said cannot be of interest to the general public, especially as it did not deal with the disappearances or with the discoveries made in the Knollys house the day before, or with any of those questions which have absorbed our attention up to this time.

That we were engaged more than five minutes in this conversation I cannot believe. I have always been extremely accurate in regard to time, yet a good half-hour was lost by me that morning for which I have never been able to account. Perhaps it was spent in the short discussion which terminated our interview; a discussion which may be of interest to you, for it was upon the action of the police.

"Nothing came of the investigations made by Mr. Gryce yesterday, I perceive," Mr. Trohm had remarked, with some reluctance, as he gathered up his reins to depart. "Well, that is not strange. How could he have hoped to find any clue to such a mystery as he is engaged to unearth, in a house presided over by Miss Knollys?"

"How could he, indeed! Yet," I added, determined to allay this man's suspicions, which, notwithstanding the openness of his remark, were still observable in his tones, "you say that with an air I should hardly expect from so good a neighbor and friend. Why is this, Mr. Trohm? Surely you do not associate crime with the Misses Knollys?"

"Crime? Oh, no, certainly not. No one could associate crime with the Misses Knollys. If my tone was at fault, it was due perhaps to my embarrassment— this meeting, your kindness, the beauty of the day, and the feeling these all call forth. Well, I may be pardoned if my tones are not quite true in discussing other topics. My thoughts were with the one I addressed."

"Then that tone of doubt was all the more misplaced," I retorted. "I am so frank, I cannot bear innuendo in others. Besides, Mr. Trohm, the worst folly of this home was laid bare yesterday in a way to set at rest all darker suspicions. You knew that William indulged in vivisection. Well, that is bad, but it cannot be called criminal. Let us do him justice, then, and, for his sisters' sake, see how we can re-establish him in the good graces of the community."

But Mr. Trohm, who for all our short acquaintance was not without a very decided appreciation for certain points in my character, shook his head and with a smiling air returned:

"You are asking the impossible not only of the community, but yourself. William can never re-establish himself. He is of too rude a make. The girls may recover the esteem they seem to have lost, but William—Why, if the cause of those disappearances was found to-day, and found at the remotest end of this road or even up in the mountains, where no one seems to have looked for it, William would still be known throughout the county as a rough and cruel man. I have tried to stand his friend, but it's been against odds, Miss Butterworth. Even his sisters recognize this, and show their lack of confidence in our friendship. But I would like to oblige you."

I knew he ought to go. I knew that if he had simply lingered the five minutes which common courtesy allowed, that curious eyes would be looking from Loreen's window, and that at any minute I might expect some interference from Lucetta, who had read through this man's forbearance toward William the very natural distrust he could not but feel toward so uncertain a character. Yet with such an opportunity at my command, how could I let him go without another question?

"Mr. Trohm," said I, "you have the kindest heart and the closest lips, but have you ever thought that Deacon Spear——"

He stopped me with a really horrified look. "Deacon Spear's house was thoroughly examined yesterday," said he, "as mine will be to-day. Don't insinuate anything against him! Leave that for foolish William." Then with the most charming return to his old manner, for I felt myself in a measure rebuked, he lifted his hat and urged his horse forward. But, having withdrawn himself a step or two, he paused and with the slightest gesture toward the little hut he was facing, added in a much lower tone than any he had yet used: "Besides, Deacon Spear is much too far away from Mother Jane's cottage. Don't you remember that I told you she never could be got to go more than forty rods from her own doorstep?" And, breaking into a quick canter, he rode away.

I was left to think over his words and the impossibility of my picking up any other clue than that given me by Mr. Gryce.

I was turning toward the house when I heard a slight noise at my feet. Looking down, I encountered the eyes of Saracen. He was crouching at my side, and as I turned toward him, his tail actually wagged. It was a sight to call the color up to my cheek; not that I blushed at this sign of good-will, astonishing as it was, considering my feeling toward dogs, but at his being there at all without my knowing it. So palpable a proof that no woman—I make no exceptions—can listen more than one minute to the expressions of a man's sincere admiration without losing a little of her watchfulness, was not to be disregarded by one as inexorable to her own mistakes as to those of others. I saw myself the victim of vanity, and while somewhat abashed by the discovery, I could not but realize that this solitary proof of feminine weakness was not really to be deplored in one who has not yet passed the line beyond which any such display is ridiculous.

Lucetta met me at the door just as I had expected her to. Giving me a short look, she spoke eagerly but with a latent anxiety, for which I was more or less prepared.

"I am glad to see you looking so bright this morning," she declared. "We are all feeling better now that the incubus of secrecy is removed. But"—here she hesitated—"I would not like to think you told Mr. Trohm what happened to us yesterday."

"Lucetta," said I, "there may be women of my age who delight in gossiping about family affairs with comparative strangers, but I am not that kind of woman. Mr. Trohm, friendly as he has proved himself and worthy as he undoubtedly is of your confidence and trust, will have to learn from some other person than myself anything which you may wish to have withheld from him."

For reply she gave me an impulsive kiss. "I thought I could trust you," she cried. Then, with a dubious look, half daring, half shrinking, she added:

"When you come to know and like us better, you will not care so much to talk to neighbors. They never can understand us or do us justice, Mr. Trohm, especially."

This was a remark I could not let pass.

"Why?" I demanded. "Why do you think Mr. Trohm cherishes such animosity towards you? Has he ever——"

But Lucetta could exercise a repellent dignity when she chose. I did not finish my sentence, though I must have looked the inquiry I thought better not to put into words.

"Mr. Trohm is a man of blameless reputation," she avowed. "If he has allowed himself to cherish suspicions in our regard, he has doubtless had his reasons for it."

And with these quiet words she left me to my thoughts, and I must say to my doubts, which were all the more painful that I saw no immediate opportunity for clearing them up.

Late in the afternoon William burst in with news from the other end of the lane.

"Such a lark!" he cried. "The investigation at Deacon Spear's house was a mere farce, and I just made them repeat it with a few frills. They had dug up my cellar, and I was determined they should dig up his. Oh, the fun it was! The old fellow kicked, but I had my way. They couldn't refuse me, you know; I hadn't refused them. So that man's cellar-bottom has had a stir up. They didn't find anything, but it did me a lot of good, and that's something. I do hate Deacon Spear—couldn't hate him worse if he'd killed and buried ten men under his hearthstone."

"There is no harm in Deacon Spear," said Lucetta, quickly.

"Did they submit Mr. Trohm's house to a search also?" asked Loreen, ashamed of William's heat and anxious to avert any further display of it.

"Yes, they went through that too. I was with them. Glad I was too. I say, girls, I could have laughed to see all the comforts that old bachelor has about him. Never saw such fixings. Why, that house is as neat and pretty from top to bottom as any old maid's. It's silly, of course, for a man, and I'd rather live in an old rookery like this, where I can walk from room to room in muddy boots if I want to, and train my dogs and live in freedom like the man I am. Yet I couldn't help thinking it mighty comfortable, too, for an old fellow like him who likes such things and don't have chick or child to meddle. Why, he had pincushions on all his bureaus, and they had pins in them."

The laugh with which he delivered this last sentence might have been heard a quarter of a mile away. Lucetta looked at Loreen and Loreen looked at me, but none of us joined in the mirth, which seemed to me very ill-timed.

Suddenly Lucetta asked:

"Did they dig up Mr. Trohm's cellar?"

William stopped laughing long enough to say:

"His cellar? Why, it's cemented as hard as an oak floor. No, they didn't polish their spades in his house, which was another source of satisfaction to me. Deacon Spear hasn't even that to comfort him. Oh, how I did enjoy that old fellow's face when they began to root up his old fungi!"

Lucetta turned away with a certain odd constraint I could not but notice.

"It's a humiliating day for the lane," said she. "And what is worse," she suddenly added, "nothing will ever come of it. It will take more than a band of police to reach the root of this matter."

I thought her manner odd, and, moving towards her, took her by the hand with something of a relative's familiarity.

"What makes you say that? Mr. Gryce seems a very capable man."

"Yes, yes, but capability has nothing to do with it. Chance might and pluck might, but wit and experience not. Otherwise the mystery would have been settled long ago. I wish I——"

"Well?" Her hand was trembling violently.

"Nothing. I don't know why I have allowed myself to talk on this subject. Loreen and I once made a compact never to give any opinion upon it. You see how I have kept it."

She had drawn her hand away and suddenly had become quite composed. I turned my attention toward Loreen, but she was looking out of the window and showed no intention of further pursuing the conversation. William had strolled out.

"Well," said I, "if ever a girl had reason for breaking such a compact you are certainly that girl. I could never have been as silent as you have been—that is, if I had any suspicions on so serious a subject. Why, your own good name is impugned—yours and that of every other person living in this lane."

"Miss Butterworth," she replied, "I have gone too far. Besides, you have misunderstood me. I have no more knowledge than anybody else as to the source of these terrible tragedies. I only know that an almost superhuman cunning lies at the bottom of so many unaccountable disappearances, a cunning so great that only a crazy person——"

"Ah," I murmured eagerly, "Mother Jane!"

She did not answer. Instantly I took a resolution.

"Lucetta," said I, "is Deacon Spear a rich man?"

Starting violently, she looked at me amazed.

"If he is, I should like to hazard the guess that he is the man who has held you in such thraldom for years."

"And if he were?" said she.

"I could understand William's antipathy to him and also his suspicions."

She gave me a strange look, then without answering walked over and took Loreen by the hand. "Hush!" I thought I heard her whisper. At all events the two sisters were silent for more than a moment. Then Lucetta said:

"Deacon Spear is well off, but nothing will ever make me accuse living man of crime so dreadful." And she walked away, drawing Loreen after her. In another moment she was out of the room, leaving me in a state of great excitement.

"This girl holds the secret to the whole situation," I inwardly decided. "The belief that nothing more can be learned from her is a false one. I must see Mr. Gryce. William's rodomontades are so much empty air, but Lucetta's silence has a meaning we cannot afford to ignore."

So impressed was I by this, that I took the first opportunity which presented itself of seeing the detective. This was early the next morning. He and several of the townspeople had made their appearance at Mother Jane's cottage, with spades and picks, and the sight had naturally drawn us all down to the gate, where we stood watching operations in a silence which would have been considered unnatural by any one who did not realize the conflicting nature of the emotions underlying it. William, to whom the death of his mother seemed to be a great deliverance, had been inclined to be more or less jocular, but his sallies meeting with no response, he had sauntered away to have it out with his dogs, leaving me alone with the two girls and Hannah.

The latter seemed to be absorbed entirely by the aspect of Mother Jane, who stood upon her doorstep in an attitude so menacing that it was little short of tragic. Her hood, for the first time in the memory of those present, had fallen away from her head, revealing a wealth of gray hair which flew away from her head like a weird halo. Her features we could not distinguish, but the emotion which inspired her, breathed in every gesture of her uplifted arms and swaying body. It was wrath personified, and yet an unreasoning wrath. One could see she was as much dazed as outraged. Her lares and penates were being attacked, and she had come from the heart of her solitude to defend them.

"I declare!" Hannah protested. "It is pitiful. She has nothing in the world but that garden, and now they are going to root that up."

"Do you think that the sight of a little money would appease her?" I inquired, anxious for an excuse to drop a word into the ear of Mr. Gryce.

"Perhaps," said Hannah. "She dearly loves money, but it will not take away her fright."

"It will if she has nothing to be frightened about," said I; and turning to the girls, I asked them, somewhat mincingly for me, if they thought I would make myself conspicuous if I crossed the road on this errand, and when Loreen answered that that would not deter her if she had the money, and Lucetta added that the sight of such misery was too painful for any mere personal consideration, I took advantage of their complaisance, and hastily made my way over to the group, who were debating as to the point they would attack first.

"Gentlemen," said I, "good-morning. I am here on an errand of mercy. Poor old Mother Jane is half imbecile and does not understand why you invade her premises with these implements. Will you object if I endeavor to distract her mind with a little piece of gold I happen to have in my pocket? She may not deserve it, but it will make your task easier and save us some possible concern."

Half of the men at once took off their hats. The other half nudged each other's elbows, and whispered and grimaced like the fools they were. The first half were gentlemen, though not all of them wore gentlemen's clothes.

It was Mr. Gryce who spoke:

"Certainly, madam. Give the old woman anything you please, but—" And here he stepped up to me and began to whisper; "You have something to say. What is it?"

I answered in the same quick way: "The mine you thought exhausted has possibilities in it yet. Question Lucetta. It may prove a more fruitful task than turning up this soil."

The bow he made was more for the onlookers than for the suggestion I had given him. Yet he was not ungrateful for the latter, as I, who was beginning to understand him, could see.

"Be as generous as you please!" he cried aloud. "We would not disturb the old crone if it were not for one of her well-known follies. Nothing will take her over forty rods away from her home. Now what lies within those forty rods? These men think we ought to see."

The shrug I gave answered both the apparent and the concealed question. Satisfied that he would understand it so, I hurried away from him and approached Mother Jane.

"See!" said I, astonished at the regularity of her features, now that I had a good opportunity of observing them. "I have brought you money. Let them dig up your turnips if they will."

She did not seem to perceive me. Her eyes were wild with dismay and her lips trembling with a passion far beyond my power to comfort.

"Lizzie!" she cried. "Lizzie! She will come back and find no home. Oh, my poor girl! My poor, poor girl!"

It was pitiable. I could not doubt her anguish or her sincerity. The delirium of a broken heart cannot be simulated. And this heart was not controlled by reason; that was equally apparent. Immediately my heart, which goes out slowly, but none the less truly on that account, was touched by something more than the surface sympathy of the moment. She may have stolen, she may have done worse, she may even have been at the bottom of the horrible crimes which have given its name to the lane we were in, but her acts, if acts they were, were the result of a clouded mind fixed forever upon the fancied needs of another, and not the expression of personal turpitude or even of personal longing or avarice. Therefore I could pity her, and I did.

Making another appeal, I pressed the coin hard into one of her hands till the contact effected what my words had been unable to do, and she finally looked down and saw what she was clutching. Then indeed her aspect changed, and in a few minutes of slowly growing comprehension she became so quiet and absorbed that she forgot to look at the men and even forgot me, who was probably nothing more than a flitting shadow to her.

"A silk gown," she murmured. "It will buy Lizzie a silk gown. Oh! where did it come from, the good, good gold, the beautiful gold; such a little piece, yet enough to make her look fine, my Lizzie, my pretty, pretty Lizzie?"

No numbers this time. The gift was too overpowering for her even to remember that it must be hidden away.

I walked away while her delight was still voluble. Somehow it eased my mind to have done her this little act of kindness, and I think it eased the minds of the men too. At all events, every hat was off when I repassed them on my way back to the Knollys gateway.

I had left both the girls there, but I found only one awaiting me. Lucetta had gone in, and so had Hannah. On what errand I was soon to know.

"What do you suppose that detective wants of Lucetta now?" asked Loreen as I took my station again at her side. "While you were talking to Mother Jane he stepped over here, and with a word or two induced Lucetta to walk away with him toward the house. See, there they are in those thick shrubs near the right wing. He seems to be pleading with her. Do you think I ought to join them and find out what he is urging upon her so earnestly? I don't like to seem intrusive, but Lucetta is easily agitated, you know, and his business cannot be of an indifferent nature after all he has discovered concerning our affairs."

"No," I agreed, "and yet I think Lucetta will be strong enough to sustain the conversation, judging from the very erect attitude she is holding now. Perhaps he thinks she can tell him where to dig. They seem a little at sea over there, and living, as you do, a few rods from Mother Jane, he may imagine that Lucetta can direct him where to first plant the spade."

"It's an insult," Loreen protested. "All these talks and visits are insults. To be sure, this detective has some excuse, but——"

"Keep your eye on Lucetta," I interrupted. "She is shaking her head and looking very positive. She will prove to him it is an insult. We need not interfere, I think."

But Loreen had grown pensive and did not heed my suggestion. A look that was almost wistful had supplanted the expression of indignant revolt with which she had addressed me, and when next moment the two we had been watching turned and came slowly toward us, it was with decided energy she bounded forward and joined them.

"What is the matter now?" she asked. "What does Mr. Gryce want, Lucetta?"

Mr. Gryce himself spoke.

"I simply want her," said he, "to assist me with a clue from her inmost thoughts. When I was in your house," he explained with a praiseworthy consideration for me and my relations to these girls for which I cannot be too grateful, "I saw in this young lady something which convinced me that, as a dweller in this lane, she was not without her suspicions as to the secret cause of the fatal mysteries which I have been sent here to clear up. To-day I have frankly accused her of this, and asked her to confide in me. But she refuses to do so, Miss Loreen. Yet her face shows even at this moment that my old eyes were not at fault in my reading of her. She does suspect somebody, and it is not Mother Jane."

"How can you say that?" began Lucetta, but the eyes which Loreen that moment turned upon her seemed to trouble her, for she did not attempt to say any more—only looked equally obstinate and distressed.

"If Lucetta suspects any one," Loreen now steadily remarked, "then I think she ought to tell you who it is."

"You do. Then perhaps you—" commenced Mr. Gryce—"can persuade her as to her duty," he finished, as he saw her head rise in protest of what he evidently had intended to demand.

"Lucetta will not yield to persuasion," was her quiet reply. "Nothing short of conviction will move the sweetest-natured but the most determined of all my mother's children. What she thinks is right, she will do. I will not attempt to influence her."

Mr. Gryce, with one comprehensive survey of the two, hesitated no longer. I saw the rising of the blood into his forehead, which always precedes the beginning of one of his great moves, and, filled with a sudden excitement, I awaited his next words as a tyro awaits the first unfolding of the plan he has seen working in the brain of some famous strategist.

"Miss Lucetta,"—his very tone was changed, changed in a way to make us all start notwithstanding the preparation his momentary silence had given us—"I have been thus pressing and perhaps rude in my appeal, because of something which has come to my knowledge which cannot but make you of all persons extremely anxious as to the meaning of this terrible mystery. I am an old man, and you will not mind my bluntness. I have been told—and your agitation convinces me there is truth in the report—that you have a lover, a Mr. Ostrander——"

"Ah!" She had sunk as if crushed by one overwhelming blow to the earth. The eyes, the lips, the whole pitiful face that was upturned to us, remain in my memory to-day as the most terrible and yet the most moving spectacle that has come into my by no means uneventful life. "What has happened to him? Quick, quick, tell me!"

For answer Mr. Gryce drew out a telegram.

"From the master of the ship on which he was to sail," he explained. "It asks if Mr. Ostrander left this town on Tuesday last, as no news has been received of him."

"Loreen! Loreen! When he left us he passed down that way!" shrieked the girl, rising like a spirit and pointing east toward Deacon Spear's. "He is gone! He is lost! But his fate shall not remain a mystery. I will dare its solution. I—I—To-night you will hear from me again."

And without another glance at any of us she turned and fled toward the house.

XXXIV

CONDITIONS

But in another moment she was back, her eyes dilated and her whole person exhaling a terrible purpose.

"Do not look at me, do not notice me!" she cried, but in a voice so hoarse no one but Mr. Gryce could fully understand her. "I am for no one's eyes but God's. Pray that he may have mercy upon me." Then as she saw us all instinctively fall back, she controlled herself, and, pointing toward Mother Jane's cottage, said more distinctly: "As for those men, let them dig. Let them dig the whole day long. Secrecy must be kept, a secrecy so absolute that not even the birds of the air must see that our thoughts range beyond the forty rods surrounding Mother Jane's cottage."

She turned and would have fled away for the second time, but Mr. Gryce stopped her. "You have set yourself a task beyond your strength. Can you perform it?"

"I can perform it," she said. "If Loreen does not talk, and I am allowed to spend the day in solitude."

I had never seen Mr. Gryce so agitated—no, not when he left Olive Randolph's bedside after an hour of vain pleading. "But to wait all day! Is it necessary for you to wait all day?"

"It is necessary." She spoke like an automaton. "To-night at twilight, when the sun is setting, meet me at the great tree just where the road turns. Not a minute sooner, not an hour later. I will be calmer then." And waiting now for nothing, not for a word from Loreen nor a detaining touch from Mr. Gryce, she flew away for the second time. This time Loreen followed her.

"Well, that is the hardest thing I ever had to do," said Mr. Gryce, wiping his forehead and speaking in a tone of real grief and anxiety. "Do you think her delicate frame can stand it? Will she survive this day and carry through whatever it is she has set herself to accomplish?"

"She has no organic disease," said I, "but she loved that young man very much, and the day will be a terrible one to her."

Mr. Gryce sighed.

"I wish I had not been obliged to resort to such means," said he, "but women like that only work under excitement, and she does know the secret of this affair."

"Do you mean," I demanded, almost aghast, "that you have deceived her with a false telegram; that that slip of paper you hold——"

"Read it," he cried, holding it out toward me.

I did read it. Alas, there was no deception in it. It read as he said.

"However—" I began.

But he had pocketed the telegram and was several steps away before I had finished my sentence.

"I am going to start these men up," said he. "You will breathe no word to Miss Lucetta of my sympathy nor let your own interests slack in the investigations which are going on under our noses."

And with a quick, sharp bow, he made his way to the gate, whither I followed him in time to see him set his foot upon a patch of sage.

"You will begin at this place," he cried, "and work east; and, gentlemen, something tells me that we shall be successful."

With almost a simultaneous sound a dozen spades and picks struck the ground. The digging up of Mother Jane's garden had begun in earnest.

XXXV

THE DOVE

I remained at the gate. I had been bidden to show my interest in what was going on in Mother Jane's garden, and this was the way I did it. But my thoughts were not with the diggers. I knew, as well then as later, that they would find nothing worth the trouble they were taking; and, having made up my mind to this, I was free to follow the lead of my own thoughts.

They were not happy ones; I was neither satisfied with myself nor with the prospect of the long day of cruel suspense that awaited us. When I undertook to come to X., it was with the latent expectation of making myself useful in ferreting out its mystery. And how had I succeeded? I had been the means through which one of its secrets had been discovered, but not the secret; and while Mr. Gryce was good enough, or wise enough, to show no diminution in his respect for me, I knew that I had sunk a peg in his estimation from the consciousness I had of having sunk two, if not three pegs, in my own.

This was a galling thought to me. But it was not the only one which disturbed me. Happily or unhappily, I have as much heart as pride, and Lucetta's despair, and the desperate resolve to which it had led, had made an impression upon me which I could not shake off.

Whether she knew the criminal or only suspected him; whether in the heat of her sudden anguish she had promised more or less than she could perform, the fact remained that we (by whom I mean first and above all, Mr. Gryce, the ablest detective on the New York force, and myself, who, if no detective, am at least a factor of more or less importance in an inquiry like this) were awaiting the action of a weak and suffering girl to discover what our own experience should be able to obtain for us unassisted.

That Mr. Gryce felt that he was playing a great card in thus enlisting her despair in our service, did not comfort me. I am not fond of games in which real hearts take the place of painted ones; and, besides, I was not ready to acknowledge that my own capacity for ferreting out this mystery was quite exhausted, or that I ought to remain idle while Lucetta bent under a task so much beyond her strength. So deeply was I impressed by this latter consideration, that I found myself, even in the midst of my apparent interest in what was going on at Mother Jane's cottage, asking if I was bound to accept the defeat pronounced upon my efforts by Mr. Gryce, and if there was not yet time to retrieve myself and save Lucetta. One happy thought, or clever linking of cause to effect, might lead me yet to the clue which we had hitherto sought in vain. And then who would have more right to triumph than Amelia Butterworth, or who more reason to apologize than Ebenezar Gryce! But where was I to get my happy thought, and by what stroke of fortune could I reasonably hope to light upon a clue which had escaped the penetrating eye of my quondam colleague? Lucetta's gesture and Lucetta's exclamation, "He passed that way!" indicated that her suspicions pointed in the direction of Deacon Spear's cottage; so did William's wandering accusations: but this was little help to me, confined as I was to the Knollys demesnes, both by Mr. Gryce's command and by my own sense of propriety. No, I must light on something more tangible; something practical enough to justify me in my own eyes for any interference I might meditate. In short, I must start from a fact, and not from a suspicion. But what fact? Why, there was but one, and that was the finding of certain indisputable tokens of crime in Mother Jane's keeping. That was a clue, a clue, to be sure, which Mr. Gryce, while ostensibly following it in his present action, really felt to lead nowhere, but which I—Here my thoughts paused. I dare not promise myself too satisfactory results to my efforts, even while conscious of that vague elation which presages success, and which I could only overcome by resorting again to reasoning. This time I started with a question. Had Mother Jane committed these crimes herself? I did not think so; neither did Mr. Gryce, for all the persistence he showed in having the ground about her humble dwelling-place turned over. Then, how had the ring of Mr. Chittenden come to be in her possession, when, as all agreed, she never was known to wander more than forty rods away from home? If the crime by which this young gentleman had perished had taken place up the road, as Lucetta's denouncing finger plainly indicated, then this token of Mother Jane's complicity in it had been carried across the intervening space by other means than Mother Jane herself. In other words, it was brought to her by the perpetrator, or it was placed where she could lay hand on it; neither supposition implying guilt on her part, she being in all probability as innocent of wrong as she was of sense. At all events, such should be my theory for the nonce, old theories having exploded or become of little avail in the present aspect of things. To discover, then, the source of crime, I must discover the means by which this ring reached Mother Jane—an almost hopeless task, but not to be despaired of on that account: had I not wrung the truth in times gone by from that piece of obstinate stolidity the Van Burnam scrub-woman? and if I could do this, might I not hope to win an equal confidence from this half-demented creature, with a heart so passionate it beat to but one tune, her Lizzie? I meant at least to try, and, under the impulse of this resolve, I left my position at the gate and recrossed the road to Mother Jane, whose figure I could dimly discern on the farther side of her little house.

Mr. Gryce barely looked up as I passed him, and the men not at all. They were deep in their work, and probably did not see me. Neither did Mother Jane at first. She had not yet wearied of the shining gold she held, though she had begun again upon that chanting of numbers the secret of which Mr. Gryce had discovered in his investigation of her house.

I therefore found it hard to make her hear me when I attempted to speak. She had fixed upon the new number fifteen and seemed never to tire of repeating it. At last I took cue from her speech, and shouted out the word ten. It was the number of the vegetable in which Mr. Chittenden's ring had been hidden, and it made her start violently.

"Ten! ten!" I reiterated, catching her eye. "He who brought it has carried it away; come into the house and look."

It was a desperate attempt. I felt myself quake inwardly as I realized how near Mr. Gryce was standing, and what his anger would be if he surprised me at this move after he had cried "Halt!"

But neither my own perturbation nor the thought of his possible anger could restrain the spirit of investigation which had returned to me with the above words; and when I saw that they had not fallen upon deaf ears, but that Mother Jane heard and in a measure understood them, I led the way into the hut and pointed to the string from which the one precious vegetable had been torn.

She gave a spring toward it that was well-nigh maniacal in its fury, and for an instant I thought she was going to rend the air with one of her wild yells, when there came a swishing of wings at one of the open windows, and a dove flew in and nestled in her breast, diverting her attention so, that she dropped the empty husk of the onion she had just grasped and seized the bird in its stead. It was a violent clutch, so violent that the poor dove panted and struggled under it till its head flopped over and I looked to see it die in her hands.

"Stop!" I cried, horrified at a sight I was so unprepared to expect from one who was supposed to cherish these birds most tenderly.

But she heard me no more than she saw the gesture of indignant appeal I made her. All her attention, as well as all her fury, was fixed upon the dove, over whose neck and under whose wings she ran her trembling fingers with the desperation of one looking for something he failed to find.

"Ten! ten!" it was now her turn to shout, as her eyes passed in angry menace from the bird to the empty husk that dangled over her head. "You brought it, did you, and you've taken it, have you? There, then! You'll never bring or carry any more!" And lifting up her hand, she flung the bird to the other side of the room, and would have turned upon me, in which contingency I would for once have met my match, if, in releasing the bird from her hands, she had not at the same time released the coin which she had hitherto managed to hold through all her passionate gestures.

The sight of this piece of gold, which she had evidently forgotten for the moment, turned her thoughts back to the joys it promised her. Recapturing it once more, she sank again into her old ecstasy, upon which I proceeded to pick up the poor, senseless dove, and leave the hut with a devout feeling of gratitude for my undoubted escape.

That I did this quietly and with the dove hidden under my little cape, no one who knows me well will doubt. I had brought something from the hut besides this victim of the old imbecile's fury, and I was no more willing that Mr. Gryce should see the one than detect the other. I had brought away a clue.

"The birds of the air shall carry it." So the Scripture runs. This bird, this pigeon, who now lay panting out his life in my arms had brought her the ring which in Mr. Gryce's eyes had seemed to connect her with the disappearance of young Mr. Chittenden.

XXXVI

AN HOUR OF STARTLING EXPERIENCES

Not till I was safely back in the Knollys grounds, not, indeed, till I had put one or two large and healthy shrubs between me and a certain pair of very prying eyes, did I bring the dove out from under my cape and examine the poor bird for any sign which might be of help to me in the search to which I was newly committed.

But I found nothing, and was obliged to resort to my old plan of reasoning to make anything out of the situation in which I thus so unexpectedly found myself. The dove had brought the ring into old Mother Jane's hands, but whence and through whose agency? This was as much a secret as before, but the longer I contemplated it, the more I realized that it need not remain a secret long; that we had simply to watch the other doves, note where they lighted, and in whose barn-doors they were welcome, for us to draw inferences that might lead to revelations before the day was out. If Deacon Spear—But Deacon Spear's house had been examined as well as that of every other resident in the lane. This I knew, but it had not been examined by me, and unwilling as I was to challenge the accuracy or thoroughness of a search led on by such a man as Mr. Gryce, I could not but feel that, with such a hint as I had received from the episode in the hut, it would be a great relief to my mind to submit these same premises to my own somewhat penetrating survey, no man in my judgment having the same quickness of eyesight in matters domestic as a woman trained to know every inch of a house and to measure by a hair's-breadth every fall of drapery within it.

But how in the name of goodness was I to obtain an opportunity for this survey. Had we not one and all been bidden to confine our attention to what was going on in Mother Jane's cottage, and would it not be treason to Lucetta to run the least risk of awakening apprehension in any possibly guilty mind at the other end of the road? Yes, but for all that I could not keep still if fate, or my own ingenuity, offered me the least chance of pursuing the clue I had wrung from our imbecile neighbor at the risk of my life. It was not in my nature to do so, any more than it was in my nature to yield up my present advantage to Mr. Gryce without making a personal effort to utilize it. I forgot that I failed in this once before in my career, or rather I recalled this failure, perhaps, and felt the great need of retrieving myself.

When, therefore, in my slow stroll towards the house I encountered William in the shrubbery, I could not forbear accosting him with a question or two.

"William," I remarked, gently rubbing the side of my nose with an irresolute forefinger and looking at him from under my lids, "that was a scurvy trick you played Deacon Spear yesterday."

He stood amazed, then burst into one of his loud laughs.

"You think so?" he cried. "Well, I don't. He only got what he deserved, the hard, sanctimonious sneak!"

"Do you say that," I inquired, with some spirit, "because you dislike the man, or because you really believe him to be worthy of hatred?"

William's amusement at this argued little for my hopes.

"We are very much interested in the Deacon," he suggested, with a leer; which insolence I allowed to pass unnoticed, because it best suited my plan.

"You have not answered my question," I remarked, with a forced air of anxiety.

"Oh, no," he cried, "so I haven't"; and he tried to look serious too. "Well, well, to be just, I have nothing really against the man but his mean ways. Still, if I were going to risk my life on a hazard as to who is the evil spirit of this lane, I should say Spear and done with it, he has such cursed small eyes."

"I don't think his eyes are too small," I returned loftily. Then with a sudden change of manner, I suggested anxiously: "And my opinion is shared by your sisters. They evidently think very well of him."

"Oh!" he sneered; "girls are no judges. They don't know a good man when they see him, and they don't know a bad. You mustn't go by what they say."

I had it on the tip of my tongue to ask if he did not think Lucetta sufficiently understood herself to be trusted in what she contemplated doing that night. But this was neither in accordance with my plan, nor did it seem quite loyal to Lucetta, who, so far as I knew, had not communicated her intentions to this booby brother. I therefore changed this question into a repetition of my first remark:

"Well, I still think the trick you played Deacon Spear yesterday a poor one; and I advise you, as a gentleman, to go and ask his pardon."

This was such a preposterous proposition, he could not hold his peace.

"I ask his pardon!" he snorted. "Well, Saracen, did you ever hear the like of that! I ask Deacon Spear's pardon for obliging him to be treated with as great attention as I had been myself."

"If you do not," I went on, unmoved, "I shall go and do it myself. I think that is what my friendship for you warrants. I am determined that while I am a visitor in your house no one shall be able to pick a flaw in your conduct."

He stared (as he might well do), tried to read my face, then my intentions, and failing to do both, which was not strange, broke into noisy mirth.

"Oh, ho!" he laughed. "So that is your game, is it! Well, I never! Saracen, Miss Butterworth wants to reform me; wants to make one of her sleek city chaps out of William Knollys. She'll have hard work of it, won't she? But then we're beginning to like her well enough to let her try. Miss Butterworth, I'll go with you to Deacon Spear. I haven't had so much chance for fun in a twelve-month."

I had not expected such success, and was duly thankful. But I made no reference to it aloud. On the contrary, I took his complaisance as a matter of course, and, hiding all token of triumph, suggested quietly that we should make as little ado as possible over our errand, seeing that Mr. Gryce was something of a meddler and might take it into his head to interfere. Which suggestion had all the effect I anticipated, for at the double prospect of amusing himself at the Deacon's expense, and of outwitting the man whose business it was to outwit us, he became not only willing but eager to undertake the adventure offered him. So with the understanding that I was to be ready to drive into town as soon as he could hitch up the horse, we parted on the most amicable terms, he proceeding towards the stable and I towards the house, where I hoped to learn something new about Lucetta.

But Loreen, from whom alone I could hope to glean any information, was shut in her room, and did not come out, though I called her more than once, which, if it left my curiosity unsatisfied, at least allowed me to quit the house without awakening hers.

William was waiting for me at the gate when I descended. He was in the best of humors, and helped me into the buggy he had resurrected from some corner of the old stable, with a grimace of suppressed mirth which argued well for the peace of our proposed drive. The horse's head was turned away from the quarter we were bound for, but as we were ostensibly on our way to the village, this showed but common prudence on William's part, and, as such, met with my entire approbation.

Mr. Gryce and his men were hard at work when we passed them. Knowing the detective so well, and rating at its full value his undoubted talent for reading the motives of those about him, I made no attempt at cajolery in the explanation I proffered of our sudden departure, but merely said, in my old, peremptory way, that I found waiting at the gate so tedious that I had accepted William's invitation to drive into town. Which, while it astonished the old gentleman, did not really arouse his suspicions, as a more conciliatory manner and speech might have done. This disposed of, we drove rapidly away.

William's sense of humor once aroused was not easily allayed. He seemed so pleased with his errand that he could talk of nothing else, and turned the subject over and over in his clumsy way, till I began to wonder if he had seen through the object of our proposed visit and was making me the butt of his none too brilliant wit.

But no, he was really amused at the part he was called upon to play, and, once convinced of this, I let his humor run on without check till we had re-entered Lost Man's Lane from the other end and were in sight of the low sloping roof of Deacon Spear's old-fashioned farmhouse.

Then I thought it time to speak.

"William," said I, "Deacon Spear is too good a man, and, as I take it, is in possession of too great worldly advantages for you to be at enmity with him. Remember that he is a neighbor, and that you are a landed proprietor in this lane."

"Good for you!" was the elegant reply with which this young boor honored me. "I didn't think you had such an eye for the main chance."

"Deacon Spear is rich, is he not?" I pursued, with an ulterior motive he was far from suspecting.

"Rich? Why, I don't know; that depends upon what you city ladies call rich; I shouldn't call him so, but then, as you say, I am a landed proprietor myself."

His laugh was boisterously loud, and as we were then nearly in front of the Deacon's house, it rang in through the open windows, causing such surprise, that more than one head bobbed up from within to see who dared to laugh like that in Lost Man's Lane. While I noted these heads and various other small matters about the house and place, William tied up the horse and held out his hand for me to descend.

"I begin to suspect," he whispered as he helped me out, "why you are so anxious to have me on good terms with the Deacon." At which insinuation I attempted to smile, but only succeeded in forcing a grim twitch or two to my lips, for at that moment and before I could take one step towards the house, a couple of pigeons rose up from behind the house and flew away in a bee-line for Mother Jane's cottage.

"Ha!" thought I; "my instinct has not failed me. Behold the link between this house and the hut in which those tokens of crime were found," and was for the moment so overwhelmed by this confirmation of my secret suspicions, that I quite forgot to advance, and stood stupidly staring after these birds now rapidly disappearing in the distance.

William's voice aroused me.

"Come!" he cried. "Don't be bashful. I don't think much of Deacon Spear myself, but if you do—Why, what's the matter now?" he asked, with a startled look at me. I had clutched him by the arm.

"Nothing," I protested, "only—you see that window over there? The one in the gable of the barn, I mean. I thought I saw a hand thrust out,—a white hand that dropped crumbs. Have they a child on this place?"

"No," replied William, in an odd voice and with an odd look toward the window I have mentioned. "Did you really see a hand there?"

"I most certainly did," I answered, with an air of indifference I was far from feeling. "Some one is up in the hay-loft; perhaps it is Deacon Spear himself. If so, he will have to come down, for now that we are here, I am determined you shall do your duty."

"Deacon Spear can't climb that hay-loft," was the perplexed answer I received in a hardly intelligible mutter. "I've been there, and I know; only a boy or a very agile young man could crawl along the beams that lead to that window. It is the one hiding-place in this part of the lane; and when I said

137

yesterday that if I were the police and had the same search to make which they have, I knew where I would look, I meant that same little platform up behind the hay, whose only outlook is yonder window. But I forgot that you have no suspicions of our good Deacon; that you are here on quite a different errand than to search for Silly Rufus. So come along and——"

But I resisted his impelling hand. He was so much in earnest and so evidently under the excitement of what appeared to him a great discovery, that he seemed quite another man. This made my own suspicions less hazardous, and also added to the situation fresh difficulties which could only be met by an appearance on my part of perfect ingenuousness.

Turning back to the buggy as if I had forgotten something, and thus accounting to any one who might be watching us, for the delay we showed in entering the house, I said to William: "You have reasons for thinking this man a villain, or you wouldn't be so ready to suspect him. Now what if I should tell you that I agree with you, and that this is why I have dragged you here this fine morning?"

"I should say you were a deuced smart woman," was his ready answer. "But what can you do here?"

"What have we already done?" I asked. "Discovered that they have some one in hiding in what you call an inaccessible place in the barn. But didn't the police examine the whole place yesterday? They certainly told me they had searched the premises thoroughly."

"Yes," he repeated, with great disdain, "they said and they said; but they didn't climb up to the one hiding-place in sight. That old fellow Gryce declared it wasn't worth their while; that only birds could reach that loophole."

"Oh," I returned, somewhat taken aback; "you called his attention to it, then?"

To which William answered with a vigorous nod and the grumbling words:

"I don't believe in the police. I think they're often in league with the very rogues they——"

But here the necessity of approaching the house became too apparent for further delay. Deacon Spear had shown himself at the front door, and the sight of his astonished face twisted into a grimace of doubtful welcome drove every other thought away than how we were to acquit ourselves in the coming interview. Seeing that William was more or less nonplussed by the situation, I caught him by the arm, and whispering, "Let us keep to our first programme," led him up the walk with much the air of a triumphant captain bringing in a recalcitrant prisoner.

My introduction under these circumstances can be imagined by those who have followed William's awkward ways. But the Deacon, who was probably the most surprised, if not the most disconcerted member of the group, possessed a natural fund of conceit and self-complacency that prevented any outward manifestation of his feelings, though I could not help detecting a carefully suppressed antagonism in his eye when he allowed it to fall upon William, which warned me to exercise my full arts in the manipulation of the matter before me. I accordingly spoke first and with all the prim courtesy such a man might naturally expect from an intruder of my sex and appearance.

"Deacon Spear," said I, as soon as we were seated in his stiff old-fashioned parlor, "you are astonished to see us here, no doubt, especially after the display of animosity shown towards you yesterday by this graceless young friend of mine. But it is on account of this unfortunate occurrence that we are here. After a little reflection and a few hints, I may add, from one who has seen more of life than himself, William felt that he had cause to be ashamed of himself for his show of sport in yesterday's proceedings, and accordingly he has come in my company to tender his apologies and entreat your forbearance. Am I not right, William?"

The fellow is a clown under all and every circumstance, and serious as our real purpose was, and dreadful as was the suspicion he professed to cherish against the suave and seemingly respectable member of the community we were addressing, he could not help laughing, as he blunderingly replied:

"That you are, Miss Butterworth! She's always right, Deacon. I did act like a fool yesterday." And seeming to think that, with this one sentence he had played his part out to perfection, he jumped up and strolled out of the house, almost pushing down as he did so the two daughters of the house, who had crept into the hall from the sitting-room to listen.

"Well, well!" exclaimed the Deacon, "you have done wonders, Miss Butterworth, to bring him to even so small an acknowledgment as that! He's a vicious one, is William Knollys, and if I were not such a lover of peace and concord, he should not long be the only aggressive one. But I have no taste for strife, and so you may both regard his apology as accepted. But why do you rise, madam? Sit down, I pray, and let me do the honors. Martha! Jemima!"

But I would not allow him to summon his daughters. The man inspired me with too much dislike, if not fear; besides, I was anxious about William. What was he doing, and of what blunder might he not be guilty without my judicious guidance?

"I am obliged to you," I returned; "but I cannot wait to meet your daughters now. Another time, Deacon. There is important business going on at the other end of the lane, and William's presence there may be required."

"Ah," he observed, following me to the door, "they are digging up Mother Jane's garden."

I nodded, restraining myself with difficulty.

"Fool's work!" he muttered. Then with a curious look which made me instinctively draw back, he added, "These things must inconvenience you, madam. I wish you had made your visit to the lane in happier times."

There was a smirk on his face which made him positively repellent. I could scarcely bow my acknowledgments, his look and attitude made the interview so obnoxious. Looking about for William, I stepped down from the stoop. The Deacon followed me.

"Where is William?" I asked.

The Deacon ran his eye over the place, and suddenly frowned with ill-concealed vexation.

"The scapegrace!" he murmured. "What business has he in my barn?"

I immediately forced a smile which, in days long past (I've almost forgotten them now), used to do some execution.

"Oh, he's a boy!" I exclaimed. "Do not mind his pranks, I pray. What a comfortable place you have here!"

Instantly a change passed over the Deacon, and he turned to me with an air of great interest, broken now and then by an uneasy glance behind him at the barn.

"I am glad you like the place," he insinuated, keeping close at my side as I stepped somewhat briskly down the walk. "It is a nice place, worthy of the commendation of so competent a judge as yourself." (It was a barren, hard-worked farm, without one attractive feature.) "I have lived on it now forty years, thirty-two of them with my beloved wife Caroline, and two—" Here he stopped and wiped a tear from the dryest eye I ever saw. "Miss Butterworth, I am a widower."

I hastened my steps. I here duly and with the strictest regard for the truth aver, that I decidedly hastened my steps at this very unnecessary announcement. But he, with another covert glance behind him towards the barn, from which, to my surprise and increasing anxiety, William had not yet emerged, kept well up to me, and only paused when I paused at the side of the road near the buggy.

"Miss Butterworth," he began, undeterred by the air of dignity I assumed, "I have been thinking that your visit here is a rebuke to my unneighborliness. But the business which has occupied the lane these last few days has put us all into such a state of unpleasantness that it was useless to attempt sociability."

His voice was so smooth, his eyes so small and twinkling, that if I could have thought of anything except William's possible discoveries in the barn, I should have taken delight in measuring my wits against his egotism.

But as it was, I said nothing, possibly because I only half heard what he was saying.

"I am no lady's man,"—these were the next words I heard,—"but then I judge you're not anxious for flattery, but prefer the square thing uttered by a square man without delay or circumlocution. Madam, I am fifty-three, and I have been a widower two years. I am not fitted for a solitary life, and I am fitted for the companionship of an affectionate wife who will keep my hearth clean and my affections in good working order. Will you be that wife? You see my home,"—here his eye stole behind him with that uneasy look towards the barn which William's presence in it certainly warranted,—"a home which I can offer you unencumbered, if you——"

"Desire to live in Lost Man's Lane," I put in, subduing both my surprise and my disgust at this preposterous proposal, in order to throw all the sarcasm of which I was capable into this single sentence.

"Oh!" he exclaimed, "you don't like the neighborhood. Well, we could go elsewhere. I am not set against the city myself——"

Astounded at his presumption, regarding him as a possible criminal, who was endeavoring to beguile me for purposes of his own, I could no longer repress either my indignation or the wrath with which such impromptu addresses naturally inspired me. Cutting him short with a gesture which made him open his small eyes, I exclaimed in continuation of his remark:

"Nor, as I take it, are you set against the comfortable little income somebody has told you I possessed. I see your disinterestedness, Deacon, but I should be sorry to profit by it. Why, man, I never spoke to you before in my life, and do you think——"

"Oh!" he suavely insinuated, with a suppressed chuckle which even his increasing uneasiness as to William could not altogether repress, "I see you are not above the flattery that pleases other women. Well, madam, I know a tremendous fine woman when I see her, and from the moment I saw you riding by the other day, I made up my mind I would have you for the second Mrs. Spear, if persistence and a proper advocacy of my cause could accomplish it. Madam, I was going to visit you with this proposal to-night, but seeing you here, the temptation was too great for my discretion, and so I have addressed you on the spot. But you need not answer me at once. I don't need to know any more about you than what I can take in with my two eyes, but if you would like a little more acquaintance with me, why I can wait a couple of weeks till we've rubbed the edges off our strangeness, when——"

"When you think I will be so charmed with Deacon Spear that I will be ready to settle down with him in Lost Man's Lane, or if that will not do, carry him off to Gramercy Park, where he will be the admiration of all New York and Brooklyn to boot. Why, man, if I was so easily satisfied as that, I would not be in a position to-day for you to honor me with this proposal. I am not easy to suit, so I advise you to turn your attention to some one much more anxious to be married than I am. But"—and here I allowed some of my real feelings to appear—"if you value your own reputation or the happiness of the lady you propose to inveigle into an union with you, do not venture too far in the matrimonial way till the mystery is dispelled which shrouds Lost Man's Lane in horror. If you were an honest man you would ask no one to share your fortunes whilst the least doubt rests upon your reputation."

"My reputation?" He had started very visibly at these words. "Madam, be careful. I admire you, but——"

"No offence," said I. "For a stranger I have been, perhaps, unduly frank. I only mean that any one who lives in this lane must feel himself more or less enveloped by the shadow which rests upon it. When that is lifted, each and every one of you will feel himself a man again. From indications to be seen in the lane to-day, that time may not be far distant. Mother Jane is a likely source for the mysteries that agitate us. She knows just enough to have no proper idea of the value of a human life."

The Deacon's retort was instantaneous. "Madam," said he, with a snap of his fingers, "I have not that much interest in what is going on down there. If men have been killed in this lane (which I do not believe), old Mother Jane has had no hand in it. My opinion is—and you may value it or not, just as you please— that what the people hereabout call crimes are so many coincidences, which some day or other will receive their due explanation. Every one who has disappeared in this vicinity has disappeared naturally. No one has been killed. That is my theory, and you will find it correct. On this point I have expended more than a little thought."

I was irate. I was also dumfounded at his audacity. Did he think I was the woman to be deceived by any such balderdash as that? But I shut my lips tightly lest I should say something, and he, not finding this agreeable, being no conversationalist himself, drew himself up with a pompously expressed hope that he would see me again after his reputation was cleared, when his attention as well as my own was diverted by seeing William's slouching figure appear in the barn door and make slowly towards us.

Instantly the Deacon forgot me in his interest in William's approach, which was so slow as to be tantalizing to us both.

When he was within speaking distance, Deacon Spear started towards him.

"Well!" he cried; "one would think you had gone back a dozen or so years and were again robbing your neighbor's hen-roosts. Been in the hay, eh?" he added, leaning forward and plucking a wisp or two from my companion's clothes. "Well, what did you find there?"

In trembling fear for what the lout might answer, I put my hand on the buggy rail and struggled anxiously to my seat. William stepped forward and loosened the horse before speaking. Then with a leer he dived into his pocket, and remarking slowly, "I found this," brought to light a small riding-whip which we both recognized as one he often carried. "I flung it up in the hay yesterday in one of my fits of laughing, so just thought I would bring it down to-day. You know it isn't the first time I've climbed about those rafters, Deacon, as you have been good enough to insinuate."

The Deacon, evidently taken aback, eyed the young fellow with a leer in which I saw something more serious than mere suspicion.

"Was that all?" he began, but evidently thought better than to finish, whilst William, with a nonchalance that surprised me, blunderingly avoided his eye, and, bounding into the buggy beside me, started up the horse and drove slowly off.

"Ta, ta, Deacon," he called back; "if you want to see fun, come up to our end of the lane; there's precious little here." And thus, with a laugh, terminated an interview which, all things considered, was the most exciting as well as the most humiliating I have ever taken part in.

"William," I began, but stopped. The two pigeons whose departure I had watched a little while before were coming back, and, as I spoke, fluttered up to the window before mentioned, where they alighted and began picking up the crumbs which I had seen scattered for them. "See!" I suddenly exclaimed, pointing them out to William. "Was I mistaken when I thought I saw a hand drop crumbs from that window?"

The answer was a very grave one for him.

"No," said he, "for I have seen more than a hand, through the loophole I made in the hay. I saw a man's leg stretched out as if he were lying on the floor with his head toward the window. It was but a glimpse I got, but the leg moved as I looked at it, and so I know that some one lies hid in that little nook up under the roof. Now it isn't any one belonging to the lane, for I know where every one of us is or ought to be at this blessed moment; and it isn't a detective, for I heard a sound like heavy sobbing as I crouched there. Then who is it? Silly Rufus, I say; and if that hay was all lifted, we would see sights that would make us ashamed of the apologies we uttered to the old sneak just now."

"I want to get home," said I. "Drive fast! Your sisters ought to know this."

"The girls?" he cried. "Yes, it will be a triumph over them. They never would believe I had an atom of judgment. But we'll show them, if William Knollys is altogether a fool."

We were now near to Mr. Trohm's hospitable gateway. Coming from the excitements of my late interview, it was a relief to perceive the genial owner of this beautiful place wandering among his vines and testing the condition of his fruit by a careful touch here and there. As he heard our wheels he turned, and seeing who we were, threw up his hands in ill-restrained pleasure, and came buoyantly forward. There was nothing to do but to stop, so we stopped.

"Why, William! Why, Miss Butterworth, what a pleasure!" Such was his amiable greeting. "I thought you were all busy at your end of the lane; but I see you have just come from town. Had an errand there, I suppose?"

"Yes," William grumbled, eying the luscious pear Mr. Trohm held in his hand.

The look drew a smile from that gentleman.

"Admiring the first fruits?" he observed. "Well, it is a handsome specimen," he admitted, handing it to me with his own peculiar grace. "I beg you will take it, Miss Butterworth. You look tired; pardon me if I mention it." (He is the only person I know who detects any signs of suffering or fatigue on my part.)

"I am worried by the mysteries of this lane," I ventured to remark. "I hate to see Mother Jane's garden uprooted."

"Ah!" he acquiesced, with much evidence of good feeling, "it is a distressing thing to witness. I wish she might have been spared. William, there are other pears on the tree this came from. Tie up the horse, I pray, and gather a dozen or so of these for your sisters. They will never be in better condition for plucking than they are to-day."

William, whose mouth and eyes were both watering for a taste of the fine fruit thus offered, moved with alacrity to obey this invitation, while I, more startled than pleased—or, rather, as much startled as pleased—by the prospect of a momentary tête-à-tête with our agreeable neighbor, sat uneasily eying the luscious fruit in my hand, and wishing I was ten years younger, that the blush I felt slowly stealing up my cheek might seem more appropriate to the occasion.

But Mr. Trohm appeared not to share my wish. He was evidently so satisfied with me as I was, that he found it difficult to speak at first, and when he did— But tut! tut! you have no desire to hear any such confidences as these, I am sure. A middle-aged gentleman's expressions of admiration for a middle-aged lady may savor of romance to her, but hardly to the rest of the world, so I will pass this conversation by, with the single admission that it ended in a question to which I felt obliged to return a reluctant No.

Mr. Trohm was just recovering from the disappointment of this, when William sauntered back with his hands and pockets full.

"Ah!" that graceless scamp chuckled, with a suspicious look at our downcast faces, "been improving the opportunity, eh?"

Mr. Trohm, who had fallen back against his old well-curb, surveyed his young neighbor for the first time with a look of anger. But it vanished almost as quickly as it appeared, and he contented himself with a low bow, in which I read real grief.

This was too much for me, and I was about to open my lips with a kind phrase or two, when a flutter took place over our heads, and the two pigeons whose flight I had watched more than once during the last hour, flew down and settled upon Mr. Trohm's arm and shoulders.

"Oh!" I exclaimed, with a sudden shrinking that I hardly understood myself. And though I covered up the exclamation with as brisk a good-by as my inward perturbation would allow, that sight and the involuntary ejaculation I had uttered, were all I saw or heard during our hasty drive homeward.

XXXVII

I ASTONISH MR. GRYCE AND HE ASTONISHES ME

But as we approached the group of curious people which now filled up the whole highway in front of Mother Jane's cottage, I broke from the nightmare into which this last discovery had thrown me, and, turning to William, said with a resolute air:

"You and your sisters are not of one mind regarding these disappearances. You ascribe them to Deacon Spear, but they—whom do they ascribe them to?"

"I shouldn't think it would take a woman of your wit to answer that question."

The rebuke was deserved. I had wit, but I had refused to exercise it; my blind partiality for a man of pleasing exterior and magnetic address had prevented the cool play of my usual judgment, due to the occasion and the trust which had been imposed in me by Mr. Gryce. Resolved that this should end, no matter at what cost to my feelings, I quietly said:

"You allude to Mr. Trohm."

"That is the name," he carelessly assented. "Girls, you know, let their prejudices run away with them. An old grudge——"

"Yes," I tentatively put in; "he persecuted your mother, and so they think him capable of any wickedness."

The growl which William gave was not one of dissent.

"But I don't care what they think," said he, looking down at the heap of fruit which lay between us. "I'm Trohm's friend, and don't believe one word they choose to insinuate against him. What if he didn't like what my mother did! We didn't like it either, and——"

"William," I calmly remarked, "if your sisters knew that Silly Rufus had been found in Deacon Spear's barn they would no longer do Mr. Trohm this injustice."

"No; that would settle them; that would give me a triumph which would last long after this matter was out of the way."

"Very well, then," said I, "I am going to bring about this triumph. I am going to tell Mr. Gryce at once what we have discovered in Deacon Spear's barn."

And without waiting for his ah, yes, or no, I jumped from the buggy and made my way to the detective's side.

His welcome was somewhat unexpected. "Ah, fresh news!" he exclaimed. "I see it in your eye. What have you chanced upon, madam, in your disinterested drive into town?"

I thought I had eliminated all expression from my face, and that my words would bring a certain surprise with them. But it is useless to try to surprise Mr. Gryce.

"You read me like a book," said I; "I have something to add to the situation. Mr. Gryce, I have just come from the other end of the lane, where I found a clue which may shorten the suspense of this weary day, and possibly save Lucetta from the painful task she has undertaken in our interests. Mr. Chittenden's ring——"

I paused for the exclamation of encouragement he is accustomed to give on such occasions, and while I paused, prepared for my accustomed triumph. He did not fail me in the exclamation, nor did I miss my expected triumph.

"Was not found by Mother Jane, or even brought to her in any ordinary way or by any ordinary messenger. It came to her on a pigeon's neck, the pigeon you will find lying dead among the bushes in the Knollys yard."

He was amazed. He controlled himself, but he was very visibly amazed. His exclamations proved it.

"Madam! Miss Butterworth! This ring—Mr. Chittenden's ring, whose presence in her hut we thought an evidence of guilt, was brought to her by one of her pigeons?"

"So she told me. I aroused her fury by showing her the empty husk in which it had been concealed. In her rage at its loss, she revealed the fact I have just mentioned. It is a curious one, sir, and one I am a little proud to have discovered."

"Curious? It is more than curious; it is bizarre, and will rank, I am safe in prophesying, as one of the most remarkable facts that have ever adorned the annals of the police. Madam, when I say I envy you the honor of its discovery, you will appreciate my estimate of it—and you. But when did you find this out, and what explanation are you able to give of the presence of this ring on a pigeon's neck?"

"Sir, to your first question I need only reply that I was here two hours or so ago, and to the second that everything points to the fact that the ring was attached to the bird by the victim himself, as an appeal for succor to whoever might be fortunate enough to find it. Unhappily it fell into the wrong hands. That is the ill-luck which often befalls prisoners."

"Prisoners?"

"Yes. Cannot you imagine a person shut up in an inaccessible place making some such attempt to communicate with his fellow-creatures?"

"But what inaccessible place have we in——"

"Wait," said I. "You have been in Deacon Spear's barn."

"Certainly, many times." But the answer, glib as it was, showed shock. I began to gather courage.

"Well," said I, "there is a hiding-place in that barn which I dare declare you have not penetrated."

"Do you think so, madam?"

"A little loft way up under the eaves, which can only be reached by clambering over the rafters. Didn't Deacon Spear tell you there was such a place?"

"No, but——"

"William, then?" I inexorably pursued. "He says he pointed such a spot out to you, and that you pooh-poohed at it as inaccessible and not worth the searching."

"William is a—Madam, I beg your pardon, but William has just wit enough to make trouble."

"But there is such a place there," I urged; "and, what is more, there is some one hidden in it now. I saw him myself."

"You saw him?"

"Saw a part of him; in short, saw his hand. He was engaged in scattering crumbs for the pigeons."

"That does not look like starvation," smiled Mr. Gryce, with the first hint of sarcasm he had allowed himself to make use of in this interview.

"No," said I; "but the time may not have come to inflict this penalty on Silly Rufus. He has been there but a few days, and—well, what have I said now?"

"Nothing, ma'am, nothing. But what made you think the hand you saw belonged to Silly Rufus?"

"Because he was the last person to disappear from this lane. The last—what am I saying? He wasn't the last. Lucetta's lover was the last. Mr. Gryce, could that hand have belonged to Mr. Ostrander?"

I was intensely excited; so much so that Mr. Gryce made me a warning gesture.

"Hush!" he whispered; "you are attracting attention. That hand was the hand of Mr. Ostrander; and the reason why I did not accept William Knollys' suggestion to search the Deacon's barn-loft was because I knew it had been chosen as a place of refuge by this missing lover of Lucetta."

XXXVIII

A FEW WORDS

Never have keener or more conflicting emotions been awakened in my breast than by these simple words. But alive to the necessity of hiding my feelings from those about me, I gave no token of my surprise, but rather turned a stonier face than common upon the man who had caused it.

"Refuge?" I repeated. "He is there, then, of his own free will—or yours?" I sarcastically added, not being able to quite keep down this reproach as I remembered the deception practised upon Lucetta.

"Mr. Ostrander, madam, has been spending the week with Deacon Spear—they are old friends, you know. That he should spend it quietly and, to a degree, in hiding, was as much his plan as mine. For while he found it impossible to leave Lucetta in the doubtful position in which she and her family at present stand, he did not wish to aggravate her misery by the thought that he was thus jeopardizing the position on which all his hopes of future advancement depended. He preferred to watch and wait in secret, seeing which, I did what I could to further his wishes. His usual lodging was with the family, but when the search was instituted, I suggested that he should remove himself to that eyrie back of the hay where you were sharp enough to detect him to-day."

"Don't attempt any of your flatteries upon me," I protested. "They will not make me forget that I have not been treated fairly. And Lucetta—oh! may I not tell Lucetta——"

"And spoil our entire prospect of solving this mystery? No, madam, you may not tell Lucetta. When Fate has put such a card into our hands as I played with that telegram to-day, we would be flying in the face of Providence not to profit by it. Lucetta's despair makes her bold; upon that boldness we depend to discover and bring to justice a great criminal."

I felt myself turn pale; for that very reason, perhaps, I assumed a still sterner air, and composedly said:

"If Mr. Ostrander is in hiding at the Deacon's, and he and his host are both in your confidence, then the only man whom you can designate in your thoughts by this dreadful title must be Mr. Trohm."

I had perhaps hoped he would recoil at this or give some other evidence of his amazement at an assumption which to me seemed preposterous. But he did not, and I saw, with what feelings may be imagined, that this conclusion, which was half bravado with me, had been accepted by him long enough for no emotion to follow its utterance.

"Oh!" I exclaimed, "how can you reconcile such a suspicion with the attitude you have always preserved towards Mr. Trohm?"

"Madam," said he, "do not criticise my attitude without taking into account existing appearances. They are undoubtedly in Mr. Trohm's favor."

"I am glad to hear you say so," said I, "I am glad to hear you say so. Why, it was in response to his appeal that you came to X. at all."

Mr. Gryce's smile conveyed a reproach which I could not but acknowledge I amply merited. Had he spent evening after evening at my house, entertaining me with tales of the devices and the many inconsistencies of criminals, to be met now by such a puerile disclaimer as this? But beyond that smile he said nothing; on the contrary, he continued as if I had not spoken at all.

"But appearances," he declared, "will not stand before the insight of a girl like Lucetta. She has marked the man as guilty, and we will give her the opportunity of proving the correctness of her instinct."

"But Mr. Trohm's house has been searched, and you have found nothing—nothing," I argued somewhat feebly.

"That is the reason we find ourselves forced to yield our judgment to Lucetta's intuitions," was his quick reply. And smiling upon me with his blandest air, he obligingly added: "Miss Butterworth is a woman of too much character not to abide the event with all her accustomed composure." And with this final suggestion, I was as yet too crushed to resent, he dismissed me to an afternoon of unparalleled suspense and many contradictory emotions.

XXXIX

UNDER A CRIMSON SKY

When, in the course of events, the current of my thoughts receive a decided check and I find myself forced to change former conclusions or habituate myself to new ideas and a fresh standpoint, I do it, as I do everything else, with determination and a total disregard of my own previous predilections. Before the afternoon was well over I was ready for any revelations which might follow Lucetta's contemplated action, merely reserving a vague hope that my judgment would yet be found superior to her instinct.

At five o'clock the diggers began to go home. Nothing had been found under the soil of Mother Jane's garden, and the excitement of search which had animated them early in the day had given place to a dull resentment mainly directed towards the Knollys family, if one could judge of these men's feelings by the heavy scowls and significant gestures with which they passed our broken-down gateway.

By six the last man had filed by, leaving Mr. Gryce free for the work which lay before him.

I had retired long before this to my room, where I awaited the hour set by Lucetta with a feverish impatience quite new to me. As none of us could eat, the supper table had not been laid, and though I had no means of knowing what was in store for us, the sombre silence and oppression under which the whole house lay seemed a portent that was by no means encouraging.

Suddenly I heard a knock at my door. Rising hastily, I opened it. Loreen stood before me, with parted lips and terror in all her looks.

"Come!" she cried. "Come and see what I have found in Lucetta's room."

"Then she's gone?" I cried.

"Yes, she's gone, but come and see what she has left behind her."

Hastening after Loreen, who was by this time half-way down the hall, I soon found myself on the threshold of the room I knew to be Lucetta's.

"She made me promise," cried Loreen, halting to look back at me, "that I would let her go alone, and that I would not enter the highway till an hour after her departure. But with these evidences of the extent of her dread before us, how can we stay in this house?" And dragging me to a table, she showed me lying on its top a folded paper and two letters. The folded paper was Lucetta's Will, and the letters were directed severally to Loreen and to myself with the injunction that they were not to be read till she had been gone six hours.

"She has prepared herself for death!" I exclaimed, shocked to my heart's core, but determinedly hiding it. "But you need not fear any such event. Is she not accompanied by Mr. Gryce?"

"I do not know; I do not think so. How could she accomplish her task if not alone? Miss Butterworth, Miss Butterworth, she has gone to brave Mr. Trohm, our mother's persecutor and our life-long enemy, thinking, hoping, believing that in so doing she will rouse his criminal instincts, if he has them, and so lead to the discovery of his crimes and the means by which he has been enabled to carry them out so long undetected. It is noble, it is heroic, it is martyr-like, but—oh! Miss Butterworth, I have never broken a promise to any one before in all my life, but I am going to break the one I made her. Come, let us fly after her! She has her lover's memory, but I have nothing in all the world but her."

I immediately turned and hastened down the stairs in a state of humiliation which should have made ample amends for any show of arrogance I may have indulged in in my more fortunate moments.

Loreen followed me, and when we were in the lower hall she gave me a look and said:

"My promise was not to enter the highway. Would you be afraid to follow me by another road—a secret road—all overgrown with thistles and blackberry bushes which have not been trimmed up for years?"

I thought of my thin shoes, my neat silk dress, but only to forget them the next moment.

"I will go anywhere," said I.

But Loreen was already too far in advance of me to answer. She was young and lithe, and had reached the kitchen before I had passed the Flower Parlor. But when we had sped clear of the house I found that my progress bade fair to be as rapid as hers, for her agitation was a hindrance to her, while excitement always brings out my powers and heightens both my wits and my judgment.

Our way lay past the stables, from which I expected every minute to see two or three dogs jump. But William, who had been discreetly sent out of the way early in the afternoon, had taken Saracen with him, and possibly the rest, so our passing by disturbed nothing, not even ourselves. The next moment we were in a field of prickers, through which we both struggled till we came into a sort of swamp. Here was bad going, but we floundered on, edging continually toward a distant fence beyond which rose the symmetrical lines of an orchard—Mr. Trohm's orchard, in which those pleasant fruits grew which— Bah! should I ever be able to get the taste of them out of my mouth!

At a tiny gateway covered with vines, Loreen stopped.

"I do not believe this has been opened for years, but it must be opened now." And, throwing her whole weight against it, she burst it through, and bidding me pass, hastened after me over the trailing branches and made, without a word, for the winding path we now saw clearly defined on the edge of the orchard before us.

"Oh!" exclaimed Loreen, stopping one moment to catch her breath, "I do not know what I fear or to what our steps will bring us. I only know that I must hunt for Lucetta till I find her. If there is danger where she is, I must share it. You can rest here or come farther on."

I went farther on.

Suddenly we both started; a man had sprung up from behind the hedgerow that ran parallel with the fence that surrounded Mr. Trohm's place.

"Silence!" he whispered, putting his finger on his lips. "If you are looking for Miss Knollys," he added, seeing us both pause aghast, "she is on the lawn beyond, talking to Mr. Trohm. If you will step here, you can see her. She is in no kind of danger, but if she were, Mr. Gryce is in the first row of trees to the back there, and a call from me——"

That made me remember my whistle. It was still round my neck, but my hand, which had instinctively gone to it, fell again in extraordinary emotion as I realized the situation and compared it with that of the morning when, blinded by egotism and foolish prejudice in favor of this man, I ate of his fruit and hearkened to his outrageous addresses.

"Come!" beckoned Loreen, happily too absorbed in her own emotions to notice mine. "Let us get nearer. If Mr. Trohm is the wicked man we fear, there is no telling what the means are which he uses to get rid of his victims. There was nothing to be found in his house, but who knows where the danger may lurk, and that it may not be near her now? It was evidently to dare it she came, to offer herself as a martyr, that we might know——"

"Hush!" I whispered, controlling my own fears roused against my will by this display of terror in this usually calmest of natures. "No danger can menace her where they stand, unless he is a common assassin and carries a pistol——"

"No pistol," murmured the man, who had crept again near us. "Pistols make a noise. He will not use a pistol."

"Good God!" I whispered. "You do not share her sister's fears that it is in the heart of this man to kill Lucetta?"

"Five strong men have disappeared hereabout," said the fellow, never moving his eye from the couple before us. "Why not one weak girl?"

With a cry Loreen started forward. "Run!" she whispered. "Run!"

But as this word left her lips, a slight movement took place in the belt of trees where we had been told Mr. Gryce lay in hiding, and we could see him issue for a moment into sight with his finger like that of his man laid warningly on his lips. Loreen trembled and drew back, seeing which, the man beside us pointed to the hedge and whispered softly:

"There is just room between it and the fence for a person to pass sideways. If you and this lady want to get nearer to Miss Knollys, you might take that road. But Mr. Gryce will expect you to be very quiet. The young lady expressly said, before she came into this place, that she could do nothing if for any reason Mr. Trohm should suspect they were not alone."

"We will be quiet," I assured him, anxious to hide my face, which I felt twitch at every mention of Mr. Trohm's name. Loreen was already behind the hedge.

The evening was one of those which are made for peace. The sun, which had set in crimson, had left a glow on the branches of the forest which had not yet faded into the gray of twilight. The lawn, around which we were skirting, had not lost the mellow brilliancy which made it sparkle, nor had the cluster of varied-hued hollyhocks which set their gorgeousness against the neat yellow of the peaceful doorposts, shown any dimness in their glory, which was on a par with that of the setting sun. But though I saw all this, it no longer appeared to me desirable. Lucetta and Lucetta's fate, the mystery and the impossibility of its being explained out here in the midst of turf and blossoms, filled all my thoughts, and made me forget my own secret cause for shame and humiliation.

Loreen, who had wormed her way along till she crouched nearly opposite to the place where her sister stood, plucked me by the gown as I approached her, and, pointing to the hedge, which pressed up so close it nearly touched our faces, seemed to bid me look through. Searching for a spot where there was a small opening, I put my eye to this and immediately drew back.

"They are moving nearer the gate," I signalled to Loreen, at which she crept along a few paces, but with a stealth so great that, alert as I was, I could not hear a twig snap. I endeavored to imitate her, but not with as much success as I could wish. The sense of horror which had all at once settled upon me, the supernatural dread of something which I could not see, but which I felt, had seized me for the first time and made the ruddy sky and the broad stretch of velvet turf with the shadows playing over it of swaying tree-tops and clustered oleanders, more thrilling and awesome to me than the dim halls of the haunted house of the Knollys family in that midnight hour when I saw a body carried out for burial amid trouble and hush and a mystery so great it would have daunted most spirits for the remainder of their lives.

The very sweetness of the scene made its horror. Never have I had such sensations, never have I felt so deeply the power of the unseen, yet it seemed so impossible that anything could happen here, anything which would explain the total disappearance of several persons at different times, without a trace of their fate being left to the eye, that I could but liken my state to that of nightmare, where visions take the place of realities and often overwhelm them.

I had pressed too close against the hedge as I struggled with these feelings, and the sound I made struck me as distinct, if not alarming; but the tree-tops were rustling overhead, and, while Lucetta might have heard the hedge-branches crack, her companion gave no evidence of doing so. We could distinguish what they were saying now, and realizing this, we stopped moving and gave our whole attention to listening. Mr. Trohm was speaking. I could hardly believe it was his voice, it had so changed in tone, nor could I perceive in his features, distorted as they now were by every evil passion, the once quiet and dignified countenance which had so lately imposed upon me.

"Lucetta, my little Lucetta," he was saying, "so she has come to see me, come to taunt me with the loss of her lover, whom she says I have robbed her of almost before her eyes! I rob her! How can I rob her or any one of a man with a voice and arm of his own stronger than mine? Am I a wizard to dissipate his body in vapor? Yet can you find it in my house or on my lawn? You are a fool, Lucetta; so are all these men about here fools! It is in your house——"

"Hush!" she cried, her slight figure rising till we forgot it was the feeble Lucetta we were gazing at. "No more accusations directed against us. It is you who must expect them now. Mr. Trohm, your evil practices are discovered. To-morrow you will have the police here in earnest. They did but play with you when they were here before."

"You child!" he gasped, striving, however, to restrain all evidences of shock and terror. "Why, who was it called in the police and set them working in Lost Man's Lane? Was it not I——"

"Yes, that they might not suspect you, and perhaps that they might suspect us. But it was useless, Obadiah Trohm. Althea Knollys' children have been long-suffering, but the limit of their forbearance has been reached. When you laid your hand upon my lover, you roused a spirit in me that nothing but your own destruction can satisfy. Where is he, Mr. Trohm? and where is Silly Rufus and all the rest who have vanished between Deacon Spear's house and the little home of the cripples on the highroad? They have asked me this question, but if any one in Lost Man's Lane can answer, it is you, persecutor of my mother, and traducer of ourselves, whom I here denounce in face of these skies where God reigns and this earth where man lives to harry and condemn."

And then I saw that the instinct of this girl had accomplished what our united acumen and skill had failed to do. The old man—indeed he seemed an old man now—cringed, and the wrinkles came out in his face till he was demoniacally ugly.

"You viper!" he shrieked. "How dare you accuse me of crime—you whose mother would have died in jail but for my forbearance? Have you ever seen me set my foot upon a worm? Look at my fruit and flowers, look at my home, without a spot or blemish to mar its neatness and propriety. Can a man who loves these things stomach the destruction of a man, much less of a silly, yawping boy? Lucetta, you are mad!"

"Mad or sane, my accusation will have its results, Mr. Trohm. I believe too deeply in your guilt not to make others do so."

"Ah," said he, "then you have not done so yet? You believe this and that, but you have not told any one what your suspicions are?"

"No," she calmly returned, though her face blanched to the colorlessness of wax, "I have not said what I think of you yet."

Oh, the cunning that crept into his face!

"She has not said. Oh, the little Lucetta, the wise, the careful little Lucetta!"

"But I will," she cried, meeting his eye with the courage and constancy of a martyr, "though I bring destruction upon myself. I will denounce you and do it before the night has settled down upon us. I have a lover to avenge, a brother to defend. Besides, the earth should be rid of such a monster as you."

"Such a monster as I? Well, my pretty one,"—his voice grown suddenly wheedling, his face a study of mingled passions,—"we will see about that. Come just a step nearer, Lucetta. I want to see if you are really the little girl I used to dandle on my knee."

They were now near the gateway. They had been moving all this time. His hand was on the curb of the old well. His face, so turned that it caught the full glare of the setting sun, leaned toward the girl, exerting a fascinating influence upon her. She took the step he asked, and before we could shriek out "Beware!" we saw him bend forward with a sudden quick motion and then start upright again, while her form, which but an instant before had stood there in all its frail and inspired beauty, tottered as if the ground were bending under it, and in another moment disappeared from our appalled sight, swallowed in some dreadful cavern that for an instant yawned in the smoothly cut lawn before us, and then vanished again from sight as if it had never been.

A shriek from my whistle mingled with a simultaneous cry of agony from Loreen. We heard Mr. Gryce rush from behind us, but we ourselves found it impossible to stir, paralyzed as we were by the sight of the old man's demoniacal delight. He was leaping to and fro over the turf, holding up his fingers in the red sunset glare.

"Six!" he shrieked. "Six! and room for two more! Oh, it's a merry life I lead! Flowers and fruit and love-making" (oh, how I cringed at that!), "and now and then a little spice like this! But where is my pretty Lucetta? Surely she was here a moment ago. How could she have vanished, then, so quickly? I do not see her form amid the trees, there is no trace of her presence upon the lawn, and if they search the house from top to bottom and from bottom to top they will find nothing of her—no, not so much as a print of her footstep or the scent of the violets she so often wears tucked into her hair."

These last words, uttered in a different voice from the rest, gave the clue to the whole situation. We saw, even while we all bounded forward to the rescue of the devoted maiden, that he was one of those maniacs who have perfect control over themselves and pass for very decent sort of men except in the moment of triumph; and, noting his look of sinister delight, perceived that half his pleasure and almost his sole reward for the horrible crimes he had perpetrated, was in the mystery surrounding his victims and the entire immunity from suspicion which up to this time he had enjoyed.

Meantime Mr. Gryce had covered the wretch with his pistol, and his man, who succeeded in reaching the place even sooner than ourselves, hampered as we were by the almost impenetrable hedge behind which we had crouched, tried to lift the grass-covered lid we could faintly discern there. But this was impossible until I, with almost superhuman self-possession, considering the imperative nature of the emergency, found the spring hidden in the well-curb which worked the deadly mechanism. A yell from the writhing creature cowering under the detective's pistol guided me unconsciously in its action, and in another moment we saw the fatal lid tip and disclose what appeared to be the remains of a second well, long ago dried up and abandoned for the other.

The rescue of Lucetta followed. As she had fainted in falling she had not suffered much, and soon we had the supreme delight of seeing her eyes unclose.

"Ah," she murmured, in a voice whose echo pierced to every heart save that of the guilty wretch now lying handcuffed on the sward, "I thought I saw Albert! He was not dead, and I——"

But here Mr. Gryce, with an air at once contrite and yet strangely triumphant, interposed his benevolent face between hers and her weeping sister's and whispered something in her ear which turned her pallid cheek to a glowing scarlet. Rising up, she threw her arms around his neck and let him lift her. As he carried her—where was his rheumatism now?—out of those baleful grounds and away from the reach of the maniac's mingled laughs and cries, her face was peace itself. But his—well, his was a study.

XL

EXPLANATIONS

The hour we all spent together late that night in the old house was unlike any hour which that place had seen for years. Mr. Ostrander, Lucetta, Loreen, William, Mr. Gryce, and myself, all were there, and as an especial grace, Saracen was allowed to enter, that there might not be a cloud upon a single face there assembled. Though it is a small matter, I will add that this dog persisted in lying down by my side, not yielding even to the wiles of his master, whose amusement over this fact kept him good-natured to the last adieu.

There were too few candles in the house to make it bright, but Lucetta's unearthly beauty, the peace in Loreen's soft eyes, made us forget the sombreness of our surroundings and the meagreness of the entertainment Hannah attempted to offer us. It was the promise of coming joy, and when, our two guests departed, I bade good-night to the girls in their grim upper hall, it was with feelings which found their best expression in the two letters I hastened to write as soon as I gained the refuge of my own apartment. I will admit you sufficiently into my confidence to let you read those letters. The first of them ran thus:

"Dear Olive:

"To make others happy is the best way to forget our own misfortunes. A sudden wedding is to take place in this house. Order at once for me from the shops you know me to be in the habit of patronizing, a wedding gown of dainty white taffeta [I did this not to recall too painfully to herself the wedding dress I helped her buy, and which was, as you may remember, of creamy satin], with chiffon trimmings, and a wedding veil of tulle. Add to this a dress suitable for ocean travel and a half-dozen costumes adapted to a southern climate. Let everything be suitable for a delicate but spirited girl who has seen trouble, but who is going to be happy now if a little attention and money can make her so. Do not spare expense, yet show no extravagance, for she is a shy bird, easily frightened. The measurements you will find enclosed; also those of another young lady, her sister, who must also be supplied with a white dress, the material of which, however, had better be of crape.

"All these things must be here by Wednesday evening, my own best dress included. On Saturday evening you may look for my return. I shall bring the latter young lady with me, so your present loneliness will be forgotten in the pleasure of entertaining an agreeable guest. Faithfully yours,

"Amelia Butterworth."

The second letter was a longer and more important one. It was directed to the president of the company which had proposed to send Mr. Ostrander to

South America. In it I related enough of the circumstances which had kept Mr. Ostrander in X. to interest him in the young couple personally, and then I told him that if he would forgive Mr. Ostrander this delay and allow him to sail with his young bride by the next steamer, I myself would undertake to advance whatever sums might have been lost by this change of arrangement.

I did not know then that Mr. Gryce had already made this matter good with this same gentleman.

The next morning we all took a walk in the lane. (I say nothing about the night. If I did not choose to sleep, or if I had any cause not to feel quite as elevated in spirit as the young people about me, there is surely no reason why I should dwell upon it with you or even apologize for a weakness which you will regard, I hope, as an exception setting off my customary strength.)

Now a walk in this lane was an event. To feel at liberty to stroll among its shadows without fear, to know that the danger had been so located that we all felt free to inhale the autumn air and to enjoy the beauties of the place without a thought of peril lurking in its sweetest nooks and most attractive coverts, gave to this short half-hour a distinctive delight aptly expressed by Loreen when she said:

"I never knew the place was so beautiful. Why, I think I can be happy here now." At which Lucetta grew pensive, till I roused her by saying:

"So much for a constitutional, girls. Now we must to work. This house, as you see it now, has to be prepared for a wedding. William, your business will be to see that these grounds are put in as good order as possible in the short time allotted to you. I will bear the expense, and Loreen——"

But William had a word to say for himself.

"Miss Butterworth," said he, "you're a right good sort of woman, as Saracen has found out, and we, too, in these last few plaguy days. But I'm not such a bad lot either, and if I do like my own way, which may not be other people's way, and if I am sometimes short with the girls for some of their d—d nonsense, I have a little decency about me, too, and I promise to fix these grounds, and out of my own money, too. Now that nine tenths of our income does not have to go abroad, we'll have chink enough to let us live in a respectable manner once more in a place where one horse, if he's good enough, will give a fellow a standing and make him the envy of those who, for some other pesky reasons, may think themselves called upon to fight shy of him. I don't begrudge the old place a few dollars, especially as I mean to live and die in it; so look out, you three women folks, and work as lively as you can on the inside of the old rookery, or the slickness of the outside will put you to open shame, and that would never please Loreen, nor, as I take it, Miss Butterworth either."

It was a challenge we were glad to accept, especially as from the number of persons we now saw come flocking into the lane, it was very apparent that we should experience no further difficulty in obtaining any help we might need to carry out our undertakings.

Meantime my thoughts were not altogether concentrated upon these pleasing plans for Lucetta's benefit. There were certain points yet to be made clear in the matter just terminated, and there was a confession for me to make, without which I could not face Mr. Gryce with all that unwavering composure which our peculiar relations seemed to demand.

The explanations came first. They were volunteered by Mr. Gryce, whom I met in the course of the morning at Mother Jane's cottage. That old crone had been perfectly happy all night, sleeping with the coin in her hand and waking to again devour it with her greedy but loving eyes. As I was alternately watching her and Mr. Gryce, who was directing with his hand the movements of the men who had come to smooth down her garden and make it presentable again, the detective spoke:

"I suppose you have found it difficult, in the light of these new discoveries, to explain to yourself how Mother Jane happened to have those trinkets from the peddler's pack, and also how the ring, which you very naturally thought must have been entrusted to the dove by Mr. Chittenden himself, came to be about its neck when it flew home that day of Mr. Chittenden's disappearance. Madam, we think old Mother Jane must have helped herself out of the peddler's pack before it was found in the woods there back of her hut, and of the other matter our explanation is this:

"One day a young man, equipped for travelling, paused for a glass of water at the famous well in Mr. Trohm's garden just as Mother Jane's pigeons were picking up the corn scattered for them by the former, whose tastes are not confined to the cultivation of fruits and flowers, but extend to dumb animals, to whom he is uniformly kind. The young man wore a ring, and, being nervous, was fiddling with it as he talked to the pleasant old gentleman who was lowering the bucket for him. As he fiddled with it, the earth fell from under him, and as the daylight vanished above his head, the ring flew from his up-thrown hand, and lay, the only token of his now blotted-out existence, upon the emerald sward he had but a moment before pressed with his unsuspicious feet. It burned—this ruby burned like a drop of blood in the grass, when that demon came again to his senses, and being a tell-tale evidence of crime in the eyes of one who had allowed nothing to ever speak against him in these matters, he stared at it as at a deadly thing directed against himself and to be got rid of at once and by means which by no possibility could recoil back upon himself as its author.

"The pigeons stalking near offered to his abnormally acute understanding the only solution which would leave him absolutely devoid of fear. He might have swung open the lid of the well once more and flung it after its owner, but this meant an aftermath of experience from which he shrank, his delight being in the thought that the victims he saw vanish before his eyes were so many encumbrances wiped off the face of the earth by a sweep of the hand. To see or hear them again would be destructive of this notion. He preferred the subtler way and to take advantage of old Mother Jane's characteristics, so he caught one of the pigeons (he has always been able to lure birds into his hands), and tying the ring around the neck of the bird with a blade of grass plucked up from the highway, he let it fly, and so was rid of the bauble which to Mother Jane's eyes, of course, was a direct gift from the heavens through which the bird had flown before lighting on her doorstep."

"Wonderful!" I exclaimed, almost overwhelmed with humiliation, but preserving a brave front. "What invention and what audacity!—the invention and the audacity of a man totally irresponsible for his deeds, was it not?" I asked. "There is no doubt, is there, about his being an absolute maniac?"

"No, madam." What a relief I felt at that word! "Since we entrapped him yesterday and he found himself fully discovered, he has lost all grip upon himself and fills the room we put him in with the unmistakable ravings of a madman. It was through these I learned the facts I have just mentioned."

I drew a deep breath. We were standing in the sight of several men, and their presence there seemed intolerable. Unconsciously I began to walk away. Unconsciously Mr. Gryce followed me. At the end of several paces we both stopped. We were no longer visible to the crowd, and I felt I could speak the words I had been burning to say ever since I saw the true nature of Mr. Trohm's character exposed.

"Mr. Gryce," said I, flushing scarlet—which I here solemnly declare is something which has not happened to me before in years, and if I can help it shall never happen to me again,—"I am interested in what you say, because yesterday, at his own gateway, Mr. Trohm proposed to me, and——"

"You did not accept him?"

"No. What do you think I am made of, Mr. Gryce? I did not accept him, but I made the refusal a gentle one, and—this is not easy work, Mr. Gryce," I interrupted myself to say with suitable grimness—"the same thing took place between me and Deacon Spear, and to him I gave a response such as I thought his presumption warranted. The discrimination does not argue well for my astuteness, Mr. Gryce. You see, I crave no credit that I do not deserve. Perhaps you cannot understand that, but it is a part of my nature."

"Madam," said he, and I must own I thought his conduct perfect, "had I not been as completely deceived as yourself I might find words of criticism for this possibly unprofessional partiality. But when an old hand like myself can listen to the insinuations of a maniac, and repose, as I must say I did repose, more or less confidence in the statements he chose to make me, and which were true enough as to the facts he mentioned, but wickedly false and preposterously wrong in suggestion, I can have no words of blame for a woman who, whatever her understanding and whatever her experience, necessarily has seen less of human nature and its incalculable surprises. As to the more delicate matter you have been good enough to confide to me, madam, I have but one remark to make. With such an example of womanhood suddenly brought to their notice in such a wild as this, how could you expect them, sane or insane, to do otherwise than they did? I know many a worthy man who would like to follow their example." And with a bow that left me speechless, Mr. Gryce laid his hand on his heart and softly withdrew.

EPILOGUE

SOME STRAY LEAFLETS FROM AN OLD DIARY OF ALTHEA KNOLLYS, FOUND BY ME IN THE PACKET LEFT IN MY CHARGE BY HER DAUGHTER LUCETTA

I never thought I should do so foolish a thing as begin a diary. When in my boarding-school days (which I am very glad to be rid of) I used to see Meeley Butterworth sit down every night of her life over a little book which she called the repository of her daily actions, I thought that if ever I reached that point of imbecility I would deserve to have fewer lovers and more sense, just as she so frequently advised me to. And yet here I am, pencil in hand, jotting down the nothings of the moment, and with every prospect of continuing to do so for two weeks at least. For (why was I born such a chatterbox!) I have seen my fate, and must talk to some one about him, if only to myself, nature never having meant me to keep silence on any living topic that interests me.

Yes, with lovers in Boston, lovers in New York, and a most determined suitor on the other side of our own home-walls in Peekskill, I have fallen victim to the grave face and methodical ways of a person I need not name, since he is the only gentleman in this whole town, except—But I won't except anybody. Charles Knollys has no peer here or anywhere, and this I am ready to declare, after only one sight of his face and one look from his eye, though to no one but you, my secret, non-committal confidant—for to acknowledge to any human being that my admiration could be caught, or my heart touched, by a person who had not sued two years at my feet, would be to abdicate an ascendency I am so accustomed to I could not see it vanish without pain. Besides, who knows how I shall feel to-morrow? Meeley Butterworth never shows any hesitation in uttering her opinion either of men or things, but then her opinion never changes, whilst mine is a very thistle-down, blowing hither and thither till I cannot follow its wanderings myself. It is one of my charms, certain fools say, but that is nonsense. If my cheeks lacked color and my eyes were without sparkle, or even if I were two inches taller instead of being the tiniest bit of mortal flesh to be found amongst all the young ladies of my age in our so-called society, I doubt if the lightness of my mind would meet with the approbation of even the warmest woman-lovers of this time. As it is, it just passes, and sometimes, as to-night, for instance, when I can hardly see to inscribe these lines on this page for the vision of two grave, if not quietly reproving eyes which float between it and me, I almost wish I had some of Meeley's responsible characteristics, instead of being the airiest, merriest, and most volatile being that ever tried to laugh down the grandeur of this dreary old house with its century of memories.

Ah! that allusion has given me something to say. This house. What is there about it except its size to make a stranger like me look back continually over her shoulder in going down the long halls, or even when nestling comfortably by the great wood-fire in the immense drawing-room? I am not one of your fanciful ones; but I can no more help doing this, than I can help wishing Judge Knollys lived in a less roomy mansion with fewer echoing corners in its innumerable passages. I like brightness and cheer, at least in my surroundings. If I must have gloom, or a seriousness which some would call gloom, let me have it in individuals where there is some prospect of a blithe, careless-hearted little midget effecting a change, and not in great towering walls and endless floors which no amount of sunshine or laughter could ever render homelike, or even comfortable.

But there! If one has the man, one must have the home, so I had better say no more against the home till I am quite sure I do not want the man. For—Well, well, I am not a fool, but I did hear something just then, a something which makes me tremble yet, though I have spent five good minutes trilling the gayest songs I know.

I think it is very inconsiderate of the witches to bother thus a harmless mite like myself, who only asks for love, light, and money enough to buy a ribbon or a jewel when the fancy takes her, which is not as often as my enemies declare. And now a question! Why are my enemies always to be found among the girls, and among the plainest of them too? I never heard a man say anything against me, though I have sometimes surprised a look on their faces (I saw it to-day) which might signify reproof if it were not accompanied by a smile showing anything but displeasure.

But this is a digression, as Meeley would say. What I want to do, but which I seem to find it very difficult to do, is to tell how I came to be here, and what I have seen since I came. First, then, to be very short about the matter, I am here because the old folks—that is, my father and Mr. Knollys, have decided Charles and I should know each other. In thought, I courtesy to the decision; I think we ought to too. For while many other men are handsomer or better known, or have more money, alas! than he, he alone has a way of drawing up to one's side with an air that captivates the eye and sets the heart trembling, a heart, moreover, that never knew before it could tremble, except in the presence of great worldly prosperity and beautiful, beautiful things. So, as this experience is new, I am dutifully obliged for the excitement it gives me, and am glad to be here, awesome as the place is, and destitute of any such pleasures as I have been accustomed to in the gay cities where I have hitherto spent most of my time.

But there! I am rambling again. I have come to X., as you now see, for good and sufficient reasons, and while this house is one of consequence and has been the resort of many notable people, it is a little lonesome, our only neighbor being a young man who has a fine enough appearance, but who has already shown his admiration of me so plainly—of course he was in the road when I drove up to the house—that I lost all interest in him at once, such a nonsensical liking at first sight being, as I take it, a tribute only to my audacious little travelling bonnet and the curl or two which will fall out on my cheek when I move my head about too quickly, as I certainly could not be blamed for doing, in driving into a place where I was expected to make myself happy for two weeks.

He, then, is out of these chronicles. When I say his name is Obadiah Trohm, you will probably be duly thankful. But he is not as stiff and biblical as his name would lead you to expect. On the contrary, he is lithe, graceful, and suave to a point which makes Charles Knollys' judicial face a positive relief to the eye and such little understanding as has been accorded me.

I cannot write another word. It is twelve o'clock, and though I have the cosiest room in the house, all chintz and decorated china, I find myself listening and peering just as I did down-stairs in their great barn of a drawing-room. I wonder if any very dreadful things ever happened in this house? I will ask old Mr. Knollys to-morrow, or—or Mr. Charles.

I am sorry I was so inquisitive; for the stories Charles told me—I thought I had better not trouble the old gentleman—have only served to people the shadows of this rambling old house with figures of whose acquaintance I am likely to be more or less shy. One tale in particular gave me the shivers. It was about a mother and daughter who both loved the same man (it seems incredible, girls so seldom seeing with the eyes of their mothers), and it was the daughter who married him, while the mother, broken-hearted, fled from the wedding and was driven up to the great door, here, in a coach, dead. They say that the coach still travels the road just before some calamity to the family,—a phantom coach which floats along in shadow, turning the air about it to mist that chills the marrow in the bones of the unfortunate who sees it. I am going to see it myself some day, the real coach, I mean, in which this tragic event took place. It is still in the stable, Charles tells me. I wonder if I will have the courage to sit where that poor devoted mother breathed out her miserable existence. I shall endeavor to do so if only to defy the fate which seems to be closing in upon me.

Charles is an able lawyer, but his argument in favor of close bonnets versus bewitching little pokes with a rose or two in front, was very weak, I thought, to-day. He seemed to think so himself, after a while; for when, as the only means of convincing him of the weakness of the cause he was advocating, I ran up-stairs and put on a poke similar to the aforesaid, he retracted at once and let the case go by default. For which I, and the poke, made suitable acknowledgments, to the great amusement of papa Knollys, who was on my side from the first.

Not much going on to-day. Yet I have never felt merrier. Oh, ye hideous, bare old walls! Won't I make you ring if——

I won't have it! I won't have that smooth, persistent hypocrite pushing his way into my presence, when my whole heart and attention belong to a man who would love me if he only could get his own leave to do so. Obadiah Trohm has been here to-day, on one pretext or another, three times. Once he came to bring some very choice apples—as if I cared for apples! The second time he had a question of great importance, no doubt, to put to Charles, and as Charles was in my company, the whole interview lasted, let us say, a good half-hour at least. The third time he came, it was to see me, which, as it was now evening, meant talk, talk, talk in the great drawing-room, with just a song interpolated now and then, instead of a cosy chat in the window-seat of the pretty Flower Parlor, with only one pair of ears to please and one pair of eyes to watch. Master Trohm was intrusive, and, if no one felt it but myself, it is because Charles Knollys has set himself up an ideal of womanhood to which I am a contradiction. But that will not affect the end. A woman may be such a contradiction and yet win, if her heart is in the struggle and she has, besides, a certain individuality of her own which appeals to the eye and heart if not to the understanding. I do not despair of seeing Charles Knollys' forehead taking a very deep frown at sight of his handsome and most attentive neighbor. Heigho! why don't I answer Meeley Butterworth's last letter? Am I ashamed to tell her that I have to limit my effusion to just four pages because I have commenced a diary?

I declare I begin to regard it a misfortune to have dimples. I never have regarded it so before when I have seen man after man succumb to them, but now they have become my bane, for they attract two admirers, just at the time they should attract but one, and it is upon the wrong man they flash the oftenest; why, I leave it to all true lovers to explain. As a consequence, Master Trohm is beginning to assume an air of superiority, and Charles, who may not believe in dimples, but who on that very account, perhaps, seems to be always on the lookout for them, shrinks more or less into the background, as is not becoming in a man with so many claims to respect, if not to love. I want to feel that each one of these precious fourteen days contains all that it can of delight and satisfaction, and how can I when Obadiah—oh, the charming and romantic name!—holds my crewels, instead of Charles, and whispers words which, coming from other lips, would do more than waken my dimples!

But if I must have a suitor, just when a suitor is not wanted, let me at least make him useful. Charles shall read his own heart in this man's passion.

I don't know why, but I have taken a dislike to the Flower Parlor. It now vies with the great drawing-room in my disregard. Yesterday, in crossing it, I felt a chill, so sudden and so penetrating, that I irresistibly thought of the old saying, "Some one is walking over my grave." My grave! where lies it, and why should I feel the shudder of it now? Am I destined to an early death? The bounding life in my veins says no. But I never again shall like that room. It has made me think.

I have not only sat in the old coach, but I had (let me drop the words slowly, they are so precious) I—I have had—a kiss—given me there. Charles gave me this kiss; he could not help it. I was sitting on the seat in front, in a sort of mock mirth he was endeavoring to frown upon, when suddenly I glanced up and our eyes met, and—He says it was the sauciness of my dimples (oh, those old dimples! they seem to have stood me in good stead after all); but I say it was my sincere affection which drew him, for he stooped like a man forgetful of everything in the whole wide world but the little trembling, panting being before him, and gave me one of those caresses which seals a woman's fate forever, and made me, the feather-brained and thoughtless coquette, a slave to this large-minded and true-hearted man for all my life hereafter.

Why I should be so happy over this event is beyond my understanding. That he should be in the seventh heaven of delight is only to be expected, but that I should find myself tripping through this gloomy old house like one treading on air is a mystery, to the elucidation of which I can only give my dimples. My reason can make nothing out of it. I, who thought of nothing short of a grand establishment in Boston, money, servants, and a husband who would love me blindly whatever my faults, have given my troth—you will say my lips, but the one means the other—to a man who will never be known outside of his own county, never be rich, never be blind even, for he frowns upon me as often as he smiles, and, worst of all, who lives in a house so vast and so full of tragic suggestion that it might well awaken doleful anticipations in much more serious-minded persons than myself.

And yet I am happy, so happy that I have even attempted to make the acquaintance of the grim old portraits and weak pastels which line the walls of many of these bedrooms. Old Mr. Knollys caught me courtesying just now before one of these ancestral beauties, whose face seemed to hold a faint prophecy of my own, and perceiving by my blushes that this was something more than a mere childish freak on my part, he chucked me under the chin and laughingly asked, how long it was likely to be before he might have the honor of adding my pretty face to the collection. Which should have made me indignant, only I am not in an indignant mood just now.

Why have I been so foolish? Why did I not let my over-fond neighbor know from the beginning that I detested him, instead of—But what have I done anyway? A smile, a nod, a laughing word mean nothing. When one has eyes which persist in dancing in spite of one's every effort to keep them demure, men who become fools are apt to call one a coquette, when a little good sense would teach them that the woman who smiles always has some other way of showing her regard to the man she really favors. I could not help being on merry terms with Mr. Trohm, if only to hide the effect another's presence has on me. But he thinks otherwise, and to-day I had ample reason for seeing why his good looks and easy manners have invariably awakened distrust in me rather than admiration. Master Trohm is vindictive, and I should be afraid of him, if I had not observed in him the presence of another passion which will soon engross all his attention and make him forget me as soon as ever I become Charles' wife. Money is his idol, and as fortune seems to favor him, he will soon be happy in the mere pleasure of accumulation. But this is not relating what happened to-day.

We were walking in the shrubbery (by we I naturally mean Charles and myself), and he was saying things which made me at the same time happy and a bit serious, when I suddenly felt myself under the spell of some baleful influence that filled me with a dismay I could neither understand nor escape from.

As this could not proceed from Charles, I turned to look about me, when I encountered the eyes of Obadiah Trohm, who was leaning on the fence separating his grounds from those of Mr. Knollys, looking directly at us. If I flinched at this surveillance, it was but the natural expression of my indignation. His face wore a look calculated to frighten any one, and though he did not respond to the gesture I made him, I felt that my only chance of escaping a scene was to induce Charles to leave me before he should see what I saw in the lowering countenance of his intrusive neighbor. As the situation demanded self-possession and the exercise of a ready wit, and as these are qualities in which I am not altogether deficient, I succeeded in carrying out my intention sooner even than I expected. Charles hurried from my presence at the first word, and proceeded towards the house without seeing Trohm, and I, quivering with dread, turned towards the man whom I felt, rather than saw, approaching me.

He met me with a look I shall never forget. I have had lovers—too many of them,—and this is not the first man I have been compelled to meet with rebuff and disdain, but never in the whole course of my none too extended existence have I been confronted by such passion or overwhelmed with such bitter recrimination. He seemed like a man beside himself, yet he was quiet, too quiet, and while his voice did not rise above a whisper, and he approached no nearer than the demands of courtesy required, he produced so terrifying an effect upon me that I longed to cry for help, and would have done so, but that my throat closed with fright, and I could only gurgle forth a remonstrance, too faint even for him to hear.

"You have played with a man's best feelings," he said. "You have led me to believe that I had only to speak to have you for my own. Are you simply foolish, or are you wicked? Did you care for me at all, or was it only your wish to increase the number of men in your train? This one" (here his hand pointed quiveringly towards the house) "has enjoyed a happiness denied me. His hand has touched yours, his lips—" Here his words became almost unintelligible till his purpose gave him strength, and he cried: "But notwithstanding this, notwithstanding any vows you may have exchanged, I have claims upon you that I will not yield. I who have loved no woman before you, will have such a hand in your fate that you will never be able to separate yourself from the influence I shall exert over you. I will not intrude between you and your lover; I will not affect dislike or disturb your outer life with any vain display of my hatred or my passion, but I will work upon your secret thoughts, and create a slowly increasing dread in the inner sanctuary of your heart till you wish you had called up the deadliest of serpents in your pathway rather than the latent fury of Obadiah Trohm. You are a girl now; when you are married and become a mother, you will understand me. For the present I leave you. The shadow of this old house which has never seen much happiness within it will soon rest upon your thoughtless head. What that will not do, your own inherent weakness will. The woman who trifles with a strong man's heart has a flaw in her nature which will work out her own destruction in time. I can afford to let you enjoy your prospective honeymoon in peace. Afterwards—" He cast a threatening look towards the decaying structure behind me, and was silent. But that silence did not unloose my tongue. I was absolutely speechless.

"Ten brides have crossed yonder threshold," he presently went on in a low musing tone freighted with horrible fatality. "One—and she was the girl whose mother was driven up to these doors dead—lived to take her grandchildren on her knees. The rest died early, and most of them unhappily. Oh, I have studied the traditions of your future home! You will live, but of all the brides who have triumphed in the honorable name of Knollys, you will lead the saddest life and meet the gloomiest end notwithstanding you stand before me now, with loose locks flying in the wind, and a heart so gay that even my despair can barely pale the roses on your cheek."

This was the raving of a madman. I recognized it as such, and took a little heart. How could he see into my future? How could he prophesy evil to one over whom he will have no control? to one watched over and beloved by a man like Charles? He is a dreamer, a fanatic. His talk about the flaw in my nature is nonsense, and as for the fate lowering over my head, in the shadows falling from the toppling old house in which I am likely to take up my abode—that is only frenzy, and I would be unworthy of happiness to heed it. As I realized this, my indignation grew, and, uttering a few contemptuous words, I was hurrying away when he stopped me with a final warning.

"Wait!" he said, "women like you cannot keep either their joys or their miseries to themselves. But I advise you not to take Charles Knollys into your confidence. If you do, a duel will follow, and if I have not the legal acumen of your intended, I have an eye and a hand before which he must fall, if our passions come to an issue. So beware! never while you live betray what has passed between us at this interview, unless the weariness of a misplaced affection should come to you, and with it the desire to be rid of your husband."

A frightful threat which, unfortunately perhaps, has sealed my lips. Oh, why should such monsters live!

I have been all through the house to-day with old Mr. Knollys. Every room was opened for my inspection, and I was bidden to choose which should be refurnished for my benefit. It was a gruesome trip, from which I have returned to my own little nook of chintz as to a refuge. Great rooms which for years have been the abode of spiders, are not much to my liking, but I chose out two which at least have fireplaces in them, and these are to be made as cheerful as circumstances will permit. I hope when I again see them, it will not be by the light of a waning November afternoon, when the few leaves still left to flutter from the trees blow, soggy and wet, against the panes of the solitary windows, or lie in sodden masses at the foot of the bare trunks, which cluster so thickly on the lawn as to hide all view of the highroad. I was meant for laughter and joy, flashing lights, and the splendors of ballrooms. Why have I chosen, then, to give up the great world and settle down in this grimmest of grim old houses in a none too lively village? I think it is because I love Charles Knollys, and so, no matter how my heart sinks in the dim shadows that haunt every spot I stray into, I will be merry, will think of Charles instead of myself, and so live down the unhappy prophecies uttered by the wretch who, with his venomous words, has robbed the future of whatever charm my love was likely to cast upon it. The fact that this man left the town to-day for a lengthy trip abroad should raise my spirits more than it has. If we were going now, Charles and I— But why dream of a Paradise whose doors remain closed to you? It is here our honeymoon is destined to be passed; within these walls and in sight of the bare boughs rattling at this moment against the panes.

I made a misstatement when I said that I had gone into all the rooms of the house this afternoon. I did not enter the Flower Parlor.

I had been married a month and had, as I thought, no further use for this foolish diary. So one evening when Charles was away, I attempted to burn it.

But when I had flung myself down before the blazing logs of my bedroom fire (I was then young enough to love to crouch for hours on the rug in my lonely room, seeking for all I delighted in and longed for in the glowing embers), some instinct, or was it a premonition? made me withhold from destruction a record which coming events might make worthy of preservation. That was five years ago, and to-day I have reopened the secret drawer in which this simple book has so long lain undisturbed, and am once more penning lines destined perhaps to pass into oblivion together with the others. Why? I do not know. There is no change in my married life. I have no trouble, no anxiety, no reason for dread; yet—Well, well, some women are made for the simple round of domestic duties, and others are as out of place in the nursery and kitchen as butterflies in a granary. I want just the things Charles cannot give me. I have home, love, children, all that some women most crave, and while I idolize my husband and know of nothing sweeter than my babies, I yet have spells of such wretched weariness, that it would be a relief to me to be a little less comfortable if only I might enjoy a more brilliant existence. But Charles is not rich; sometimes I think he is poor, and however much I may desire change, I cannot have it. Heigho! and, what is worse, I haven't had a new dress in a year; I who so love dress, and become it so well! Why, if it is my lot to go shabby, and tie up my dancing ringlets with faded ribbons, was I made with the figure of a fairy and given a temperament which, without any effort on my part, makes me, diminutive as I am, the centre of every group I enter? If I were plain, or shy, or even self-contained, I might be happy here, but now—There! there! I will go kiss little William, and lay Loreen's baby arm about my neck and see if the wicked demons will fly away. Charles is too busy for me to intrude upon him in that horrid Flower Parlor.

I was never superstitious till I entered this house; but now I believe in every sort of thing a sane woman should not. Yesterday, after a neglect of five years, I brought out my diary. To-day I have to record in it that there was a reason for my doing so. Obadiah Trohm has returned home. I saw him this morning leaning over his fence in the same place and in very much the same attitude as on that day when he frightened me so, a month before my wedding.

But he did not frighten me to-day. He merely looked at me very sharply and with a less offensive admiration than in the early days of our first acquaintance. At which I made him my best courtesy. I was not going to remind him of the past in our new relations, and he, thankful perhaps for this, took off his hat with a smile I am trying even yet to explain to myself. Then we began to talk. He had travelled everywhere and I had been nowhere; he wore the dress and displayed the manners of the great world, while I had only a hungry desire to do the same. As for fashion, I needed all my beauty and the fading sparkle of my old animation to enable me to hold up my head before him.

But as for liking him, I did not. I could admire his appearance, but he himself attracted me no more than when he had words of angry fury on his tongue. He is a gentleman, and one who has seen the world, but in other ways he is no more to be compared with my Charles than his pert new house, built in his absence, with the grand old structure with whose fatality he once threatened me.

I do not think he wants to threaten me with disaster now. Time closes such wounds as his very effectually. I wish we had some of his money.

I have always heard that the wives of the Knollys, whatever their misfortune, have always loved their husbands. I do not think I am any exception to the rule. When Charles has leisure to give me an hour from his musty old books, the place here seems lively enough, and the children's voices do not sound so shrill. But these hours are so infrequent. If it were not for Mr. Trohm's journal (Did I mention that he had lent me a journal of his travels?) I should often eat my heart out with loneliness. I am beginning to like the man better as I follow him from city to city of the old world. If he had ever mentioned me in its pages, I would not read another line in it, but he seems to have expended both his love and spite when he bade me farewell in the garden underlying these bleak old walls.

I am becoming as well acquainted with Mr. Trohm's handwriting as with my own. I read and read and read in his journal, and only stop when the dreaded midnight hour comes with its ghostly suggestions and the unaccountable noises which make this old dwelling so uncanny. Charles often finds me curled up over this book, and when he does he sighs. Why?

I have been teaching Loreen to dance. Oh, how merry it has made me! I think I will be happier now. We have the large upper hall to take steps in, and when she makes a misstep we laugh, and that is a good sound to hear in this old place. If I could only have a little money to buy her a fresh frock and some ribbons, I would feel perfectly satisfied; but I do believe Charles is getting poorer and poorer every day; the place costs so much to keep up, he says, and when his father died there were debts to be paid which leaves us, his innocent inheritors, very straitened. Master Trohm has no such difficulties. He has money enough. But I don't like the man for all that, polite as he is to us all. He seems to quite adore Loreen, and as to William, he pets him till I feel almost uncomfortable at times.

What shall I do? I am invited to New York, I, and Charles says I may go, too—only I have nothing to wear. Oh, for some money! a little money! it is my right to have some money; but Charles tells me he can only spare enough to pay my expenses, that my Sunday frock looks very well, and that, even if it did not, I am pretty enough to do without fine clothes, and other nonsense like that,—sweet enough, but totally without point, in fact. If I am pretty, all the more I need a little finery to set me off, and, besides, to go to New York without money—why, I should be perfectly miserable. Charles himself ought to realize this, and be willing to sell his old books before he would let me go into this whirl of temptation without a dollar to spend. As he don't, I must devise some plan of my own for obtaining a little money, for I won't give up my trip—the first offered me since I was married,—and neither will I go away and come back without a gift for my two girls, who have grown to womanhood without a jewel to adorn them or a silk dress to make them look like gentlemen's children. But how get money without Charles knowing it? Mr. Trohm is such a good friend, he might lend me a little, but I don't know how to ask him without recalling to his mind certain words long since forgotten by him perhaps, but never to be forgotten by me, feather-brained as many people think me. Is there any one else?

I wonder if some things are as wicked as people say they are. I——

Here the diary breaks off abruptly. But we know what followed. The forgery, the discovery of it by her suave but secret enemy, his unnatural revenge, and the never-dying enmity which led to the tragic events it has been my unhappy fortune to relate at such length. Poor Althea! with thy name I write finis to these pages. May the dust lie lightly on thy breast under the shadow of the Flower Parlor, through which thy footsteps passed with such dread in the old days of thy youthful beauty and innocence!

THE END